Also by Mary Ellenton

FLIPPING

Critical Praise and Reviews

"In Mary A. Ellenton's debut novel, "Flipping," readers will find a most unexpected financial criminal: a woman."
-Cristina Merrill, *The International Business Times*

"In her debut novel, Mary Ellenton manages to make the mortgage industry seem as sexy as it does scandalous. Ellenton deftly weaves realistic details of the industry into the narrative making the reader nearly complicit in Fay's rise and fall.
-Nathalie Hardy, columnist and editor of *Nathalie's Notes*

"Ellenton provides very realistic details about the creative financial loopholes within the lending market and oddly does it with a woman at the helm. I was quite surprised that I enjoyed this book so much.
-*Chic Lit Plus*

"Wow. When I first read the synopsis for this book I thought that it would be a light, fluffy chick book. I was so wrong and I'm so glad."
-*The Minding Spot*

"If you like complex characters and three-dimensional plots, this book will surprise you."
-Alla Salatnovich, *Celebrity Books Reviewer*

"What I found fascinating about this book is that the story revolves around the ethical and mortal dilemma of making money an its personal impacts"
-Aloisa Santos, *Guiltless Reader*

The Psychic is a work of fiction. Name, characters, businesses, organizations, places, events and incidents are either the product of the author's imagination or are used fictitiously. Any resemblance to actual persons living or dead, events or locales is entirely coincidental.

Copyright ©2017, Mary A. Ellenton. All rights reserved.
Published by MAE Productions, New York
978-0-9839065-1-3

Printed in the United States of America

For C and Jack's lady

We are never deceived;
we deceive ourselves.

Johann Wolfgang von Goeth

THE PSYCHIC

A Novel
by
Mary A. Ellenton

MAE
PRODUCTIONS

1

$\mathcal{M}$iriam Stemple, the hostess of the psychic reading party, sat on her sofa in suburban Long Island chewing a cube of Jarlsberg and rearranging the configuration of the cheese platter on the coffee table for the third time. The watery ice cubes in her second Tanqueray rattled in her glass as she sprang to her feet when she heard a car door slam. She stubbed out her Newport and darted to the window only to spin back around to satisfy compulsive, ritualistic tapping on the end table and poked her nose out of the corner of the living room drapes just as the taxi was pulling away. It was her. The psychic had arrived.

She watched the woman's rotund figure emerge though the cloud of exhaust the cab left behind on the frigid December night, swigged the last mouthful of her cocktail and hurried to the kitchen. She had been counting down the days for weeks for this night.

When Miriam had previously had a reading with the psychic, Mrs. Habbibi, at a similar gathering hosted by a woman she'd met through her bereavement group, she was stunned to tears when Mrs. Habbibi accurately pieced together that her twenty-three-year-old son, Garrett, had recently died from a heroin overdose. Garrett's message to her through Mrs. Habbibi on that evening, that he was happier than he had ever been in the physical world, was as far as they got. Miriam had been so overtaken with emotion both she and Mrs. Habbibi agreed it was best to end the reading.

Since that night, waiting for a second chance to consult with the gifted psychic again was the only reason Miriam could think of to continue living. Richard, her husband of twenty-five years had filed for divorce a week after their son's funeral. In truth the marriage had been faltering for years and the obligations of Richard's commercial flooring business, inherited from Miriam's father, conveniently required frequent travel.

Miriam set her glass down into the sink just as the bell rang and took off towards the door, abruptly rounding back, past the supermarket crudités platter on the kitchen counter to tap, tap, tap the curve of the faucet. *Would Mrs. Habbibi be able to contact her Garr-Garr for her again tonight? Did her extreme emotional response frighten him away forever?* There were so many questions she had for him. She blinked away the liquid grief burning her eyes, gave herself a bracing slap across the face and tapped, tapped, tapped the knob with the pads of her fingers before opening the door for the enchanted woman waiting on the other side.

"Hello, Miriam." Mrs. Habbibi stood motionless in the doorway. The soft, unhurried, manner of her speech and her lilting Middle Eastern accent gave even the simple greeting deeper meaning. It was a voice that cast a spell, a voice meant for telling fairytales.

Miriam could not contain her relief and lunged forward to embrace her.

"Please." The elegant older woman took a graceful step backwards. "For the integrity of the readings this evening—" she placed a light, dignified hand on her heart. "Comply with my requests."

"I'm sorry. Right." Miriam snatched her hands up to her chest in self-admonishment. "No physical contact. Follow me. It's this way." She spun on her heel and led the way to the room she had prepared as per instructions in a phone conversation earlier in the week.

Mrs. Habbibi silently followed through the wake of the woman's over sprayed floral perfume.

"Excuse the boxes, some of my husband's things. Did you have trouble finding the address? The temperature really has dropped out there. I wonder if we'll get our first snow. I was so worried I wouldn't be able to get another appointment with you." The hostess prattled on over her shoulder.

"And now, I am here." Mrs. Habbibi, a bit bottom heavy, waddled after her down the hallway of the gaudy home, shopping bag in hand, her floor-length, saffron skirt swaying beneath the hem of her overcoat.

There were advantages to hostessing one of Mrs. Habbibi's psychic parties. The hostess was charged half the usual two hundred dollar reading fee and was given the last reading of the evening, allowing for a more relaxed experience, if the client was capable. Many were too shaken by her insights. But most enticing, it was the quickest way to secure an appointment with Mrs. Habbibi who was steadily booked weeks in advance. The hostess's duties were to collect Mrs. Habbibi's fee from each guest upon their arrival and provide refreshments for them to enjoy while they waited their turn for a reading.

"It was my husband's office. I cleared off the desk for you and took all of the photographs down off of the walls just like you asked."

"Thank you. It will do perfectly."

"It's such an honor to have you in my house. Do you need anything else, Mrs. Habbibi? Can I get you some water, something to eat?" the homeowner slavishly fawned.

"No. Just please, no interruptions while I prepare. I will take the first person at seven o'clock."

"Right. Seven," Miriam said and nodded dutifully.

"And please keep our guests a considerate distance from this door until their appointment time."

"Yes. Right. I remember." Miriam touched a bony finger to her temple and turned to leave the room.

"And Miriam…"

The woman's angular shoulders hunched and she spun around, her eyes starving for anything the psychic would offer.

Mrs. Habbibi's peaceful smile revealed the caricature-like gap between her front teeth that somehow served to enhance her mystical charm. "There is love all around you tonight. I felt it the instant I stepped into your home."

The weary dam keeping the woman's heartache at bay began to fail and she wiped at her eyes. "Thank you, Mrs. Habbibi. I felt better as soon as I saw you." She sniffled and backed out of the room.

The psychic pressed a gentle palm against the door to make certain it was completely shut. She closed her eyes and after a long purposeful exhale, slowly turned, and stood perfectly still in the silence of the strange surroundings, assessing the room and its energy.

Her auburn hair was set and heavily sprayed, and after a customary primp, she passed her hands through the air, "I seal myself in the chamber of goodness and fill this room with the protective white light of the Christ," she commanded and set off to work.

The dark draperies and heavy furniture gave the room a dominant, masculine feel. The psychic took her position in the tufted, upholstered armchair behind the imposing, claw-footed desk and reached down inside her canvas shopping bag. She pulled out a gold-colored damask runner, spread it across the smooth, cherry finish of the desktop and then placed two stout pillar candles on opposite ends; one white, the other purple. Next, out came her pad and pencil, a small alabaster bowl, a plastic bag containing a tangle of herbs and a box of Kleenex.

After neatly folding her coat and placing it into her bag, she struck a wooden match and lit both candles. The white candle for purity, purple for spiritual wisdom and then tapped out a clump of the fresh sage into the small bowl and dropped the match into it. Instantly, the fragrant smoke began to rise, dense, into the air of the low-ceilinged room.

"I cleanse this dwelling of all dark spirits. I cast out all negative energy and ask that it be surrounded in the golden light of God's grace."

She lifted the smoldering saucer and made a clockwise pass through the room with it held at her eye level, flipping off the switch to the harsh lighting of the overhead fixture.

Too dark. She set the bowl down and padded across the thick burgundy oriental to the far side of the room, clicked on a small table lamp next to the tweed sofa and dragged a side chair to the opposite side of the desk and settled at her post for the evening.

As she dropped her head in meditation, centering, clearing her mind of all thoughts, she could hear the house grow fuller with each distant ring of the doorbell, her clients' voices high in excitement, failing early in their conversations with each other to keep their initial hushed tones. And then, the first knock of the evening, timidly rapped upon her door. She checked her watch; exactly seven o'clock.

"Come in please." She pushed her eyeglasses further up on the bridge of her nose and sat erect, hands folded atop each other, fully aware of the effect her powerful presence would have on the person entering the room.

"I am Mrs. Habbibi."

"Wendy...Wendy Waxman."

The platinum-haired woman in her thirties was impeccably dressed with the type of formidable face that stares back from a commercial hair color box on a drugstore shelf. Awkward seconds passed while the psychic waited to see if her glamorous client would take the seat without permission. Most of them approached her with the same reserved demeanors, but it was futile—too thin a veil for the anticipation the evening conjured. Their nervous energy changed the vibration of the room the instant they entered. She didn't judge; even those of the most composed nature became jittery with the prospect of hearing from a departed loved one or stealing a glimpse into their future.

Walking through her door was raising an ominous cocktail to the lips, equal parts hopefulness and dread with a twist of fear that rendered the emotional equilibrium askew before they even committed to the seat across from her. The conditions were a loaded deck for Mrs. Habbibi to work with in spite of her great intuitive gifts.

"Please sit, Wendy." Her covert scanning was already under way, her friendly invitation deliberately displaying the imperfection of her smile, aware that it made her presence less fateful.

She registered the ring of paler flesh on the woman's fourth finger of her left hand. The attempt to miser away clues from her revealed more of the client than the jewelry would have itself, but it wasn't any superficial article or lack of one that Mrs. Habbibi relied on to aid her assessments. Her level of observation skills were of a far more elevated rank. It was organic clues she was looking for. It was the condition of the hands, themselves and the shape of its fingers that silently assisted in choosing the best approach for each client; square finger tips; good work ethic, methodical. Long fingers; indecisive, creative. Narrow nail beds in males; a propensity towards unfaithfulness. The body was her silent informant, giving up secrets that required the rigors of a relationship for the lay person to discover. Even the ears unwittingly conspired with her; flat against the head, self-critical. Bulbous lobes; goal-oriented, self-assured, naturally lucky. If face reading was an art form, experience had made her one of the great masters.

Wedding ring or not, this client was not here for insights on romance. It was loss, easily detectable in the area between the brows, even on the young. Uncomfortable with the stillness that had descended upon the room, her client folded her arms across her body and began unconsciously petting her elbows.

"Are you cold, Wendy?"

"Oh, no. No. I'm not cold. Just nervous. What kind of accent is that?"

"I am Persian."

"I've never been to a psychic before. But I guess you already know that." She nervously laughed at her own quip. "Wasn't sure I was going through with it until I was in the car. What's that smell? Incense?"

"You shouldn't be nervous. The pain that brought you here will be soothed tonight."

"Pain?"

"I have been listening to piano music since the moment you walked through the door? Who has been playing for us? Is this your mother?"

"Oh, my God!" The woman clasped her hand over her mouth. "How do you know that?"

The psychic tilted her head at the woman whose posture had become ramrod straight.

"There is also a very prominent dark star looming over you. It separates you from your money attraction power. It has been in place for quite some time." Mrs. Habbibi bowed her head, and her eyes squinted in concentration. "I'm sensing some type of transgression." Her hands fondled the air. "A betrayal... a deception of some kind."

Wendy sat frozen with intrigue, her attention now honed on the mystifying seerer.

"Was there a divorce or broken business alliance?" The psychic took her time, leveling her gaze to meet the astonishment in her client's eyes.

"My partner walked out of our salon last year with half of the staff and clientele behind my back, he even –"

The psychic stopped her with a gently raised hand. "What's important now is that you allow yourself to be released from this event. Only a fool trips over what is behind them."

There was a subtle drop in the woman's shoulders.

"The emotional toll of this violation has manifested in a spiritual imbalance that has closed you off from your abundance flow. It keeps you from your most desired pursuits."

Wendy nodded with understanding.

"But you have nothing to fear." Mrs. Habbibi made deeper eye contact.

"Your prosperity energy is strong and it is very clear that a star is on the rise for you. You are entering a most favorable time to act on new business opportunities. Be watchful. Take notice of the situations that will present themselves or perhaps already have. Do not hesitate. Although this favorable phase is fleeting, if acted on with confidence it will move you out of the negative cycle and has the potential to secure your future."

Mrs. Habbibi noticed the good tidings caused Wendy's leg position to shift; an involuntary reaction to an increased heart rate. She seized the moment.

"Time to get comfortable with your destiny, Miss Wendy." Her eyes widened, the charm of her smile lighting her face. "You are going to be wealthy."

Wendy Waxman took an audible breath, her eyes alight with excitement.

"There are specific crystals that can be aligned with your own energy that are very effective in expediting the reversal of money blocks and opening cash flow-lines; jade, tiger-eye, garnet—worn against your body their effect is quite remarkable. But do act before the window of favor closes."

"When is the window closing?" Wendy panicked.

"Difficult to say."

"Where can I get these crystals?"

"I offer personal aligning services. I will be happy to make an appointment to pair you with the proper stone, but right now the presence of your mother is coming through so powerfully, perhaps it's best we concentrate on her, yes?" The psychic's eyelids batted as she softly smiled.

"Yes," the woman meekly agreed, clearly thrown off balance by the abrupt shift of emotional gears.

The psychic offered her palms across the table. "I need your hands, please."

Wendy complied and immediately began to tear up the instant her hands were resting in the warmth of Mrs. Habbibi's. She sat transfixed as the psychic's eyes scoured her palms.

"Too, too much sorrow, Wendy." The psychic ticked as she continued studying the woman's hands. She looked up. "But there is no need. Your mother is with loved ones, she is blissful, and precisely where she needs to be in the journey of her soul." She observed in silence as tears began to trickle down the woman's flushed cheeks. "Don't be ashamed. Tears are the soul's healing balm. Trust in the wisdom of your higher self. It serves as your ardent guide if you allow it. It is the very impetus that brought you here tonight, in spite of your ambivalence, yes?" She returned again to the woman's palms, studying with intent.

"What do you see? What is it?"

Mrs. Habbibi's disregard of the question further established her command of the reading. "I want you to relax with me, Miss Wendy. We need to prepare to receive your mother's message. I need you to close your eyes and imagine the highest good you are capable of." Her voice was low and hypnotic, inducing a soporific effect in the growing warmth of the low- ceilinged room, still redolent with smoky sage. "Let this image fill your consciousness. That's very good. Now pull in a deep breath…another…we will do it together… let it fill you with purest of white light, the protective light of the Christ."

The woman's eyes snapped open scattering the serenity that had begun to descend on the darkened room.

"I'm a Jew. I can't …"

"He does not discriminate—and His power is infallible. I am sorry if I have offended you."

"I'm not offended. It's just that…"

"I understand—can you fill yourself with the Divine goodness of the All?"

"I can do that…but is all this necessary?"

"Very."

"Why?"

"There is a departed soul who wishes to contact you." The psychic's voice took on a militant tone. "In order for me to receive their message we will be piercing the other world. The world beyond our natural realm."

"Stop. Stop!" Wendy Waxman yanked her hands from Mrs. Habbibi's. "You're scaring the shit out of me, now."

Mrs. Habbibi smiled, amused at the woman's candor. "There is nothing for you to fear as long as you state that your intentions are pure. You will be protected."

"Protected… from what?"

"Discarnate souls…lower energy forms."

"What? What lower energy forms?" Wendy pushed away from the desk and her arms clutched around her body.

Mrs. Habbibi remained motionless in the dimly lit room, and then abruptly sat up. She rested her elbows on the wide desk, interlacing her fingers and after a deliberate pause, she looked squarely into the woman's eyes just an arm's length across from her. She pushed her glasses further up the bridge of her nose. "Your mother has passed. She has come to you in your dreams. Thrice in the last months. This is why you have come to me, yes?"

Wendy's eyes seemed to double in size.

"She is desperate to make contact with you." She observed the woman struggle to swallow the lump of grief and terror that had lodged in her throat.

"Her death was sudden, am I correct? Perhaps there is something she wishes you to know and I would like to retrieve her message on your behalf. But first you need to understand something."

The intensity of Mrs. Habbibi's glare and the severity in her tone prompted a nod from Wendy who was now too frightened to speak.

"To receive this message we are delving into the other plane. It is not of the physical realm and it is perfectly understandable if you are not comfortable participating with my level of reading and opt not to continue." Mrs. Habbibi leaned back in her chair.

"No, no. I do."

"So, in this, the other plane, often there are souls who have not fully crossed over."

"Why wouldn't a soul cross over?"

"Many reasons." The psychic voice turned compassionate. "Some are too intensely attached to the physical world. Perhaps there is unsettled emotional business that tethers them here. Sometimes, in a sudden, untimely death, the departed does not even realize that they have passed," she smiled empathetically. "They are confused, lost, and unable to transition."

"Is my mother lost?"

"No she is not. She has fully crossed over."

"Then why are you telling me all of this?"

"Because there are others who have not."

"Others?"

"They dwell between the realms of the living and the dead and in their fear and anxiety they sometimes attach themselves to whoever is receptive and," she hesitated, "some of these energy forms are dark."

"Dark?"

"Or inhuman."

"Oh, God!" the woman gasped.

"Exactly, my dear." Mrs. Habbibi casually sucked at her teeth. "Shall we proceed with the prayer of protection?"

Struggling to summon the courage to continue, the woman nodded.

The psychic again offered her open palms toward Wendy and closed her eyes. "Pull in a deep breath, filling yourself with the highest good. The divine protection of the All. Slowly release it. Very good." Her voice dropped in volume.

"Again, but this time as you breathe in I need you to concentrate on the essence you know to be your mother's."

Mrs. Habbibi's face strained, resisting the impulse to grimace as her fingers were squeezed tight from the intensity of her client's grip as she dared pull in another breath.

In the foreboding stillness that descended on the room, Wendy sat frozen; her eyes riveted on Mrs. Habbibi, the candle flame dancing in the lenses of her glasses, the sepia shadows playing on the smoothness of her olive skin.

"Again, please," Mrs. Habbibi commanded, eyelids twitching, her brow furrowed in concentration.

Just as Wendy heaved in another breath against the tightness constricting her chest, Mrs. Habbibi's eyes opened and widened and she whispered. "She is here with us, now."

"Mom?" The heartbreak in Wendy's tear-choked voice challenged even Mrs. Habbibi's focus at the task at hand.

Four hours and many readings later in the shadowy room, which had grown uncomfortably warmer, Mrs. Habbibi rested her head in her hand on a bent elbow. She took off her glasses and carefully rubbed her eyes. She was uncharacteristically tired. It had been a long night of particularly emotional readings—and now Miriam Stemple. She could hear her on the other side of the door, ushering out the last guest, emphatically prodding the person to take a tray of leftover sandwiches. The psychic leaned back in her chair and closed her eyes, palms rested down on the table as she worked to reconnect with her calm.

"Mrs. Habbibi?" Miriam softly knocked.

"Come in Miriam." Mrs. Habbibi adjusted her posture.

The reek of stale cigarette smoke layered with sinus-pinching perfume that arrived with the reed-thin woman was inescapable in the warm, enclosed room. Mrs. Habbibi massaged her temples.

"Here's everyone's money, Mrs. Habbibi. I put it all in size order for you." She anxiously slid the bulging envelope across the desk as she sat, sending a few bills lazily drifting down onto the thick nap of the carpet. "Oops. I'm so sorry," Miriam bent to retrieve them, fumbling to return the money back onto the ample pile.

The psychic shoved the envelope down into her shopping bag ending the awkward moment.

"I think you need a bigger envelope or a rubber band, or something…" Miriam's voice trailed off, her fingertips drumming against her chin.

"Thank you, Miriam. And thank you for hosting the readings tonight. The room was perfect. How have you been? I know our first reading was challenging for you. It is always difficult for those who are working through grief. Difficult, yet comforting, yes?"

"Yes. But the next day was the best I felt since he left me." She smiled; her freshly-reapplied scarlet lipstick bled onto the skin around her mouth and clung to a front tooth. "Just knowing he was okay, being able to feel him so close again…"

"I'm pleased. Our loved ones are always near us. They are within us. They are the fiber of our hearts." Mrs. Habbibi spoke carefully, her voice a soothing drawl of tenderness.

"I'm ready to talk to him again. There is something I have to know. I know I'm ready now."

"I will try my best, but demanding a contact would be like commanding a butterfly to light on your finger."

"You don't understand. I have to speak with him tonight. You're the only one who can help me," she spoke in rapid fire. "I don't know what else I can do—please." She lurched herself forward.

Mrs. Habbibi's eye lids fluttered, shielding herself from the woman's alcohol-laced spittle. "Try and stay calm. The need for urgency is past. Your son has let you know he is at peace and under God's protection." She held open her palms. "Let's touch hands and quiet our minds. Prepare to open and accept the love surrounding us. We will work from there."

"I have to know something only Garrett can tell me," she persisted. "Please, Mrs. Habbibi."

The psychic withdrew her empty hands. "What is it that is troubling you so, Miriam?"

"My husband—my soon to be ex-husband." She shook her head with a scornful huff. "He stopped by to get some of his things and started pressuring me again to sell the house. My parents bought it for us and Garret was born in this house. We fought and he told me I was impossible and he wouldn't be surprised if Garrett's death was a suicide. I went crazy. He left the house running for his life." She picked at a loose thread on the seam of her dress. "And to think it was my father who started him up in business," she snorted. "Miserable bastard, putting that in my head. It was his fault if it was anyone's— always taking off somewhere. Never being here for his son or me. The business was double the size when my father was alive and he never traveled nearly as much." She began twirling a wisp of her hair around a finger and tugging at it. "Garrett was always difficult." She looked away. "I couldn't handle him on my own when he'd get in one of his moods and take it out on me."

Before Mrs. Habbibi had the chance to consider a response, Miriam leaned further across the desk, pushing her face close with desperation. "I need to know. Don't you understand that I need to know?"

"Yes. I do."

"I don't sleep anymore. I never considered the possibility and now that's all I can think about."

"Words. The power of words. If only the sweet ones had the lasting effect on us as the bitter ones do," the psychic lamented.

"Why would Garrett do that? What could have been so bad? Why would he want to leave me?"

Mrs. Habbibi stared off in contemplation and after an artful pause returned. "It is said that we each will our own deaths. In the deepest subconscious, where our cosmic intelligence resides, our soul knows when our work on this plane is done. So couldn't it be said that every death is a suicide?"

The woman pondered for a moment, but her grief stood close guard, refusing to allow her to even consider the poignant response. "I want to know. I won't have peace until I know."

"Peace?"

"Yes. Peace," Miriam said defiantly.

"How bold are we to expect both peace and motherhood? These are the two most divine states that one can hope to possess in our physical world. Don't you see you have been given both?"

Miriam huffed.

"What else could ever hurt more than being separated from the soul that took form in that of your child? What else could you possibly fear? As painful as this reality is, you will come to realize your experience together has met its purpose. Perhaps it has cleared the path for you to attain your divine purpose."

"Why? Why does it have to be this way?" Miriam twisted away from the desk and began weeping.

"The human existence, turbulent with its complex emotions is a mystery I do not claim to comprehend. But I cannot accept the struggles we endure in this, our physical form, are without purpose. Perhaps the lessons earned are payment for passage to spiritual evolution."

The woman scoffed, hopelessly impenetrable from heartache. "You

certainly have a way with words, Mrs. Habbibi. I have to say that much."
She snatched a tissue from the box on the desk and blew her nose.

"It pleases me that you find comfort in our exchanges, but there is
something I need to tell you, Miriam," the psychic deftly shifted her
approach.

"What?' The woman's head jerked in her direction.

"I was hoping it would disburse, but I sense there is harmful discord around you. I felt it as soon as you sat down—the effect of your
husband's destructive words, an incubus? I cannot say, but it means to
harm you. Its presence may be the very thing blocking contact tonight."

"Can you try again?"

"Ha. I will try if you'd like, but just as important, your protective
aura needs to be fortified."

"I don't follow what you're saying."

"I believe that you have sustained a psychic breech. I've seen it occur
before. It's quite common in people who have suffered an emotional
trauma or are under prolonged psychological stress. Would you say that
applies to you?"

"Yes."

"These conditions make one highly susceptible to these types of astral attacks. But I don't want you to worry. There are methods to coun-
teract this type of damage and shield the victim from further infiltra-
tion. As long as the subject is capable of being receptive, that is."

"I can be receptive." Miriam puffed up in defense. "How does it
work?"

"A daily candle. I can burn a meditative candle with the intention
of your spiritual healing and strengthening your psychic self-defense
to deflect the negative powers at work against you. The treatment is
quite powerful. But ultimately its success will depend on the subject. It
requires their full intent to manifest."

"Okay. How much does it cost?"

"I have never put a fixed price on the service. As the conduit, the
positive energy of a successful treatment flows directly back to me, a

compensation in itself. So I have learned that the practice is most effective when I let my client determine its value."

"That's so beautiful. You're a good woman, Mrs. Habbibi." Miriam rested her palms over her heart. "What do other clients offer you?"

"Generally the fee for three readings, although it requires far more time and intensive application."

"That seems fair. And how long does it take to see results?"

"One lunar month. Twenty-eight days. And if reinforced with strict adherence to the personalized daily meditations I will subscribe along with sufficient exposure to open air, within ten days there is usually a marked lightning of the aura."

"Is there any way to speed it up? I can't wait that long to hear from my son again. "

"When you are lying in the sun do you presume to hasten the effectiveness of its rays?"

Miriam blinked in confusion.

"It is a natural process. These things cannot be rushed."

"I've already waited so long to get my appointment with you. I can't wait that long again," she begged.

"Let me ease your fears, Miriam. What if I promise to let you host my readings here in your home again within a month so your appointment is secured? By then, your aura should be cleared and we can try another contact."

"Okay." Miriam sat up with hopefulness. "Do you really think this treatment will work for me?" She nibbled furiously at her nails, stopping herself abruptly when she took notice of Mrs. Habbibi observing her.

The psychic's face lit up and her eyes bore into Miriam's. "I will make sure it does."

Miriam Stemple sat up with a giggle bolstered by Mrs. Habbibi's confidence in her methods.

"So the evening is not a total disappointment to you…" Mrs. Habbibi reached down into her shopping bag and carefully removed her deck from its silk pouch. "Let's see what the Tarot wants to share with you tonight." She shuffled with style.

"The train station, please." Mrs. Habbibi let her body go limp against the taxi's worn upholstery before it even jerked into reverse. The driver completed his maneuver out of the driveway, passing Miriam Stemple's silhouette, a motionless figure in her front door watching as the car pulled away from the house. "Would you mind turning the heater off, please?" She removed her eyeglasses.

The solitude became a haven even in the stale air of the beat-up cab. In the darkness of the backseat she wiggled her mouthpiece loose and ran her tongue over her top teeth. The taste of the adhesive made saliva pool at her jaws. She spit into a tissue and stared off into the night through the window, dotted with the remnants from earlier rain until a pothole challenged the worn shocks, jolting her back to the present. She leaned her head back and closed her eyes for the rest of the short ride. Mrs. Habbibi never drove herself to appointments; it was always a cab to the train station.

She stood high above street level over the Long Island Rail Road station, a lone passenger in the late hour, bracing herself against a gust of vindictive wind that whipped across the elevated concrete platform and darted down the endless vista of lonely track. She eyed her Camry sitting in the municipal lot below as her breath rose and disappeared into the frigid air. She contorted the shape of her mouth; *human smoke signals,* she laughed to herself, and it wasn't too long before a train rumbled into the desolate station. Its destination didn't matter; she would be getting off at the next stop; a practice that would make it difficult for anyone following her to go unnoticed. There had been situations.

As squeaking brakes and hissing engines brought the 11:25pm to a gradual stop she looked behind with practiced casualness and glided inside the train the instant its doors rolled opened. The car was empty. She sat. The doors slid closed. She allowed herself to exhale as the train rocked left and right, slowly rolling out of the lonely station. There was just enough time to pop out her contact lenses, slip off her shoes and change into her Nikes before the next stop.

She trotted down the dark stairwell coated in pigeon droppings and disappeared into the waiting room, slipping into the public restroom. Flipping the latch on the stall door, she made quick work of her routine. She gently peeled off the prosthetic nose and carefully removed her wig; expensive, made of human hair, she shook it out and hung it on the stall hook. Leaning forward, she emancipated her long, dark hair with audible relief as she scratched her scalp with vigor.

She swung her head up and pulled her hair back in a loose ponytail and stepped out of the padded skirt. Black running tights clung to her thighs and her tee-shirt rode up as her arms went over her head to wiggle out of the boxy, over-sized, sweater. Jozette Moreau was forty-one years old, but favorable genes and obsessive personal upkeep permitted her to pass for younger. She pulled a fashionable, thigh-length jacket from the shopping bag and replaced it with the items she'd just shed.

At the sink, she swished a mouthful of water, spit, and began the systematic process of swabbing her face clean of expertly applied make-up with a packet of high-end facial wipes, tossing each sienna-stained cloth into the trash. She dabbed her face dry, lovingly lost in her reflection and then, as if jolted from a daydream, abruptly turned and whisked out the door.

She spryly took the stairs two at a time back up onto the platform to catch the next train, reversing the direction she had just come from. She leaned against a billboard, peeling off her press-on nails, casually flicking them onto the tracks while she waited.

2

The Previous Summer

It was well after eleven o'clock on a suffocating, hot July evening when Josie arrived at her elderly mother's home. It was a two-story, salt box sized house in an old neighborhood in Midwood Brooklyn that had belonged to her mother's fourth husband. It was the only possession the unassuming, retired bus driver had left to his name when he died that Vera hadn't swindled out of him during their short marriage.

Inside, Josie's older sister, Simone sat in the living room beading a bridal veil for a private client. Her two Dachshunds, snoring at her feet, came alive barking when they heard the rapping on the kitchen door.

"Trixie, Darla!" Simone tried to shush them as she carefully laid the headpiece on the arm of her recliner. But it was too late—her mailman husband, Raymond was watching her from across the living room where he had fallen asleep in front of the television.

She mashed out her cigarette in an Atlantic City souvenir ashtray and stumbled over the dogs weaving between her bare feet as all three of them scurried for the door.

Twelve years apart, each sibling born from different fathers, the sisters' lives were eternally bound together by the events of their tragic childhood. Simone, the eldest, was a gifted seamstress; she also worked weekends as a manicurist at a local shop. Jozette, the family's shining star, held a continuous string of odd jobs, her latest and most consistent to date, a beauty consultant at a popular Brighton Beach hair salon. Marilla, the youngest, a shift supervisor for a freight forwarder, had long ago distanced herself from the hard luck family.

In the kitchen, Simone peered through the split in the curtains and unlocked the door to a duet of worn hinges and wind chimes.

"Hello, pretty little girlies. You're so happy to see your, Auntie Jo?" She knelt in the doorway, affectionately cooing to the bouncing Dachshunds as if it were midday.

"Keep your voice down. Do you know what time it is? What are you doing here?"

"Is that any way to greet a guest?" Josie stood, swaying across the cramped, dated kitchen.

"We just finally got her into bed. She had another bad day." Simone gestured towards the front porch which had been converted to a bedroom for Vera when she became too ill to make the stairs any longer.

"I told you—have her doctor prescribe something to knock her out for the night."

"She's already on too many medications. I'm afraid of the interactions."

"Does it matter at this point?" Josie dropped into a chair and slid a fold of bills across the kitchen table; her sister's cut of the evening's profits from the unsuspecting clients Simone funneled to her, posing as Miss Ruby, the psychic.

Simone snatched up the money and stuffed it down into her bra, nudging her chin toward the living room.

Josie's rolled her eyes with indifference.

"And why did you bring that in here?" Simone whispered, referring to the shopping bag containing her Miss Ruby paraphernalia.

"I need you to hold onto it here for me. Tommy's been acting up and I wouldn't put it past him to snoop in the trunk of my car. I don't need any problems from him."

Simone snatched the bag and hastily shoved it into an overstuffed cabinet with her knee.

"Hey, be careful," Josie scolded her, pulling a bottle of Evian water out of her purse.

Simone sat at the table and peeled the wrapper off of a fresh pack of

Merit Lights. "So what's the latest drama with psycho Tommy?"

"Let's just say it's not working out between us." Josie took a swig of water to wash down a Valium. It was her new drug of choice to combat chronic anxiety after her latest attempt to kick her anti-depressant addiction resulted in an emergency room visit for a seizure.

"What a surprise." Simone held a lighter to her cigarette. "And I don't like to see you still eating those things."

"I'm good, Simmy. Worry about yourself. Do you know how bad those cigarettes are for your skin?" Josie grimaced.

Simone exhaled into the air above her head. "So I thought you said this one was a great guy?"

"Great guy? He left his wife and a newborn to be with me."

"That didn't bother you when you let him move in with you."

"I can always count on you to throw me under the bus." Josie swatted at the passing cloud of cigarette smoke. "That was before I knew he was a paranoid lunatic." She glanced up from rummaging in her handbag. "And, he offered to take over my rent payments. I was able to start up my Restylane shots again." She swept her finger tips up over her cheek bones.

Simone glanced up at the cat-shaped wall clock, its tail, wagging off the seconds against the faded print of the wallpaper. "Where does he think you are now?"

"At my monthly make-up party. And he's not home anyway." She tilted her head back to squeeze in eye drops. "It's his four-year-old's birthday and he promised to spend the night back in his house with the fam for the brat—Oh, hi, Raymond." Josie's voice took on the lazy drawl she reserved for males.

"What's she doing here?" He stumbled over to the refrigerator, adjusting his pants over his doughy belly.

"What are you asking me for?" Simone bristled.

"I came to see my mother. I heard she's had a few bad days."

"Right." He said, pushing a slice of leftover meatloaf into his mouth.

"I was telling Simmy, I think we should ask her doctor to prescribe something to help her sleep –"

He cut her off, and turned on his wife. "Don't let me find out that you're still in on it with her. I swear I'll call the cops myself." He switched off the feeble air conditioner grinding away in the peeling frame of a kitchen window.

"Really Raymond?" Simone cocked her head at him. "Don't forget to tell them about all the mail you swiped for us when you get them on the phone." She reached around, reviving the aged appliance with a defiant twist of her wrist and went back to her cigarette.

"I made a mistake." He plucked a splotch of meat and gravy off of his undershirt and popped it back into his mouth. "I got a pension to lose if someone goes to the cops on her."

"You weren't worried about that when you ordered your premium package TV or when you were eating your steak house dinners."

"Ever hear of quittin while you're ahead, bird brain?"

Simone began to turn towards him with the lethal calm of an alligator.

"Come on you two, cut it out," Josie headed them off before it could escalate to Simone hurling dishware. "We have a solid client base now. It's steady income if we all just stay cool."

"I told you, I'm out." Raymond turned his back to her. "Do you ever think of what could happen if she messes with the wrong person?" he drilled Simone.

"What wrong person? We know who all of the clients are—and she's finally starting to pay back the money she borrowed from us, so where's the problem?"

Josie dropped her water bottle back into her purse. "I didn't come here to make any trouble. I just want to peek in on Vera and I'm leaving."

"Good. Good-bye." Raymond stalked out of the kitchen. "Don't be an idiot your whole life, Simone…" His voice faded as he climbed the stairs to the second floor. "She's gonna screw you one way or the other."

"At least someone is," she called after him, pushing her hands through her own thick, dark hair, cropped far shorter than Josie's and rogue with grays. "Sorry-ass, schnook. He never did have any balls." She ground down the butt into the ashtray.

Josie grinned. "Forget it. Let it go. Lots of people lose their nerve when real money starts coming in – go figure." She hoisted her handbag over a shoulder as she stood. "I could never put up with that from a man."

"Or anything else from any man you've ever been with."

"I've never had to," Josie coolly referred to her beauty, still disarming at forty-one.

Simone watched her disappear down the dark hallway.

The sisters shared the same dramatic bone structure, but a broken nose suffered when she was a teen marred Simone's natural beauty. She also walked with an uneven gait from a fractured ankle that had gone untreated. Both maladies and a nervous twitch were permanent reminders of a childhood stolen by a tyrant, drunkard stepfather, Martin, Vera's fourth husband.

Simone left home at seventeen, stranding herself in a loveless marriage due to a teenage pregnancy and over the years, had stowed away all of life's disappointments around her midsection, unlike Josie, whose used her figure, and every asset she could manipulate as an effective seductive device.

Josie stood in the doorway watching her mother sleep in the faint glow of the nightlight casting the tiny room in shadows. It was as if she was checking in on a baby; the blankets tucked neatly under her chin, lying peacefully, alone in the tiny room.

Her sister's voice carried from the kitchen. "Please, God, don't wake her, you get to go home," Simone complained over the clanking of dry dog food hitting the metal bowls she shook from an oversized bag.

The Valium was kicking in. The stifling warmth in the compact space and the droning hum of the oxygen machine made her feel woozy. She grabbed hold of the bed rail to regain her balance. The pungent odor of urine left in the rental commode stung her nostrils as she stepped between the single bed and the walker to the unframed photo Vera kept at the bedside, leaning against a lamp.

It was a faded image of what presumably was her mother's fondest memory. A life that never exceeded the illusion the camera had borne witness to. Josie picked up the timeworn snapshot. The past stared back; Simone, holding Marilla's hand in front of the house on St. John Street on a summer day, looking on while Vera struck a glamorous pose, sitting on the front steps in a broad-brimmed hat, her head tilted back in a carefree laugh, baby Isabelle held in her arms and Josie at her hip, gazing up with star struck wonder at the larger-than-life beauty who was their mother.

Josie looked down at the sleeping old lady, searching for a trace of the woman in the photo and then her thoughts went to the man holding the camera. She put the photo back in its place and returned into the brightness of the kitchen. "I'll be back for my bag in a few days."

The wind chimes tinkled as she left the house.

Her headlights illuminated Tommy's burly frame as she pulled into the parking lot of her apartment building. He strode towards her as she stepped out of her car, being tugged in her direction by her dog, Pharaoh.

"How long have you been out here?" she snapped at him, kneeling to meet the overjoyed Doberman Pincer's eager welcome. "Aren't you supposed to be at your daughter's birthday party?"

"The bitch started in with me. I had to get the hell outta there."

"And you couldn't think of anything else to do but wait for me out here?" She rose, snatching Pharaoh's leash from him.

He followed closely behind her.

"I stopped by to see my mother." She started and then spun around sensing his encroachment. "Are you sniffing me you head case?" She stalked ahead into the building.

An hour later Tommy was sitting up in her canopy bed, naked, hard, and waiting for her when she finally emerged in a shampoo-scented cloud of steam from the bathroom. His imposing size, shaven head and the menacing brawn of his body looked ridiculously out of place in the decisively feminine decor of her bedroom.

She dropped her towel and slipped under the sheet.

"You smell good." He leaned into her, running his hand over the smooth curve of her hip.

She jerked away from him.

In a single motion, as if she were as weightless as a rag doll, he pulled her across the bed and up on top of him.

"Let's just forget it for tonight," she said, looking up at the ceiling.

He yanked her down against his body. "Let's not."

His thick arms snaked around her as she tried to wiggle away, crushing her closer and closer into his massive chest. Her thighs bumped against his strong erection as she thrashed to free herself from his powerful hold, but he only squeezed tighter, systematically compressing the air from her lungs with his rib-crushing constrictions. She fought him until the lack of air rendered her motionless.

"Tommy," she finally begged in surrender, her eyes squeezed shut against the suffocating pressure.

He waited several heartbeats before releasing her and before she could draw a breath he jerked her upwards, setting her down onto his hips with a neck-snapping jolt. His eyes twinkled in the erratic shadows of the television light, his face awash in sadistic delight as he watched her gulp in air.

She spat in his face and glared with amusement as his expression flitted from shock to rage and threw her head back, bursting into a fit of wild laughter.

His face contorted with confusion before he let himself join her, running his hand through her damp hair, down the side of her flushed face, pinching her lips between a firm thumb and forefinger. "You are one crazy bitch." He laughed with deranged affection.

She let her body go limp, catching her breath in the soft, thick forest of his chest and slithered downward.

Weeks Later

A rainy July lagged into August and an oppressive humidity pressed down on the city, discouraging activity and forcing most to retreat indoors for refuge in air conditioning.

The night air did not offer much relief as Miss Ruby wearily climbed out of a cab, shopping bag in tow. Feeling particularly anxious, it felt good to be on her feet again, back under her own steam. She had performed her usual prayer of protection after the evenings reading which was usually effective in dissipating the residue of her clients' energy, but uneasiness still nagged this night.

She decided on a Valium and to walk the last few blocks to the train to help ease her anxiety.

She paused to swipe at the perspiration trickling between her breasts, taking notice of the full moon soundlessly exacting reverence, suspended in the heavens above her. *A colossal circle of parchment paper covering a giant light bulb,* she observed; nature was always a friend in centering her.

The sticky asphalt released up the day's heat around her ankles as moved through the eerily quiet streets, taking note of the discordant energy that seemed to own the night: the distant whining of a car alarm carrying from blocks away, a faulty street light buzzing overhead, flickering for help, and the sooty innards of a disabled city bus exposed, stranded at the curb. She turned her thoughts to the cool shower and sitcom reruns waiting for her when she arrived home. Tommy was spending the next few days with his four-year-old. It would be just her and sweet Pharaoh snuggling in the crisp sheets.

"Missus, Missus. Wait, please." A thick Russian accent in a cheerful tone stopped her midstep. She had no idea where they had appeared from, two burly phantoms in dark clothing.

"Missus, wait–" they were rushing towards her.

On her left, her eye caught a white van rolling up the opposite end of the street at an oddly slow pace. The tsunami of adrenaline flooding her body made it hard to think. She ran through a few quick scenarios. Should she stop and face them? Should she run? She eyed the park on the other side of the station and twisted the straps of her canvas bag higher up around her wrist in preparation.

"Hey, come on Missus, stop. I just want please to talk to you." They were trotting now.

She turned. Panic ensued the moment she made eye contact with the hard-featured, scowling Russian. She pushed back her rising terror and kicked out of her low-heeled sling backs and took off running.

The stockier one of the pair lunged for her. The seconds the men stood gaping at the wig clenched in his fist gave her a lifesaving head start. Arms pumping, legs digging in, she sprinted across the expanse of the spotty lawn in her long skirt and stocking feet, her bulky shopping bag slapping against her leg in an incidental rhythm. She headed for the dark backdrop of trees looming in the distance backlit by the incandescent moon, majestic and ever indifferent to the goings on it illuminated far below.

She knew better than to look back. An avid runner fueled by fierce vanity; she knew how to meld into her pace, to become fused with it, faster and faster. She was just hitting stride when the distant vengeful voice cut through the moist, heavy air heralding her successful escape.

"Suka! (Bitch) We're going to find you."

"What the hell happened to you?" Simone scanned Josie's disheveled mop of dark hair and her face glistening with sweat. "Get in here." She stuck her head out the door, checking both directions before locking it.

Josie hopped across the kitchen and fell into a chair, dropping her bag onto the floor.

"What happened to your face?" Simone squinted at scratches tracked across her sister's cheek. "Tommy?"

"Bushes." She pushed out of her sneakers revealing tattered stockings, bloodied and covered with mud.

"Oh, jeez." Simone jerked her head away when Josie turned up the sole of her foot.

"What the hell happened?" Her voice rose in panic. "Do you want to go to the hospital?"

"Now, there's an idea." Josie glanced up through cutting eyes and continued to tentatively peel off her knee-high stocking.

"Did someone get a hold of you?"

"No. I probably wouldn't be sitting here if they had." She pulled another chair closer to prop her foot on. "I got it running through the park. Just get me a glass of water and some paper towels, would you, please?"

Simone scrambled to the counter.

Josie reached into her purse and popped a Valium into her mouth. "Arrrgh." She winced facing the injury her body had already known was serious.

"You shouldn't have come here." Simone stood over her, water glass in hand.

Josie's head jerked up. "Really?" She glared.

"That's not how I meant it." Simone lowered her voice to a whisper, looking towards the living room. "You should have called me. I would have met you somewhere else—Trixie! Darla! Git! Get outta there." Simone shooed her dogs that had begun licking at the blood dripping onto the worn linoleum.

"Oh, boy, that's deep." She folded her arms across her breasts as she stood looking on.

Raymond staggered into the kitchen, blinking against the light, while smoothing down his hair. "What's going on?" He squinted across the room at Josie working on her foot.

Even hunched over in pain, bleeding, she still managed a calm, casual ease in her greeting. "Hi, Raymond."

"What the hell happened to her?" he demanded.

Simone chewed her lip in silence.

He stuck his beefy face up into Josie's. "What'd someone chase you down, Jo?"

"I thought I might have been being followed by some creeps at the train station. I took some detours just to be sure—it's nothing, Ray."

"Nothing?" He cringed at her blood-soaked sneaker lying on its side. "And she came here? How does she know she wasn't followed?"

"Would you just please go up to bed, Raymond? This has nothing to do with the readings."

Both of their eyes darted to the shopping bag on the floor near the table.

"I warned you." He thrust a finger up into his wife's face. "She's not going to be satisfied until somebody kicks the door in on us." He spun and bent at the sink slurping from the faucet.

"That's never going to happen." Josie looked up from probing at her foot. "You know how careful I am. I know what I'm doing."

"Right." He smirked at the growing puddle of blood pooling beneath her chair, wiping his mouth with the back of his hand. "Why can't you just leave us alone? Get yourself straightened out. Has it ever crossed your mind you can't spend money from a jail cell or with a bullet between your eyes?" He jammed his finger into the bridge of his nose.

"There's always a risk factor in any entrepreneurial venture."

"Do you hear that?" His palms went up to the sides of his head. "She's sitting there bleeding and that's what she has to say. She's out of her mind. Just like the bunch of you."

"Keep screaming Raymond. Hopefully you'll give yourself a heart attack." Simone sat at the table.

"That's it!" His fleshy arms crisscrossed his body like an umpire making a close call at home plate. "I don't want her back in this house! She's got nothing to lose and she's taking you along for the ride."

"*You* don't want her back? This is my mother's house. I decide who stays or goes." The veins bulged in Simone's neck.

"You do that." He stormed out of the kitchen, his voice booming as he climbed the stairs. "I'll finally be rid of you and your whole crazy family."

Simone shot out of her chair.

"Sit down, Simmy, would you please?" Josie sighed. "You're going to give yourself a stroke." She continued to work whatever was imbedded in her foot closer to the surface.

Simone sat and held a lighter to her cigarette with a shaking hand. "Maybe I'll get lucky and he'll be on the same shift when someone goes postal and sprays the place." She scooted her chair closer into the table pulling in a long, lung inflating drag of her cigarette. "So let's hear it."

Josie lowered her voice to a whisper, her eyes shifting to the staircase. "I was trailed to the station after the readings tonight."

"Who do you think it was?" Simone's voice was hushed. "Not one of mine, I hope."

"No. One of mine and I don't think, I know who it was."

Simone gave a nudge of her chin, blowing a stream of smoke out of the side of her mouth.

"Elena, the esthetician at the salon." Her voice dropped even lower. "It had to be her boyfriend, Yuri's people."

Simone's face tightened with fear. "How do you know that?" The end of her cigarette glowed with her nervous inhale.

"Two over-sized goons with Russian accents trying to get me to stop for them."

"Could it just have been foreigners needing directions? Maybe you overreacted?"

"When was the last time someone who wanted directions from you grabbed for your throat and then chased you across a park?"

"Josie!" Simone hushed, her voice a combination of fear and sympathy.

"It's bad. I know."

"Out of all the people. Why would you even consider giving Elena a reading knowing who her boyfriend was, let alone a second and third?"

"She just needed to hear she could trust her intuition."

"Did you really just say that? You're taking this whole Miss Ruby thing too seriously. I think you're starting to enjoy it a little too much." Simone pushed up from the table and ran her cigarette under the faucet.

"I got an extra three-hundred dollars out of her on her first visit to burn a protection candle. So yeah, I am enjoying it." Josie gathered her hair at the back of her neck. "And who do you think goes to a psychic, people who don't have problems? It's desperate people looking for somebody else to make their decisions for them."

"Oh, is that right? Well, making this stupid Russian bitch's decisions for her could have had you in two pieces of fish food tonight." She pulled a box of first aid items out of a cabinet and handed Josie a tweezers. "What was her problem?"

"I had already read her twice before. She left messages this week offering double and then triple to move up another appointment. She was frantic. Torn over staying here or breaking off her engagement and going back to Russia." Josie gritted her teeth, drawing a jagged shard of amber glass out of the fleshy split in her heel. She held it up between her fingers. "Beer bottle."

"Hold your breath, Jo." Simone squirted antiseptic into the angry gash. "So why'd she want to call off the wedding?" She steadied Josie's heel now cascading bubbling peroxide and watery blood.

Grimacing, Josie spoke behind bared teeth. "She realized that Yuri was an animal."

"Like she didn't know that before she said 'yes' to him? Everybody at your place knows that he's mobbed up. How'd she think that slob became the owner? His love of hairstyling?" She propped her sister's foot on her thigh and began to bandage it.

"I guess she started to find out more about him than she would have liked. She's only been in the country for about a year or so. But the thing that drove her to the psychic was when a friend of theirs mysteriously stopped coming around. She was in denial, but it was eating her up. She knew that Yuri had something to do with it."

"Really?" Simone smiled with amusement and tore off a strip of first aid tape from the roll with her teeth. "That's some exciting little shop you work in, over there in Little Russia."

"And then, when the missing guy's girlfriend came to them begging for help finding him, knowing that Yuri was the last person he was with before he went missing....Elena knew for sure, but she didn't let on."

"Do you think this Elena was dumb enough to tell Yuri she was going to a psychic?"

"I'm thinking, no. Elena's English may not be so *goods,* but she's no dope. I've eaten lunch with her a few times at the shop. She probably started acting weird and he picked up on it and had her followed."

"She was one of your clients tonight?"

"Yeah. She brought me the missing guy's favorite watch. The girl-friend gave it to her to see if it could help me find out if he was dead or just in hiding."

"Dumb bitches. You asked her to bring it to you?"

"Not the watch, exactly—a piece of jewelry or a personal possession belonging to the missing party. It's a great hook and it gets me another reading out of 'em."

"What'd you do with it?"

"I told her to leave it with me—I needed to..." she donned her thick, exotic Miss Ruby accent, *"clear the many shades of death the possession already had attached to it with a cleansing ceremony* before I would know for sure."

Simone shook her head with a smirk. "How do you come up with that stuff?"

A smile spread across Josie's angular face. "I scare myself sometimes."

"What kind of watch was it?"

"A Rollie, of course. These Russians love American status symbols. Here, I'll show it to you." She reached down into her bag and handed her sister the weighty arm piece.

"Yowza." Simone bobbed the diamond-encrusted watch up and down in her palm. "I can't believe this woman left this with you. How stupid could these Russian bimbos be?"

"It wasn't stupidity. It was fear. Fear makes people do stupid things."

"So what are you going to do with it?"

"Don't think I'll be reading Elena again anytime soon," she smirked. "You hold on to it. Maybe we'll sell it. The resale on a mid-range Rolex is eighteen grand. That model has the diamond bezel. Enjoy it in the meantime."

Simone clipped the watch on her wrist. "Gotta get a link or two taken out." She rotated her wrist, admiring the ostentatious piece.

"Nice. I think the chunky look of a man's watch is sexy on a woman." Josie flexed her ankle, testing her sister's bandaging job.

"How's it feel?"

"Good. I'm just worried about how I'm going to stand all day tomorrow without this thing splitting open on me. You know how busy Fridays are."

"You're going into work tomorrow? That's a mistake." Simone shook her head. "What if you're right and those were Yuri's guys tonight? He's got creeps in and out of that place all the time. What if the wrong person notices you limping around, the scratches on your face…"

"I'd bring more attention to myself if I wasn't there, and the only thing they have is a wig." She shook her head and ticked. "A damn expensive one—and a pair of old lady's sandals."

"How'd they get your sandals?"

"I was running for my life. You can't run in sling backs. I had to kick out of them."

"An old lady who can outrun a man… I gotta tell you, Josie, I got a bad feeling about this." She stood.

"Well, thanks for that."

"Raymond was right. We should have quit while we were ahead." She slid the first aid box back into the cabinet.

"You're getting the yips on me, now, too?" She looked up at the floor above them. "There is absolutely no possible connection to us." She caressed the top of her foot. "I'm just going to tape this thing up real good and wear a funky dress that works with my cowboy boots. Covering these scratches is the easy part. And besides, I want to see if Elena shows up tomorrow. Maybe I can get a feel for what's going on."

"And what if she doesn't show up? Simone bent to her dogs' water bowl and refilled it at the sink.

"It's out of our hands. They're barbaric immigrants. It's like Chicago in the 1930s here for them."

"You're out of business, Josie. You know that, don't you? You can't give anymore readings."

Staring off, Josie ran a soft touch over her lips, lost in thought.

"They'll slit your throat if they ever find out it's you," Simone whispered.

The startling ring of Josie's cell phone at the late hour in the quiet kitchen sent the metal water bowl in Simone's hand crashing onto the kitchen floor.

"Relax, would you? It's my private number." Josie glared at her, masking her own jangled nerves as she dug in her bag. She looked at the phone. "It's just Tommy."

Simone placed her hand on her chest with relief, the metal bowl wobbling to a stop in a puddle at her feet.

Josie shook the hair from her face with a quick toss of her head as if preparing to speak publicly. "Hi, baby. I stopped to see my sister. Are you serious? You really need to get a grip on yourself." She held the phone out. "Say hello, Simmy." Josie rolled her eyes.

"Hi, Tommy."

"I didn't realize the time. I stopped by after work to give her a hand with my mother and we dropped a glass, I stepped on a piece. …Yeah it went in pretty deep. We're just finishing up, bandaging it. Okay, I didn't think you'd be home until Sunday night. I'm leaving right now." She snapped the phone shut and began to gather her belongings.

"You're afraid of him aren't you?"

"Let's just say it's time to leave."

"I'd be careful how you exit this one. I only met him that once, but I could tell that he wasn't all up there." She twisted her finger at her temple.

"I know how to handle him."

"What are you gonna do?"

"Nothing for right now. I have to be smart and ease myself out of there *and* the salon.

"And go where?" Simone sat, wet dish towel clutched in her hand.

"Maybe I'll ask to stay at Marilla's until I can figure something out. Long Island is loaded with salons."

Simone looked as if she just drank sour milk. "Marilla? Her and that creepy Charlotte. Charles, Charlie—whatever she calls herself."

Josie managed a grin. "She did better with Charlotte than any man she could have ever hoped to snatch up, that's for sure."

Simone shook off a chill.

"It's a mother figure thing for Mimi, how don't you get that?"

"You've been dipping into too many of those psychology books and I don't care what it is. I'd rather take my chances with the Russians than ask Marilla for any favors."

"It's not the Russians I'm worried about."

3

The South Shore of Long Island

"The view is as incredible as ever." Josie stood on the second floor deck of the beach house her younger sister Marilla shared with her partner, Charlotte, a retired school psychologist. The rays of the midday, October sun struggled to give warmth, but shimmered brilliantly off of the subdued Atlantic and played in the soft violet hues in both sisters' dark hair; the breeze combing it back off of their impossibly-flawless skin.

Josie zipped up her jacket and pulled in a full breath of crisp, sea-salted air. "You don't know how grateful I am, Mimi."

"Grateful to me? I'd rather you were grateful for escaping another deadly relationship. And it was Charlee who talked me into letting you stay here." She walked to the corner of the deck and stared off further east, down the hazy Long Island shoreline at the Jones Beach inlet that jutted out into the ocean.

Josie pressed a kiss on the older woman's weathered cheek.

"I didn't have a problem with you staying inside." Charlotte took a hand out of the pocket of her khaki-colored cargo pants and ran it through her shorn, graying hair. It's just my boys ..."

"We didn't want to chance your baby snacking on Charlee's Siamese." Marilla referred to Pharaoh waiting patiently in the car. "And we knew you wouldn't let him sleep alone, so we set you two up in the guesthouse." Her sister gestured across the lower deck.

"The pool house?" Josie snorted an incredulous laugh.

"You've got a better offer?"

The three women clumped down the wooden stairs to the ground level, dotted with patio furniture safety tucked in with plastic covers for their winter sleep. They passed a rock fountain silenced for the season. In warmer weather it flowed into the swimming pool, now sealed with a taut, green tarpaulin.

"You'll need to come up into the house when you want to use the kitchen, but you'll have your own bathroom and your privacy out here." She handed Josie a single key hanging on a dolphin keychain.

"I'll make it work. You've helped me out of a bad spot. "

"It's not the first time. I'm sure it won't be the last." Marilla propped up a fallen wind catcher.

"I've already found a job, so I'll be gone most of the day. And you don't have to worry about the pussy cats. You know what a chicken Pharaoh is, he'd be more afraid of them."

"A job already? That's impressive," Charlotte complimented.

"I'm not surprised," Marilla said. "Jozette presents very well. Where this time?"

"Up on the North shore, Salon 99. Ever hear of it?"

"No. There are slews of salons up there. Salons, overpriced boutiques and snooty restaurants to show it all off in. You're going to be right at home."

"That's her way of complimenting me." Josie winked at Charlotte.

"Do you need help unloading your car?"

"No, thanks. I left most of my things at my mother's house. Simone made room in the garage for me. I'm not planning on staying long."

Marilla's tone became terse at the mention of their sister's name. "You know that I work nights a few shifts a week. Charlotte is usually home in her studio, but if she's not," she pointed to the upper deck. "There's a key on top of the lantern over the sliders. And Jozette, I don't want to get into any family discussions while you're here." She busied herself straightening a stack of empty flower pots.

"You won't. But, just let me tell you, Vera's not doing well. I don't want you to have any regrets."

Marilla spun around her tone defiant. "It's not me who has to worry about having regrets. I have to get ready for work." She turned her back and headed towards the stairs.

"I'll get started bringing in my things."

"You can stay as long as you need to. The main concern is your safety." Charlotte gave Josie's shoulder a friendly pat and followed after Marilla.

Josie mouthed a humble thank you and watched them climb the stairs back into the house, the shade dropping on the patio doors as soon as they disappeared inside.

Marilla flung herself into a chair and covered her head with her arms like a child on the kitchen table.

"What's wrong?" Charlotte took the seat across from her.

Marilla straightened. "Why can't they just leave me alone? I'm so annoyed with myself for letting you talk me into allowing her to stay here."

"Why? It was the right thing to do. It could be an opportunity for the two of you to reconnect; especially now with your mother's condition. How long has it been now, over six years? You proved your point. Think of the future. That's your family."

"My family: a delusional, alcoholic mother who tossed her kids aside for an unattainable modeling career; one sister who is a violent, loose cannon and the other an impetuous, destructive narcissist. All of them scrounging for anyone they can pour their misery onto."

"It was tough on all of you, but treating Josie like a stray animal is not helping you or her. I wish you would try and be a bit more sympathetic. You were younger than your sisters. You were spared a lot of the abuse they suffered. To be honest with you, I think we should let her stay in the guest room. I can keep the boys upstairs."

"Don't even mention it." Marilla bolted, upright. "Everyone who has ever tried to help Jozette winds up regretting it. I'm going against my better judgment letting her stay in the pool house. You have no idea what you're dealing with." The petite woman pressed her fingertips to her eyelids. "And now I'm going to be a wreck until she's out of here."

"Don't blame her for that." Charlotte looked away from her. "Are you crying? What's wrong?"

"Just seeing her still on the run, after all these years, so unsettled. It just makes me so sad." Marilla wept into her hands.

Charlotte moved to the other side of the table and wrapped her arms around her as she cried. "I'm sorry, Mim. If I realized having her here was going to have this effect on you…"

Marilla twisted away, wiping at her tears. "It's not like I'm unsympathetic, I just get a sick feeling in the pit of my stomach whenever she's around. It's like I'm always waiting for the other shoe to drop."

"I understand. There is a feeling of desperation about her."

"She works so hard at coming off in control, but I've always known that something terrible is going to end up happening to her," she sobbed deeply. "And I feel horrible because I just don't want to know about it."

Charlotte kissed her cheek as she pushed herself up from the table. "I'm going to make you a cup of tea."

"I just don't get it." Marilla stood and began to pace. "Why does she have to be so reckless? Everything about her." She held her hand to her forehead. "It's almost as if she thrives on turmoil. Just look at her choice of pet. Isn't that breed notorious for turning on their owners?"

"Counter phobic," Charlotte said quietly as she filled the kettle at the sink.

"What?"

"A person who overcompensates for their fears by putting themselves right in harm's way."

"Huh?"

"I know; it seems to defy logic. Think of it as a subconscious defense mechanism to manage chronic anxiety. You know her history. It's pretty obvious."

"Then how come I'm not one?"

"Everyone responds to emotional trauma differently and everyone is not as resilient as you are." Charlotte's smile was tender.

"Jozette, not resilient? Don't let her act fool you." Marilla sat down at the table. "My sister would be the lone survivor of the Zombie Apocalypse." She couldn't help but grin at her partner's contagious giggle.

"She is a complex character, that's for sure." Charlotte said, laughing. "But it's just a temporary situation. You're doing the right thing. I'm proud of you." She patted Marilla's hand. "We'll do just what we can to be supportive while she's with us."

Exhausted from hauling boxes into the pool house all afternoon as she attempted to turn the small space into her home, Josie stood at the window as the last of the daylight was slowly backing out of the wood-planked room pulled by the sovereign sun, slipping down behind the dark edge of the ocean. *Slipping, slipping, always something slipping away.* She pulled in a deep breath to head off the quiet anxiety building as she stood alone in the darkening room.

The exodus of light affected her physically, as could any random event; a perpetual ebbing and flowing wave, a pressing jumbled mix of homesickness and desperation that had loomed ever since she could remember. She began self-medicating in high school which at first offered reprieve, but the cure soon spiraled out of control continually taking more than it gave, including a marriage to a decent man and her five-year-old son after she drove under the influence of painkillers head-on into a corner delicatessen sending several bystanders to the hospital including her son.

She pulled out the sofa bed and tucked in clean sheets while waiting for the medication to mute her symptoms. The broad windows showed the western sky now painted with bold brush strokes of moody purples and mauves. She smoothed a comforter into place and eased down onto the mattress. Pharaoh instantly hopped up next to her, curling inside the curve of her body. She rubbed her face into his sleek coat. She could smell her own scent on him, her shampoo and skin cream. It calmed her. They cuddled under the nautical-print comforter, closing their eyes and softly, they drifted off.

Soon, Josie found herself sitting between Simone and Marilla on the front steps of their childhood home on a dusty, hot afternoon. The sounds of buoyant laughter of other children playing in the streets floated up, away, into the summer sky above the house on St. John Street. They were restricted to its confines by their stepfather, while he and Vera were gone during the day; baby Isabel sleeping peacefully in her stroller next to them.

Although she was Martin's daughter, Isabel was their little sister, an angelic toddler with the signature wavy dark hair the sisters had inherited from Vera. The girls shamelessly doted on the adorable eighteen-month-old who they called Belle.

Lost within the recurring nightmare, her body tossed restlessly in the sheets while Pharaoh stood stiff legged on the bed barking an insistent alarm at the wind rattling the windowpanes of the dark, drafty pool house.

It was a lucky night, they were still awake. She could hear the creaking of his stumbling footsteps, erratic, but coming closer and closer, up the stairs while she and Simone frantically struggled with the heavy, double-hung window at the end of the hallway. It was summer; high in the tree tops, out in the open air, safety was a magical refuge under the shadows of hanging leaves in the moonlight. In winter, the roof, slick with ice, their night gowns feeble against the midnight cold, was a treacherous mission waiting out his clumsy retreat back down the stairs or the thud of his collapse onto the floor into unconsciousness.

She jolted awake, damp with sweat, disoriented in the darkness of the strange surroundings, not sure if it was morning or night. She checked her watch; just past six, pm. Her heart still racing, she eased herself back down on the bed, stroking Pharaoh, waiting out the ghosts of her childhood to retreat back into their hiding places.

Out under the stars, Josie turned her body against the vicious wind as she jiggled the key out of the stubborn pool house lock. She could hear the waves crashing out beyond the lonely berm of swaying beach grass in the darkness as she looked up to the beckoning golden glow of the lights from inside the house and with no other actual destination, found herself starting up the stairs.

Joni Mitchell crooned from somewhere behind the glass doors of the kitchen and she rapped on the them several times before the sound was turned down and Charlotte appeared in a leather apron, soldering iron in hand.

The older woman slid the door open. "Everything okay?"

"I'm heading out to get myself some Chinese, wanted to know if you'd like me to bring back some for you. I fell asleep and woke up starving."

"Thoughtful." Charlotte smiled and after a brief hesitation, invited her in. "I've got a pot of vegetable barley soup going. You're welcome to some."

"It does smell pretty good in there." Josie poked her nose further inside. "One problem." She tugged at Pharaoh's leash, pulling him into sight. "I can't leave him alone until he gets used to the new place. He'd get hysterical."

Charlotte's head tilted with affection and pity at the gentle giant staring into her face and held up a finger. "Hold on while I put the boys in the bedroom." She slid the door closed and disappeared back into the house.

The cold wind whipping in off of the ocean blew Josie's hair in every direction as she waited high above the protective dunes on the second floor balcony. "We're going to have a home- cooked meal tonight, baby." She knelt down to Pharaoh mussing his ears.

Charlotte reappeared. *"Entréz s'il vouz plaît."*

Josie stepped into the welcoming, rustic kitchen breathing in rich cooking smells. "Marilla sure hit the jack pot with you, Charlotte."

"You can call me, Charlee. And trust me; it's not an everyday occurrence. Autumn just puts me in the mood to cook. I baked some cornbread, too."

"Good timing on my part. Is it always so windy out there?" She smoothed down her hair.

"Every front has a back, my dear. In the summer we beg for the breeze off of the water."

"What are you working on in your studio these days?" Josie asked, leaning over the simmering soup pot, breathing in a deep whiff.

"Stained glass."

"No more jewelry?"

"Still making my jewelry. Just trying something different. The craft fairs are glutted with vendors selling jewelry. How's your new job going?" Charlotte untied her apron.

"These Long Island women aren't afraid to spend money, I've learned that much." She took a seat at the farmhouse-style table, Pharaoh plunking down on the wide-planked wooden floor at her feet. "But so far so good. I pitched the owner to expand my sales area, bring in some more foot traffic to the place. She was all over the idea. I think she may go for it."

"You must have been convincing."

"Not really. I just think she took a shine to me."

"Aren't we the modest innovator?" Charlotte reached up into a cabinet, taking out two terracotta-colored crocks.

"Fake it, until you make it," Josie quipped. "I've been setting up accounts with costume jewelry wholesalers for this new place. Once I get established maybe I could feature some of your stuff at the salon."

"And a networker, too. Those are natural gifts you have. You would have made a great CEO. I can only wonder what you'd achieve in the corporate world with your business prowess."

"You and me both." Josie bit into one of the breadsticks from the basket Charlotte had set on the table. "You had parents bankrolling your dreams, am I right?"

"Ah, ha." Charlotte nodded. "Education was a priority in our home." She ladled out the steaming soup into the bowls. "My father was a tax attorney and my mother was a maternity ward nurse."

"Mine were drunks. But I always dreamed of being a screenwriter or a movie director."

"And?'

"And you know the story."

"I've heard a few. Which story are you referring to?"

"The one where my drunken stepfather regularly wiped up the floor with us while our mother was out trying to be the next Elizabeth Taylor and then slowly loses her mind after he sets the house on fire with Isabel asleep inside."

Charlotte carefully put her ladle down and leaned across the counter looking squarely at Josie. "Those events have already happened. You are your own person now. What are you getting out of allowing them to still be your road blocks?"

"That's the million dollar question. Any answers, doctor?" Josie flippantly asked.

"For starters, you should get yourself to an Al-Anon meeting." She peered over the top of her glasses. "And it's not too late to pursue a writing career if that's what you want."

"That ship has left the dock. I need to make money." She handed her breadstick to Pharaoh. "Did you always know you wanted to be a psychologist?" Josie's voice returned to a casual conversational tone.

"Always. You and I are lucky. Some people never discover where their passion lies." She pulled a bottle of red out of a wine rack and took a corkscrew to it. "I like a glass of wine with my meals, you?"

"Sure."

"It's a Jordon from Sonoma. Drinks like a cab from Napa, half the price."

"You're quite the versatile little lady, aren't you?"

"I'm retired. I have the time now to indulge my passions."

"You could still see a few private clients if you wanted, couldn't you?"

"I had my own practice on Central Park South before I went to work in the New York City school system. I have no shame in admitting I burnt myself out. "

"Aren't the taxes on Long Island beachfront property epic? What about finances?"

"State pension—and my father was a very smart man. He was investing for me since before I could walk. Bought this house in the seventies. It's worth about a million more now than what he paid for it. Money has never been something I worried about and at sixty-three I'm not going to start now."

"Sounds like you don't have to, and you sure don't look sixty-three."

"Why thank you, Mon cher Amie." She held a fancy goblet up to the light, assessing the composition of the wine before handing it to her guest. "Time has been a stranger to your face as well. I've only seen your sister, Simone that one time, but it seems that all of you have been kissed by Aphrodite."

"Thanks. You should have seen our mother back in her day. What a knockout. Her husbands wound up hating her for it, but that's the thing with men and beautiful women, isn't it?" She took a swallow of wine. "Buyer's remorse."

"It's probably not fair to group all men under that declaration."

"All the men I've ever been with."

"Could it be possible that you're the one weaponizing your own beauty?"

"I thought you said you were too burnt out to practice?"

"Just a thought." Charlotte grinned, taking a seat at the table across from her. "What's the matter?"

"There are only two bowls."

Charlotte looked at Pharaoh who was staring back at her, ears at attention. "Of course." She laughed. *"Pardon moi."* She rose to fetch another bowl.

"What's with all the French, *cherie?"*

"Brushing up. We're planning a trip to Paris in the spring for our tenth anniversary."

"I'd be content with staying put right here. If this were my place, I'd never leave." Josie gazed up to the exposed beams and the bedroom loft above them. "It's perfect."

"Your sister gets the credit for that. She redesigned the entire place herself. Now that's a versatile woman."

"Why is she still working, if you don't mind me asking? Don't you get lonely, eating dinner by yourself?"

"It's not every night and I have a lot of hobbies to keep me occupied. Marilla is younger than me. She's still climbing in her career."

"Classic over-achiever syndrome." Josie reached for a square of corn-bread.

"TransAir is one of the biggest international freight forwarder in the world now. She's the managing supervisor at JFK."

"Well, isn't that just the perfect position for her? Looking over other peoples' shoulders showing them how much better she can do their job."

"Give her credit. She started out as a freight-forwarding agent. I would never ask her to sacrifice her career for me."

Josie rolled her eyes. "You're just too good to be true, Charlee. And you make a mean vegetable barley, too."

They were in the living room; Charlotte in her recliner enjoying the last of the wine, Josie sitting on the floor in front of the stone fireplace, flipping through the glossy pages of another one of the books scattered on the cocktail table.

"You're really enjoying yourself, Jozette?"

"I am." She looked up with a genuine smile. "I always loved books, the way they feel in your hand, the way they smell." She gestured to the wall of book lined shelves. "You've read all of them?"

Charlotte nodded.

"You're an interesting lady. I could learn a lot from you."

"And I, from you. Your insights are impressive."

"It's the job." Josie pulled in her knees, stroking snoozing Pharaoh, his fur warm to the touch from the cozy fire.

"Your work must keep your people reading skills in top form."

"You need to win over a woman before she'll relax enough to let you into the world of her vanity."

"Women and their vanity." Charlotte gazed peacefully at the last splash of ruby-colored wine she swirled in her glass.

"The contents of a woman's cosmetic bag will tell you everything you need to know about her."

"You're practicing psychology and you don't even know it," Charlotte cackled.

"Oh, I do." Josie tossed her head back joining her laughter. "I do know it."

Still laughing, the women pointed at each other as if acknowledging their unspoken bond.

"Do you mind if I ask you about your son? Marilla mentioned he's about fifteen now. Do you get to see him often?"

Josie pushed herself up from the floor and walked over to the book-lined wall of shelves. "Ethan is fifteen." She kept her head turned away. "And I haven't seen him at all this year. His father still has full custody and makes it as difficult as possible for me to spend time with him." She dragged her finger along the spines of the books.

"He can try all he wants. You have rights."

"Moving him to LA hasn't helped and he can afford lawyers who still require that all my visits are supervised, which of course further demonizes me in my son's eyes. Like most everything in this life, it just comes down to finances."

The older woman shook her head with sympathy. "Unfortunately.

That must be frustrating for you."

"He'll be eighteen in just a few short years." She slipped a book out of the tightly-packed section. "We'll make up for lost time and fall in love with each other then. By that time I should have socked away enough money from my other business to buy a house for us."

"What other business?"

"Maybe some other time."

"If you say so." Charlotte casually dropped the subject.

Josie fanned thorough the book's pages. "Okay if I take this down to the pool house with me?"

"What have you got there?" Charlotte took her glasses from the top of her head. "*The Art of Being.* Interesting choice. I wouldn't have pegged you for an Erich Fromm fan." She handed the book back to her house guest.

"Does that surprise you?"

"A little. I have to tell you, I've been sitting here all night, trying to figure out what it is that makes talking with you so intriguing."

"It might be that third glass wine."

"No." The older woman grinned. "Have you ever been enjoying a swim in the ocean, maybe out further than you're comfortable with? And then unexpectedly the water temperature takes a sudden drop?"

Josie had to laugh.

"It usually prompts the swimmer to get out of the area quickly." She picked up her glass. "I've always been the type who likes to stay and find out what's down there."

"You're not afraid that it could be dangerous?"

"Maybe it's thinking the same about me?"

"I'd say that you're probably pretty harmless."

"You're not."

The woman's words stunned her as if she needed to recover from an unsuspected blow. Josie managed a cavalier laugh and deftly dodged the comment. "I'm not going to find a bill under the pool house door in the morning am I?"

"Two. One for the soup."

Josie grinned and tapped her thigh prompting Pharaoh to his feet. "I won't keep your book too long."

"I'll be waiting."

Josie winced against the cold, Charlotte's book tucked under her arm as she scurried down the stairs back to the pool house. The plastic covers on the patio furniture whipped wildly in wind that had picked up, recklessly vaulting and swooping in the ink-black infinity of the cold sky over the Atlantic. She fought with the pool house lock, finally catching it just right as a powerful gust swept in from the ocean and barged past her, then taking flight into the night just as she slipped inside.

Across town, the crowded movie theater trembled as the score climbed to its crescendo, waltzing the 8:00 showing to its close. Joan Bruno gathered her coat and purse and quietly slipped out of her aisle seat before the house lights came up. A widow being spotted alone at the movies on a Friday night causes an awkward situations for both parties. Her husband, Vinny, a fifty-six year old mechanic had died of a heart attack ten months earlier.

There were always plenty of sincere invitations from their friends, an assortment of couples in their forties and fifties, but she was alone by choice. The awkwardness of dinner conversations taking obvious swerves on her behalf and then squabbling with a friend's husband to let her pay her own way when the check arrived, ended even a pleasant evening on a pitiful note. She had also detected an unfamiliar distance from the women on these occasions as well, but maybe it was her imagination. She couldn't trust her perception of anything anymore. She wasn't sure if it was the grieving process or another subversive symptom of menopause carrying out its insidious plans for her systematic ruin, but something seemed to be fogging all her brain functions just enough to keep her wondering.

It didn't take too many invitations to demonstrate that the practicality of the former relationships had died along with her husband. And although all pretended otherwise, those gatherings around restaurant tables only served to identify its corpse. She had figured out that being alone most of the time was better off for everyone.

Stepping into the klieg-light brightness of the popcorn-perfumed lobby, she blinked at her watch, *not even eleven yet*. She pulled on her coat as she padded across the wildly swirling patterned carpet, past the red velvet rope that corralled the fidgety crowd waiting for the late show. She kept her focus on the oasis of anonymity on the other side of the exit doors across the lobby, but she could feel the their eyes on her, searching her face for a review as she prayed that there wasn't anyone in the line she knew.

She pressed her body weight against the glass doors with relief, and fought the cold wind that winter seemed to be riding into town, bullying her all the way to the parking lot. She let out a yelp against an angry gust and broke into a trot thinking Vinny would have laughed at her reaction as she threw herself into her car. She was hungry, and while she waited for the car to warm up she thought about places where she would have liked to have gone for a snack; share a pizza right out of a coal oven and a glass of wine or maybe a slice of tiramisu and a cappuccino in a warm cozy café. *Too many calories anyway* and she backed out of the space and settled for calling her older sister, Francie to keep her company on her ride back home. There were already three missed calls from her.

"Where were you, Joanie? I was so worried."

"Worried? For what? I was just at your house a few hours ago."

"You didn't answer your phone."

"I turned it off. I was at a movie."

"You didn't tell me that you were going to the movies."

"I didn't know I was going."

"Who'd you go with?"

"A friend from tennis."

"You're lying. You could have come to paint night with me and Aunt Dee."

"Don't turn worrying about where I am into a hobby, Francie. Don't you have your hands full taking care of Mom?"

"I was just concerned for you. Don't get pissy."

"I'm sorry. I'm out of sorts. I just feel like my situation makes me so highly visible to everyone. I wish there was somewhere I could go and disappear."

"I could only imagine how you feel."

"No. You couldn't. I hate when you say that. And the weekends are the worst. I feel like if I don't have something planned, I need to make something up to avoid the conversation we're having now."

The silence on the other end of the phone made her catch herself. "I'm sorry."

"You don't have to apologize, but I don't like what all of this is doing to you. If you won't go to counseling, at least reconsider trying the bereavement group."

"Just what I need—to join up with a sewing circle of terminally- depressed widows."

"Don't be so thickheaded. I'm sure they'll be plenty of women your age who are experiencing the same feelings that you are. Women you can relate to."

"I don't want to relate to anyone who's feeling like me."

Francie laughed at her sister's familiar sarcasm. "If you won't do it for yourself, do it for me then."

"I'll think about it. See you in the morning. I'll bring bagels."

"Don't bring anything for Mom. She can't have any solids yet."

"I know. I know."

THE PSYCHIC

Back at home in her pajamas Joan stood in the light of the refrigerator in the dark kitchen eyeing the possibilities. She nudged a takeout carton of leftover salad from her lunch with the girls from her tennis league, considered the container of cottage cheese and then her eyes honed in on the Ring Dings. She fought the urge for a fleeting second then tore into the box. She knew that all twelve individually wrapped representatives of various emotions disguised as snack cakes were living on borrowed time once she recklessly threw them into her shopping cart that afternoon.

She sat at the kitchen counter and at the sight of the empty chairs around the table in the dark dining room she pushed away, desperate for relief from the crushing stillness shrieking the reality of her lonely existence and headed for the front window. They had lived in their home for twenty-four years. In her mind's eye she could imagine the exact shadows the Japanese maple branches in their front yard would be casting over the lawn. She walked to the window and staring out, even the sky above seemed finite. She checked the locks on the front and back doors again and then lay on her side of their bed staring up at the shadowy ceiling, sucking chocolate off her teeth, weeping.

4

$\mathcal{J}$osie was making the best of the red traffic light touching up her eyeliner when her cell phone rang.

"Why haven't you returned my calls?" Simone snapped. "I'm having some problems over here. I thought you were supposed to call me once you got settled in?"

"That's because I'm not settled in yet," Josie said, staring into the rear view mirror, her mouth hanging slightly agape as she traced the inside rim of her eyelid with the pencil.

"How long does it take to settle into beach front living?"

"Glamorizing my crisis isn't going to help either one of us. What's the problem? I'm wrung out from this new job. I'm just leaving there now. What time is it, seven?"

"She's getting worse. We woke up last night to her trying to get out the front door. She's accusing us of stealing from her. Not to mention stripping herself. I don't know how much longer I can do this." Her voice trailed up in desperation.

"You're not. You have an aide helping you that I'm paying for."

"I think we have to start looking into a nursing home."

"We agreed we weren't going to do that. You knew this day was going to come. You and Raymond have been living there dirt cheap for years. Figure something out."

"That's all you have to say to me?"

"Would you like to hear about my problems? Do you have any idea what my life has been like? I'm working ten hours a day, six days a week trying to build up a clientele, sleeping in a moldy pool house cleaning up dog diarrhea because Pharaoh hates it as much as I do."

"They wouldn't let you stay in the house? Marilla, that witch. Serves you right for going there."

"It's not her. Charlotte has two cats."

"I'd buy Pharaoh a T-bone if he went to work on them," her voice strained on the inhale of her cigarette.

"I just have to make it work until I build up some cash and get myself an apartment. The energy it's taking to get this cult of high-maintenance, Long Island shrews to warm up to me is soul draining." She sighed. "I should have just stayed in Brooklyn."

"Don't martyr yourself. You couldn't have. You're hiding from the Russian mafia and you're on the run from a nut job ex who's gunning for you."

"What are you talking about? And what do you mean, gunning for me?"

"If you'd pick up one of my calls I would have told you."

Simone could hear the volume of the talk radio Josie always listened to become lower.

"That's right. He was here last week. I caught him peeking into the garage window and then he was back again, a few days ago. Almost broke the glass in my back door pounding on it so hard. Did you know that he owns a gun?"

"He's a corrections officer. They all carry guns, so what? Did he open fire on you, Simmy?"

"Don't try to make small of it, you weren't here."

"Tell me."

"I felt like I had to be careful not to set him off. He was sweating, gritting his teeth when he talked and he made good and sure his jacket was open so I could see he was carrying. Lucky for you Raymond wasn't home. He would have put him right on to you."

"You told Raymond where I'm staying?"

"You didn't say not to."

Josie huffed with irritation. "You never could keep your mouth shut.

So what actually happened? I'm on way to an appointment."

"I told him I had no idea where you were. Of course he didn't believe me and he doesn't believe that you're still in California visiting your son. Did you borrow money from him?"

"He offered. I didn't ask."

"How much?"

"Five grand."

"Don't you think you should have let me know that? Didn't you figure this would be the first place he'd come looking for you?"

"I'll give him a call. I know how to handle him."

"He doesn't want to be handled. You already broke up the guy's family. Just give him his money back."

"I will. He's just going to have to wait. He has a demolition business on the side and he's partners in a scrap metal yard. It's not like he's struggling."

"And I should deal with him in the meantime? That's just so *Jozette* of you," her voice was thick with irritation.

"Trust me; he's going to get tired of coming around. He has his hands full getting dragged in and out of court by his wife. I just need you to play dumb and stall him for a little while longer. I was going to wait to tell you, but I've started up the readings again."

"Oh, Josie. Why can't you just leave it alone? You're good at so many things. I thought this was going to be a fresh start for you?"

"It's just going to be until I can build up a nice cushion for myself, a down payment on a nice condo some place warm. I have a new system. Your little sister is a genius." Josie could hear a commotion in the background and her mother shrieking. "I'm actually on my way now to do some research and development. We'll get together so I can fill you in. Gotta go. Bye."

The bereavement group met in a basement room of an elementary school across street from a local church. Joan adjusted her stance to conquer the weight of the castle-like wooden door and slipped inside with relief, leaving the spinning collection of dried leaves and litter whirling on the other side. She was keeping the promise she made to her sister, but the reality was she just had nowhere else to go on a Wednesday night in December. She looked up at the gothic entranceway as she pulled off her gloves, wondering how the school children managed its heft.

As she padded down the quiet, deserted hallway, the universal scent of school corridor, unique and indiscernible, instantly evoked images of her two adult sons in their grade school years and through the sense of smell and its power of time travel, she was her nine- year-old self again, too.

The blare of a basketball coach's whistle brought her back to the present as she passed a team practice. The squeak of sneakers on the sheen of auditorium floor echoed down into the empty stairwell where she paused before a door with a handwritten sign taped to it: HEALING HEARTS.

Here you go, Joanie. You can do this. And she opened the door into a room that looked like it once was a small cafeteria now refurbished with commercial carpet and a dropped ceiling with harsh, fluorescent lighting. Standing in the doorway, observing the strangers gathered in clusters in the dull, charmless room, she fought the impulse to turn around and flee.

"Healing Hearts?" a neatly dressed older gentleman asked. "I'm John. I guide our gatherings."

"Joan. My first time."

"It's good to meet you Joan." He offered her a pamphlet. "We'll be starting soon. There's some juice and cookies if you like. Grab yourself a seat."

She scanned the semi-circle of folding chairs and sidestepped into a row, avoiding a stringy-haired woman who seemed to be suffering from a cold and then steered clear of a young couple, knees touching, holding hands who she assumed had lost a child. As she sat, skimming through the pamphlet she couldn't help overhearing a women in the row behind her going on and on to some others about a gifted psychic she had visited when a strikingly attractive woman appeared in the door way. Joan tugged her blouse down over her midsection as the dark haired beauty appeared to be heading for the empty chair right next to her.

"Can I?" The stylish stranger confidently looked her straight in the eye, with a subtle twist of her frosted lips.

"Of course." Joan removed her purse from the chair.

"I'm Fiona Price." The bangles on her wrist jingled when she held out a neatly-manicured hand. "Hello, ladies," Fiona warmly returned the greetings from the women in the other row as she peeled off her brown leather jacket and hung it on the back of the chair. "I don't think I've seen you here before," she said and sat, her pleasing fragrance claiming the space as her own.

"Joan Bruno. It's my first time. My sister forced me to give this a try and I definitely didn't expect someone like you to be here."

"Someone like me?" She titled her head with a grin.

"You look like you should be selling perfume at Neiman Marcus."

She laughed. A good, hearty, one-syllable bark that did not seem to match the polished image she projected. "You're funny."

"Is that allowed here?"

"It's a help group. Laughing helps."

Joan leaned into her. "I'm so glad you sat next to me. I was dreading that it would be all senior citizens."

"I've been back a few times. This group is mostly all our age."

"Our age? I must have ten years on you."

"Don't be so sure. I'm forty-five," Fiona said.

Joan laughed. "Thanks. I wish. Fifty-four."

"Really?" Fiona peered closer. "You must live at the gym."

"No. Just good genes, I guess. And a tennis league. How do you keep in such great shape?"

"I've just started running again after a foot issue. It feels good to be back. I've been playing with the idea of training for next year's marathon."

"Go for it."

Fiona placed a light touch on Joan's wrist. "That's gorgeous. I've never seen that style Cartier before."

"My husband surprised me with it for my fiftieth." Joan's fingers stroked the sleek watch.

John politely cleared his throat and took the center of the room, now alive with animated conversations. "Welcome everyone. If you could all find a seat, please. We have some new faces here tonight. How we like to get started is by pairing off and taking a few minutes to get to know each other. If you already know the person sitting next to you, please move on down the line to get to know someone new."

Amid the clumsy clank of metal folding chairs and scuffling feet, Fiona turned her chair into Joan's. "Me and you?"

"Sure, you want to go first?" Joan offered.

"Why not?" Fiona volunteered. "My mother passed a few months ago. We didn't have the greatest relationship. She had a drinking problem ever since I can remember so I was surprised to find myself having a harder time with her not being here than I thought I would. I'm kind of a private person, so this group works for me. It lets me be anonymous and it's on the way home from work," Fiona ended with a shrug.

"My husband, Vinny. About a year ago—fifty-six. He was working on his vintage Camaro in our driveway. He came in for a beer and dropped to the kitchen floor in front of me."

Fiona rested a compassionate hand on Joan's arm. "Oh, no. You poor thing."

"Massive coronary. He died in the ambulance on the way to the hospital."

"Any children?"

"Two boys, twenty-seven and thirty-one. You?"

The room had become clamorous as the exercise succeeded in loosening up its participants.

"A fifteen-year-old son from a marriage I had in my twenties. He lives out of state with his father." She began to dig in her purse. "But

that's a whole other story I don't think we have time for," she said, casually reapplying her lipstick as if she was in her bathroom mirror. "Great
shade, isn't it?" Fiona smacked her lips together.

"Yes. It is, actually."

"Here. This is for you." She pulled another tube from her over-sized
bag.

Joan hesitated.

"Go ahead. It's yours. It's a sample. I can get a hundred more. I sell
it, apply it, mail orders and costume jewelry too. I work at Studio 99.
Ever hear of it?"

Joan shook her head. "Sorry, no."

"It's a few towns over. You should stop in. Exceptional stylists. I'll
do your makeup for you. What do you do, Joan?"

"Right now, nothing besides going out of my mind from boredom.
I used to manage Vinny's front office, but once his partner officially
took over the business I knew it was time for me to leave. But I always
wanted to have a little business of my own."

"Really?"

"We were married right out of high school and then the kids came."

"So he was the only man you've ever been with?"

"Ye…yes." The question took Joan by surprise.

"What kind of business were you interested in?"

"A clothing store or a little boutique. You know, jewelry, gifts, pretty
soaps."

John stepped into the center of the room again. "Chairs forward
now, please. We are going to begin our group share. Pat has volunteered
to start. Hearing other's grieving experiences is helpful; you'll find that
emotions you thought were unique are a normal part of the process.
And that's what grieving is: a process." He gestured to a reserved looking, middle-aged woman still clutching her Styrofoam coffee cup. "Pat?"
he gave a reassuring grin turning the room over to her.

The woman cleared her throat. "This has actually been my best week
since my mother passed. It's been three months," she said in a weak,

barely audible voice. "Her name was Lucy. Lulu to her friends. And she had a ton of them." Pat gestured with an open palm punctuating her pride. "She lived with us. The sandwich generation, you know?" she continued on with growing confidence, encouraged by the commiseration from others in the group. "I know she lived a long life, but what's so difficult for me is that even though she was eighty-three and really sick at the end, she didn't want to go. It was so hard for me to watch. She was still playing bridge with her friends up till the end. Or Solitaire, she loved her games. Some afternoons I swear I still hear cards shuffling in her room. And I think to myself, am I going crazy?"

"That's a common thing," John comforted her. "Thinking that you see or hear your loved one shortly after they've passed."

A chorus of assenting voices verified this experience.

"It won't happen as much as time goes on." A gravelly-voiced woman wearing a pink crochet cap topped with a pom-pom, sympathetically offered, "I used to think I'd see my husband, Chester, in his bathrobe unloading the dishwasher."

Joan and Fiona had to look away from each other like two high school girls misbehaving in the back of class; Joan biting her lip.

"Don't. Stop it," Fiona urged under her breath, discreetly elbowing her partner in crime in her ribs, but it was too late. Joan's giggling fit had already overtaken her, escalating with the bizarre details being shared by others in the group.

"Is she okay over there?" John asked his face wrinkled with concern as he looked over at Joan, her face buried in her hands, her body shaking uncontrollably.

"Just a little overwhelmed." Fiona took Joan by the arm and began to lead her out of the room. "I'll take her out to get some air."

Someone handed Joan a tissue amid the hushed murmurs of pity and concern as Fiona ushered her out of the room, pulling the door shut behind them.

She yanked Joan into the stairwell. "They all think that you were crying." Fiona exploded with laughter.

"I know. I couldn't stop myself." Joan gasped. "You must think I'm some kind of a nut."

"I don't. The rest of them probably do."

They perched on the stairs gaining their composure and bursting back into hysterics again every time they looked at each other.

"Chester…" Fiona teared up with laughter.

"It was the hat. That hat is what did me in." Joan choked. "That's the most I've laughed since I can remember and at a bereavement group!" She wiped at her eyes with the donated tissue, shaking her head. "I couldn't stop myself. I'm more screwed up than I thought."

"It was just nervous energy. It was good for you."

"I'm too embarrassed to go back in there. Would you mind getting my bag for me?"

"Sure." Fiona was still laughing as she pushed herself up from the step.

"And my coat too, please." Joan called after her, sitting alone looking around the stairwell that seemed as if it was built to withstand a nuclear holocaust. "I'm just going to call it a night," she said to herself wiping at her eyes.

Fiona returned with Joan's coat draped over her arm, and handed her the purse. "You sure you don't want to come back in?"

"I'll give it another try next week. And I apologize. I'm so embarrassed."

"Don't apologize. I think it was a hoot. I need to get back in there. Take my card. I want you to stop by the salon. We should get to know each other better. I could use a friend who still gets the giggles. I'll be there all day Saturday."

Joan accepted the business card. "See you Saturday."

Feeling as if she had drunk several cups of coffee, Joan accelerated past her exit. The thought of sitting home by herself in her empty house was not an option even though the wet snowflakes floating onto the windshield were quickly multiplying. For the first time since she had become a widow, she felt authentically herself and needed to share the phenomenon with someone she loved.

"What's wrong?" Her cherub-faced older sister Francie whisked open her front door.

"Nothing. Why do you always think something is wrong?' She stepped into the warmth of Francie's well-lived in home.

"Did you go to the meeting?" Francie stepped backward staring into her sister's face as they passed through the living room.

"Yes. I told you I was," Joan said, shaking her arms out of her coat and tossing it on the Jet's throw draped over the couch. "Mom still up?"

"No. She went to bed right after dinner. Bob sacked out too. Let's go into the kitchen. I made apple cobbler for dessert. Soo-o good."

The scented candle flickering on the counter filled Francie's kitchen with the homey smell of cinnamon on the wintery night. Joan sat at the table rummaging through the basket of her mother's prescription bottles while her sister pulled out a surplus stack of paper goods from Thanksgiving. She set two cornucopia-imprinted plates down on the table and turned only to make an abrupt stop.

"What's wrong?" Joan asked her.

"Nothing." She continued to the refrigerator. "Did you ever forget what you were doing for a minute?"

"All the time. I call it having *a room away.*"

"A room away?"

"I'm just a room away from remembering what I came in there for."

Her sister's familiar, zany laugh made Joan smile. "And now with this hellacious menopause plaguing me it's an everyday occurrence."

"Been there." Francie jiggled the extra girth at her hips and heaped the plates of cobbler with a scoop of Häagen-Dazs Vanilla. "So let's hear about your meeting."

"It wasn't what I had expected."

"See! I told you." Francie's face lit up reacting to her sister's positive tone as she settled at the table with her.

"Well, it was going pretty good until I had a giggling fit while some poor soul was pouring her heart out to the group over her dead husband." She clipped off a taste of the ice cream with the edge of her spoon.

Her sister stopped mid-bite. "You didn't?"

Joan nodded, savoring the cold, sweetness of vanilla. "I did. Full-tilt, hunched over, rocking, shaking and making a fool of myself. " She pushed away the plate.

Francie put her hand over her mouth in disbelief and swallowed a mouthful of cobbler. "So what happened?"

"Luckily, the woman I was sitting next to escorted me out of there before they called 911 for me."

"She must have thought you had a screw loose. What did she say to you?"

"Nothing. It didn't bother her. She was laughing her head off, too. She invited me to the salon where she works. She wants to do my make-up for me."

"Sounds like a nice person."

"She was. And fun, too. Not to mention gorgeous with a figure to die for. I'm meeting her there Saturday."

"That's great." Francie nudged her sister's arm with an encouraging swipe. "Aren't you glad you listened to me? And why aren't you eating your cobbler?"

Studio 99 took up half a block in the snooty Beacon Hill shopping district, an affluent suburb on Long Island's North Shore. It was the only beauty parlor Joan had ever visited that offered valet parking and it looked just like a place she'd imagined Fiona would spend her work days. Joan found herself second-guessing her outfit before she even reached for the bronze handles of glass and scrolled iron doors of the two-level salon and spa.

She stepped into a bustling cacophony of privileged, North Shore women whose animated conversations were drowned out by the endless whining of blow dryers wielded by a small army of stylists whose attire seemed more suited for Mardi Gras than cutting hair. If Studio 99's objective was to create an atmosphere of pretentiousness, it succeeded from the very first step inside.

Unable to spot a make-up counter and having no clue where it might be located within the posh, enormous salon, Joan approached the team of stylishly dressed young women, breasts pouring out the tops of their blouses, who were commandeering the hotel-sized reception area.

"Hi, I'm looking for Fiona," she said over the jungle-like clamor and bass-thumping sound system.

"That way. Just past color," one of the receptionists pointed returning her attention to the good-looking Latino stylist who had just swayed up to the counter.

Joan proceeded unnoticed amid the chaotic energy as she braved the alternate universe. She walked through a hive of self-important aliens flipping through magazines and bent over their cell phones, their heads springing with aluminum foil antennas, the idle rich inhabitants of the strange planet, Studio 99's hair coloring section, and just beyond, there was Fiona.

In leather pants, ankle-high boots and a print scarf glamorously wrapped around her head, she stood over her white leather chair, kissing close to a client, one hand on the woman's chin, and the other applying mascara with surgeon-like concentration, a liner pencil held between her teeth.

"Come on over. We're just about done here." She seemed to sense Joan's presence by intuition.

The client sitting in the chair appeared visibly irritated by Fiona's attention being distracted away from her, and proceeded to inspect Joan from top to bottom with a condescending smirk.

"Hi, I'm Joan. You're makeup looks absolutely fabulous."

Thrown by the confident and friendly greeting, the woman stammered out a thank you and Fiona spun the chair around to the oversized, ornate mirror.

"She's right. Look at you. You do look fabulous."

The woman angled her head, admiring her reflection and rose from the chair. "That's why I love you, Fia." She planted an audible kiss on Fiona's cheek. "See you next week, lovey," she called over her shoulder, tablet in hand, designer coffee cup in the other, as she shuffled away trying not to dislodge the sponge separators between her toes.

Fiona beamed at Joan with her hands on her hips. "What a team. I knew I liked you."

"Twenty years in customer service." Joan presented her with a ribbon-tied tray of homemade cookies. "Give me a hug. Thanks for asking me by and giving me a chance to prove that I'm not a kook."

"You're not? I retract the invitation." Fiona's infectious laugh was interrupted by her cell phone. She placed the cookies dismissively off to the side.

While Fiona took her call, Joan perused the selection of jewelry and trinkets that corralled Fiona's work area, artfully displayed and as beautiful and unique as the woman who was selling them.

"Sorry, it's insanity here on Saturdays. Have a seat." She patted her white leather chair. "Come on," she prodded.

Joan sat. "I just came for a visit…"

"Shh-hh." Fiona leaned the chair back and began to smooth Joan's cheeks and forehead with confident fingers. The calming strokes put Joan at ease even amid the frenetic setting.

"You have near-perfect skin. Nice tight pores." Her demeanor turned serious and professional. "Doesn't mean you can get away with as little makeup as you wear now. Is this how you usually go out?"

"You ask that like I should be answering *no.*"

"I think you're a beautiful woman, but I can't even guess why you're not playing up your features. None of us are eighteen anymore, honey."

A younger woman leaned into Fiona's station. "Wish me luck, Fia. Hope I'll have good news to tell you next week. Have a great weekend."

"Good luck, sweetie." Fiona held up crossed fingers while still examining Joan's skin. "Invitro injection therapy. I don't know what's going on with the young girls today. When I was her age, not getting pregnant was the problem. I don't mean full-face makeup for you. I like your natural style, but just a little something to even out your tone. You have great hair too, but you've probably been wearing that same style for decades, am I right?"

"Fiona?" A heavily made-up, statuesque woman purposefully approached Fiona's station trailed by a workman wielding a tape measure. "Do you have a minute for me?"

"Sure, Wendy." Fiona smiled. "Joan, this is Wendy Waxman. She's the owner of the salon."

"Pleasure to meet you—I apologize for the interruption, but the men are here to take the measurements for the new cases. They won't be in your way, will they?"

"No, of course not." Fiona placed a palm over her heart. "I'm so excited, Wendy."

"Me too. It's going to be great." Wendy beamed and spun on her designer heels, her shoulders squared with confidence as she strutted back into the chaos of her salon.

"Hectic place," Joan said smoothing her hair in the mirror, considering the effect of the bronzer her new friend had applied.

"Busiest salon I've ever worked in. She's expanding my retail area for me."

"Congratulations. That was nice of her."

"I thought so. I have a client coming in a few, but I would love to reshape your brows."

Before Joan could even register a reply, Fiona was pulling her out of the chair, leading her to a private room just beyond her work station.

"You have to. You owe me. It won't take long. Lay back." She swung the door closed behind them with the heel of her boot.

Back at her chair Fiona gave Joan a hand mirror. "Look how that opened the whole eye area and brightened up your entire face."

Joan furrowed her newly-shaped brows in the mirror.

"And the higher arch." Fiona put her hand on her hip admiring her work. "Very sexy. You look like you're thinking about something. Now you'll always have everyone wondering what it is."

"Hmmm…" Joan assessed the improvement, raising and lowering her brows.

"I wish I could get out of here and grab a bite with you." Fiona watched her next client approaching. "Too jammed today. Are you free tomorrow? It's my day off. I can stop over after my run."

"Ah, sure. Tomorrow works. I'll have the coffee waiting."

"A plan. Give me your address. And the makeup and brow waxing are my treat."

"Fia!"

She leaned in the opposite direction and offered her cheek accepting the affectionate peck from her next client. "Hey Stacy, we're just finishing up here. How are you, honey? How's the house hunting going?"

On her drive back home, Joan spent equal time admiring her newly shaped brows in the rearview mirror and trying to figure out how it all happened so fast. It was unlike her to be so spur-of-the-moment about a change, especially one regarding her appearance. Fiona was over the top and pushy, presumptuous and bawdy, but there was something about her that not only made it okay, it made you want more of her.

Early the next morning Fiona was peering through the etched glass windows flanking the door into Joan Bruno's tidy home. The entry foyer looked as if it had been staged for a scene on a greeting card. The shafts of morning sun lay across the high polished oak floors. A tufted bench stood on a pale rose area rug, and a single umbrella leaned in a stand in a corner. It's controlled, orderly charm reflected the woman who lived there. A bronze plaque reading, *The Brunos* hung above the doorbell.

"It's open." She heard Joan's pleasant voice call from somewhere inside.

Fiona poked her head in and slowly inched open the door. "Someone's baking," she sang, following the smell into the kitchen.

"I'm making a cake for my mother's eightieth birthday party this afternoon," Joan said closing her oven door.

"I have a friend with me, is that okay?"

Joan turned around cake batter-dipped toothpick in hand.

"Joan, meet Pharaoh."

Joan stepped back, her palms flattened against the cabinet. Her arms froze at her sides at the sight of the leashless Doberman Pincer; his head clearing Fiona's waist.

"Relax. He's as docile as a bunny rabbit. Lay down for Mommy, baby."

Joan watched the threatening beast flop onto his side on top of Fiona's running shoes.

"Come on over and say hello. Pharaoh loves kisses."

Joan reluctantly approached. "You sure?"

As Joan knelt, Pharaoh's long black toenails made a flurry of frantic clicks on the kitchen's tiled floor as he hopped to his feet to greet her.

Joan shrieked, jumping backwards.

Fiona laughed at her. "He just excited to meet you. You're going to hurt his feelings. Look at this." She put her hand into Pharaoh's mouth.

As soon as Joan was on her knee, the black and tan titan lovingly butted his head against hers, nuzzling into her neck.

"Woo-hoo, it tickles. He's darling." She giggled as Pharaoh won her over. She kneaded his ears. "Scary looking as hell, but what a mush."

"Told ya. He's not so crazy about men, but I've gone through some phases of feeling that way myself," she said, laughing. "I didn't have the heart to leave him alone again today. I've been working for six straight days."

Pharaoh's paws were now on Joan's shoulders, her head buried in his broad chest.

"I knew you'd love him. And he's good company, too."

"And what a handsome collar." Joan tugged on the thick, rhinestone-studded leather cuff he was sporting. "I miss having a dog. We had to put our Golden down a few years ago. Can I give him a treat?"

"Pharaoh loves treats. What ya got?"

"Does he like Ring Dings?"

"What are you doing with Ring Dings?"

"Good question."

Fiona handed Joan a silver gift bag with Studio 99 printed in purple ink. "Here. This is for you, tinted moisturizer. Trust me; you're going to love it." Fiona twirled around the kitchen with outstretched arms. "What a great feel this house has. Everything is in the exact perfect spot, but it looks like it happened accidentally. That's the sign of someone who's got an eye for decorating." She pointed at Joan.

"Thanks, Fiona."

"Call me Fia. Everyone does. This is one of those homes you want to belong to," she swayed around the homey kitchen. "It's got a good feel, and trust me, you get to see a lot of homes in my line of work."

"You make house calls?"

"Of course. Bridal parties, bar mitzvahs. And my standing weeklies."

"Standing weeklies?"

"For a lot of women, an application of full-face makeup substitutes for a soul." She shifted the topic. I bet when your kids were little this was the house that all the neighborhood kids gravitated to." Fiona stopped in front of a restaurant- sized espresso machine and ran her hand over its chrome and copper finish. "Beautiful. It's got to be an import?"

Joan nodded. "One of Vinny's toys. I think we used it a total of six times. He was a gadget freak."

Fiona fussed with the cords of a lopsided Roman shade. "That's better."

"I can't believe you just fixed that. I was waiting for a service call."

"When we were kids, my sisters and I lived across the street from two seamstresses. They taught us to use the magic in our fingers. I just seem to have a knack for that type of thing."

"Did you ever think of doing it for a living?"

"No. My older sister made a career out of it, but sewing beads on other women's wedding dresses doesn't do it for me. Can we sit?"

She tapped at her thigh and Pharaoh followed as she walked across the room and plopped into the overstuffed sofa. "I've been standing all week."

Joan sank into the chair across from them and watched Pharaoh drop onto the sisal rug at Fiona's feet. "He doesn't leave your side, does he?"

"Never. He's like a jealous boyfriend, but he's loyal."

"How did you get him to be so attached?"

"He was a shelter dog. He knows what I saved him from."

"Interesting pick," Joan commented as Fiona stroked the angular wedge of a Pharaoh's head, resting on her thigh.

"I didn't pick him. He picked me." She smiled looking into the invisible past, pulling Pharaoh up by his front paws and cradling his head against her belly.

"Tell me." Joan pulled her knees into her chest.

Fiona stroked the sheen of the dog's muscular neck. "Two years ago I was going through a rough time. The guy I was engaged to abandoned ship."

"You don't have to go into it."

"I was in a bad way for a while—everything in my life seemed wrong, but even I knew I needed to take some time before I got involved again. I wound up at the animal shelter, which I knew was a bad idea in my emotional state, but that didn't stop me. So there I am, kneeling at the cages to get a feel for each innocent prisoner, every muscle in their bodies squirming for the chance to show how much love they had to give. But being in the position of choosing one and disappointing all the others, it was just too much for me. I had to get out of there. I started walking out and someone calls me back."

Joan pointed to Pharaoh who was gazing up at Fiona as if he was listening to the story too.

"It was a deliberate, one-syllable bark. Like a command, as if to stop me. I turned around and he was on his hind legs, paws against the bars."

"So not only is he manly, he's the assertive type too."

Fiona laughed. "Very. When I knelt in front of his cage he laid down, closed his eyes and then looked right in my face and stood straight up again as if to show me what a good boy he would be."

"Swear?"

"Swear. We left together that afternoon, went home and fell asleep in my bed until the next morning. I guess we both had been through a bad time." She massaged his neck. "The next day I made pancakes for us and we spent the rest of the day in the park."

"Aw, I love happy endings," Joan cooed. "But, didn't you consider that a dog so lovable was turned over to a shelter for a reason. An incident maybe…"

"I'm sure who ever left him in that place had their story. But we'll never know his version."

Joan nodded sympathetically.

"I knew it would work with us." Fiona's tone turned upbeat, as if someone had changed a radio station. "He's a Leo."

"How do you know?"

"I can't document it, but I just know that he has to be a Leo or has a Leo rising sign. The regal air about him, his self-importance. Got to be. Your cake smells done."

"My cake!" Joan hopped off the chair.

"This is some view of the water you have here, Joanie." Fiona called from the living room as she stood enjoying the stark beauty of winter on the bay. Joan joined her and they stood in silence watching a solitary boat out on the lonely stretch of water make its way past the wall of glass patio doors that ran the length of the house.

"Is that yours?" Fiona motioned to an impressive-sized boat resting in a cradle at the dock, the morning sun reflecting off of its burnished chrome trim.

"Vinny's baby. He got just one season out of it." She began to tear up. "He wanted us to spend his retirement boating. I know eventually I will have to sell it. We took out a mortgage on the house for it and, financially, I'm worse off than when Vinny was alive. I just haven't been able to bring myself to go through with it yet." Her voice cracked. "And seeing it just sitting out there every day…"

Fiona watched Joan's face contort as she struggled for command of her emotions.

She fussed with a strand of her hair. "I swear, it's not who I am." She lost the battle with her tears.

"Come on. Put your coat on." Fiona pulled her away from the view. "We're going for a walk. Being outdoors always cuts problems down to size."

Joan allowed herself to be led away, spurred by a wistful intuition that a rescue party had been sent for her in the form of this fairy-like, ethereal soul sister. "Would you like to come to a birthday party this afternoon?"

"We'd love to."

5

*I*t didn't take long for Josie to endear herself to Joan's extended family. She quickly became a surrogate member; loved and revered by all for bringing their beloved Joan back into the world of the living again, restored to her old self and then some.

It was Super Bowl Sunday and Francie's home was the site of another lively family get-together, a bubbly mix of relatives, neighbors, and her son's friends, home from college.

"Your friend Fiona is no wallflower, that's for sure," Francie's sister-in-law said to Joan, chomping on a chicken wing as they observed Fiona comfortably move from the young group watching the halftime show to the circle of men standing around talking second half strategy.

"And we hardly get to see Joanie anymore since she's taken up with her," Francie said, stirring a half-empty tray of chili. "She's missed the last two months of our book club because she's always out gallivanting with Fiona somewhere."

"I thought you said you liked that about her?" Joan bristled.

"She's a little too fast for me—and maybe you, too." Francie glanced down at the high-heeled boots Joan had taken to wearing, similar to Fiona's in style.

"First you complain I'm not having enough fun, now I'm having too much. Make up your mind, Francie." Joan took a sip of her nephew's homemade sangria from her over-sized plastic glass.

"Don't get upset. Your sister is just overprotective of you. Has been for as long as I've known you two."

"I didn't mean anything by it," Francie apologized. "It's just that there's something about her I can't put my finger on, that's all." She shrugged. "Come on, girls. Help me refill these trays."

Joan didn't follow. Instead she stayed and finished her drink. She watched Fiona from across the crowded, noisy rooms until she stepped away from the party and leaned against a wall, a finger plugged into one ear taking a phone call.

"This better be good, Simmy. This is the fifth call I've gotten from you in the last hour. I'm at a party."

"Oh, I'm so glad you're having a good time. Guess who was just at my house? This time with a friend."

"What friend?"

"Oh, you'd remember him if you met him. Crazy eyes. Neanderthal-looking."

"Wait a minute, I'm going outside." She slipped out of the kitchen door, stepping through a group of college kids lingering around a fire pit, smoking cigarettes.

They returned her congenial smile.

"Okay, so what happened?" She paced the sidewalk along the car-lined street in front of the house, shivering in the gray February cold.

"Luckily, Raymond was at the bar watching the game. I had Vera's Jamaican aide tell Tommy that I wasn't home through the door. Do you know that he told her it was okay to let him in? That he was my brother? Can you believe that? Tell me what I'm dealing with here."

"Don't overreact. He probably just wanted to see if my things were there, if I was staying with you."

"Overreact? Why is he still coming here and trying to get into my house and bringing backup with him? What did you say to him when you called him?"

"I didn't call him."

"Why not?"

"I've been busy and….well, it's a little more than a couple grand that he lent me."

"Like how much more?"

"Fifteen grand more."

"What did you do with fifteen grand?"

"I had bills. I paid off the surgeon who redid my implants, paid down a few charge cards. I can't rent anything with bad credit."

"Well that explains a lot. And what did you think? That he was just going to just forget about it?"

"Don't you get that I know what I'm doing?" She lowered her voice, glancing back at the house. "You don't come out ahead in these situations by being in a hurry. It takes strategy."

"And you're okay with me getting stuck dealing with him and Raymond *and* our mother while you test out strategy?"

"It's found money. You don't even know a score when it's already sitting right in your lap."

"I know a nut job when I see one. You tell him that I'm calling the cops if he comes here again. That's my strategy."

"I'm not going to threaten him with that. Trust me, it will only make things worse for you."

"For me?" Simone screamed.

Josie pulled the phone away from her ear. "The cops aren't the way to go. Think about it. Do we need to be talking to the police about anything? Think chess, not checkers. I could be on to something really big with the readings here and I'm going to need your help soon."

"And you're still bent on messing with that again?"

"It's a different system this time. Wait till you hear."

"Whatever you say, Josie. Just call him and tell him whatever you have to, to keep him away from here."

Josie spotted Joan approaching, her coat draped over her shoulders. "I gotta go. I'll call you tomorrow and we'll meet during the week so I can fill you in. I'll have some cash for you, too. Bye."

"It's freezing out here. Everything alright?" Joan shivered, her arms clutching her coat around her body.

"Scheduling problem with a photographer that I'm working with tomorrow. You have no idea how impossible some of these clients can be."

"Come on, let's get back inside." Joan tugged her towards the house. "They're starting to pull the box winners for the quarter."

The sound of clanking dishes and the busy noise of the open kitchen filled the small luncheonette in the seaside town of Long Beach where Josie waited in a booth flipping through the *New York Post.* She slowly lowered her tea as Simone approached holding Vera firmly by an arm.

Simone smirked with glib satisfaction as Josie gaped in controlled horror at the decline in their mother's condition. The woman who was all but consumed by vanity throughout her entire life, who never left the house in shoes without heels or a purse that didn't match her outfit, shuffled along in rubber-soled orthotics and a shapeless cardigan that hung off her gaunt frame.

"Hello, stranger," Simone said smugly, guiding Vera into the booth and slipping in next to her.

"Hi, Mom," Josie hesitantly greeted her mother.

"Hi, Renee."

Simone met her sister's uneasy glance.

"Why is she carrying a doll?" Josie closed the newspaper.

"The aide suggested it. It keeps her calm—most of the time." She pulled off Vera's ski cap.

"What have you got there?" Josie sweetly asked, reaching to touch the wide-eyed, plastic baby doll her mother held protectively against her chest.

"Don't!" Simone warned.

But she was too late.

Josie yanked her hand away as if the doll was electrified as Vera, her hair disturbingly askew, began shrieking. She watched in dismay as Simone went into action, cupping her hand over the old woman's mouth and waving a plastic bag of Oreos she pulled from her purse, hastily pushing one into Vera's hand which abruptly silenced her shrill screams.

"Jeez," Josie looked away. "When did this all happen?"

"It has been almost two months since the last time you saw her."

"What do her doctors say?"

"Eventually she'll get to a point where she'll have to be put into a nursing home."

"We agreed we weren't going to do that."

"You don't live with her."

A waiter arrived.

"Chicken salad on a bagel and a coffee," Simone told him.

He nudged his chin at Vera.

"She's good." Simone waved him off.

"Here, Simmy, take this." Josie dipped into her bag and peeled off several bills. "Get another aide to stay nights with her."

Simone plucked the money from the table.

Josie glanced sideways at the irritating clacking sounds coming from Vera, who was happily scraping the filling from the cookies with her teeth like a distracted toddler, saliva and chewed Oreo running down her chin.

"Take this, too." She reached back into her purse and peeled off several more bills from the fold. "Go get your hair done or a massage or something."

"Thanks." Simone stuffed the money down into her bag. "You're looking good, Josie. It seems like Long Island is treating you right. "

"It is. There's a lot of money to be made here, even legitimately."

"So be legitimate. Why are you even bothering with the readings? You didn't learn your lesson from last summer?"

"With my new angle, they've taken off so incredibly that it's just too good to pass up."

"So let's hear it," Simone sighed. "What's this new angle?" She passed her mother another cookie and shifted in her seat.

"Are you ready?" Josie raised her tea to her lips and whispered. "Bereavement groups."

A smile slowly spread across Simone's face as the concept registered. "I love it," she squealed.

"Shhh-hh." Josie cautiously scanned the room.

"What gave you the idea?"

"Well, I am working alone and necessity is the mother of invention."

"What are you calling yourself?"

"Mrs. Habbibi," she whispered, her eyes shifting left and right.

"Where'd you come up with that one from?"

"Do you remember the Arab family that used to own the convenience store on the avenue when we were kids? Every time we went in there, it was every other word out of their mouths–thank you, habibi, have a nice day, habibi, be careful crossing the street habibi…"

"What's it mean?"

Josie shrugged. "I don't know–darling, sweetie or something. But I like the effect."

"You're so imaginative. It's too bad that you never did make it to film school. So what's your approach?"

"I'm a widow, or I've lost my mother, a younger brother to a drunk driver. I've been to more meetings than I can count. I'm working so many towns now that I've got myself booked three months out."

"How much are you taking?"

"Two-fifty."

Simone shook her hand at the wrist.

"It's nothing to this North Shore crowd—and that's not including extras that I'm tacking on during the sessions."

"I'm proud of you, Josie." Simone poured a long stream of sugar into her steaming mug of coffee. "Vera always said that you were destined for greatness."

Josie looked over at the old woman. "Vera…" she shook her head. "Did you ever think you'd see the day? Promise that you'll shoot me if that ever happens to me."

"Promise."

"I've built a pretty good base at the salon; it's a gold mine in itself, full of my favorite type— loaded, self-absorbed and too much time on their hands. But there's one in particular I have my eye on." Josie's finger traced the rim of her teacup. "She has the potential to be a long-term score so the hook has to be perfect. That's why I need you for this one."

"Go on." Simone blew across the top of her cup.

"Her name is Andrea Petrakas. A new widow. From what I hear at the salon, she and her husband own more real estate than you have hair on your head, plus old family properties on the banks of the Mediterranean in Greece worth millions. I took a ride past their house a few days ago." Josie's eyes widened. "And, wow."

"Really loaded, huh?" Simone drank her coffee.

"Jaw dropping," Josie said. "Long Island's Gold Coast meets the Parthenon."

Simone leaned in.

"I've been asking around about the husband and no one has a good word to say about him. The girl that colors Andrea's hair told me that the two sons moved their families out of state. So what does that tell you?"

"How'd the old bastard die?"

"Fell five stories with a day laborer when a terrace on one of his decrepit rental buildings in Far Rockaway collapsed."

"Whoopsie." Simone shrugged. "And what's she like?"

"Old school. Wouldn't walk from here to there without her husband's permission, still giving two-dollar tips to the shampoo girls. "You know the type; they have everything and nothing."

"You think she'll go for it?"

"I'd say that she's perfect. People who are that cheap are paranoid by nature. They think everyone is out to get them. And now that she's on her own, lying awake, wringing her hands over what the future has in store for her..."

"I like it." Simone eyes lit.

"And we have a violent, sudden death to work with, the estranged sons, no support system." Josie pretended to lay a hand of cards on the table. "Royal flush."

Simone giggled." How long before you're ready to pounce?" She passed Vera another cookie.

"I'm still in the wooing phase with her. When I first chatted her up I got her talking about her country, it really took her walls down. She thinks she has a new best friend. A few more weeks and she'll be ready for a baiter. That's where you come in."

"I'm ready."

"I'll have her in for a facial, complimentary if it has to be, and you'll already be in my chair when she gets there, laying it on thick to me about Mrs. Habbibi, this incredible psychic that you went to see. Helped you out so-ooo much."

"No problem. I know exactly what to say."

"If my setup session is good enough and I play this right, I'm shooting to get a couple of months out of her. Maybe even a year if I stay put. They were slumlords. He left her with more money than she could spend in five lifetimes." Josie pulled a tube of hand cream out of her bag. "We're talking a nice condo in Cali, a shark lawyer to get custody back." She gently rubbed her hands against each other, working in the lotion.

"Are you so sure that's the best thing for you or Ethan at this point?" Simone suggested.

Josie stopped. Her jaw clenched and she glared across the table. "What makes everyone think that I give a shit about what they feel is best for me and my son?" she snarled.

"Alright, alright. Don't get upset. You just better start laying off the pills if that's what you're planning—that's all I'm saying. The court is going to make you submit blood work to prove that you're clean."

"I'm not worried." She changed the subject. "I don't want to get ahead of myself, but I've heard of operators getting their marks to sign over deeds. You ready to move?" Her demeanor took on an abrupt cheerfulness.

Simone returned her sister's playful grin. "Maybe Mrs. Habbibi should learn a little Greek."

"Thanks. You're a genius, Simmy," Josie dismissed her. "Don't you think I'm all over that already? I've been listening to one of those instructional CDs while I drive. And I still remember a few phrases I picked up from some idiot I dated a few years ago. It's not going to be a problem. I've got it covered."

"Speaking of idiots you've dated. I took care of a problem for us myself," Simone proudly announced.

"What problem is that?" Josie's eyes narrowed.

"Tommy. He showed up at the house again with the Neanderthal."

"Yeah. And?"

"I offered him the Russian's Rolex. He looked it over, turned and left."

"What?" Josie pushed her cup and saucer away. "Do you know how much that watch was worth? That was my emergency fund." She slapped her palm down on the table.

Vera jumped, globs of speckled mush falling out of her mouth as she screamed.

"It's okay, Mom. It's okay." Simone attempted to calm her down while the curious diners sitting nearby tried their best to pretend not to notice the scene.

"All you had to do was stall him a little while longer." Josie turned her head away while Simone tried to push the lumps of chewed Oreo back into Vera's mouth. "You never did know how to finesse a situation."

"How do you finesse a steroid freak who was swindled out of fifteen grand?" She dunked a napkin into a water glass.

Josie waved for the check and leaned across the table. "I thought you knew me better. Didn't you know that I would have a little insurance policy just for this type of situation?"

"So what were you waiting for?" She dabbed at Vera's chin.

"The right time."

"Well, it was the right time for me. Do you see what I'm living with?" Simone's eyes darkened, a crimson flush climbing up her neck as she shoved her untouched sandwich away.

"Okay. Okay. It's done. Let's just forget about it." Josie held up her palms. "What's that smell?" Her nose wrinkled.

"She must have went." Simone mopped her own forehead with the wet napkins clutched in her fist.

"You're joking, right?" Josie looked over at Vera still chewing blissfully, gazing around the luncheonette. "Come on, I can't do this." She grabbed her purse. "Let's get her out of here."

Out in the parking lot Josie leaned inside her sister's car window. "I didn't realize she'd gotten so bad."

Simone blew a cloud of smoke up into the air. "And who knows how long this could go on for? Up until last year she was swimming three days a week at the rec center."

Josie bit her lip.

"I swear this family is cursed. God forbid anything should ever go easy for us."

"Shh-hh. Don't talk like that in front of her."

Simone glanced at Vera and the plastic doll in her rearview mirror. "She's not there." Her voice was low with dejection.

Josie laid her hand on her sister's arm. "I know all of this is no picnic. But just be patient and have a little faith in me. You're going to be a rich old lady, lying on the beach all day drinking those flavored wine coolers you like."

"Right." Simone allowed herself to smile and pulled away.

6

*F*rozen mounds of snow lined the Belgian block streets of down-town Manhattan, stubborn remnants of a stormy winter. Fiona and Joan were among the bundled throngs strolling the crowded sidewalks of Soho, merrily popping in and out of its one of a kind shops and galleries on the blustery, sunny Sunday afternoon in the shoppers' paradise.

They stopped, standing shoulder to shoulder, admiring the eye-catching selections in the window of a trendy shoe store.

"Ooh, look at those," Joan said, pointing to a pair of pretty leather ballerina flats. "Come on, I want to try them on." She tugged Fiona inside.

Joan sat and slipped off her boots while Fiona strolled around the airy, austere design of the showroom, perusing the inventory while they waited for the sales girl to return with Joan's request.

She soon reappeared empty handed and apologetic. "Sorry. No more size eights." She frowned. "We have another store not too far from here, in Nolita. Let me give them a call for you."

Fiona moved toward the counter while the clerk made her call and as soon as the young woman turned her back, Joan caught Fiona nonchalantly slip a can of suede protector from the display near the cash register and drop it into her purse so quickly that she doubted that she had even witnessed the low and off-putting deed.

"Sorry. They don't have an eight, either." The woman ended the call and walked back into the center of the brightly lit store. "I can order them for you and have them shipped if you like."

"No. That's okay, but thank you very much for your help." Joan pulled her boots back on, her head down, trying to process the unsettling event she'd observed.

"Are we ready, Joanie?" Fiona was standing over her and as they began to walk out of the store together the clerk's voice stopped them at the door.

"Excuse me."

They turned back to her.

"You might want to try Bloomingdales on Broadway. Their shoe department sometimes carries a few styles from that company." She smiled at them.

Back outside, bold, abstract, hand-painted murals adorned the sides of the brick buildings that loomed over the teeming streets below. Indie authors and Bohemian artists peddled their creations along the curbsides amid the delightful aromas floating out of the cafes and independent coffee houses into the streets.

Joan permitted the pleasures of the day to slowly dilute her concern over her friend's earlier, disturbing behavior. And when Fiona allowed herself to be dipped and twirled by a homeless man in the crowd who was also swept into the moment by the a street performer's lively African beats drummed out on empty plastic buckets, it was easy to let the episode fade into irrelevance.

Joan handed Fiona back her share of the colorful shopping bags when she returned from her dance partner and they held on to each other as they stepped over an exhaust-topped heap of old snow as dusk fell and they ducked into a noisy tapas bar for warmth and an early dinner.

As they settled in, sitting elbow to elbow with fellow diners at a community table, Joan began to unwind from around her neck the new, royal blue scarf she'd bought from a street vendor. Watching the lively eatery fill with others retreating in from the darkening city streets, she realized that she too was a part of the ceaseless energy that was Manhattan. She was overcome with a wave of gratitude.

"I love all of these out-of-the-way places you take me. How do you find them?"

"I used to live down here for a few years when I was in my twenties."

Joan pulled the menu down and away from Fiona's face. "Thank you."

"Sure. For what?" Fiona grinned back at her and returned to the list of daily specials.

"If it weren't for you, I'd be getting into my pajamas at this time on a Sunday night." She took Fiona's hand, blinking back unanticipated tears. "Thank you for everything you've done for me."

Fiona reached over and playfully grabbed a handful of Joan's hair. "Even for this fabulous new cut you let me pressure you into?"

"Did I have a choice?" Joan asked, laughing.

"Of course you did and you chose correctly. Didn't I tell you Fredrico was an artist? This look is so smart on you, fresh, sexy…"

"My sister hates it."

"She's just afraid of the new you."

"So am I," Joan blurted, taking joy in Fiona's throaty and now familiar bray.

"Good. It means you're having fun." She patted Joan's hand and went back to the menu. "Oh, I wanted to ask you something." Fiona lowered the menu. "Wendy, the woman who owns the salon is buying into another place and asked me if I was interested in expanding with her. I haven't given her an answer yet. I'm not sure if I want to take it on, but if I did, would you be interested in helping me out, two or three days a week? You don't have to answer me this minute."

"Are you kidding me?" Joan leaned across the table. "I would love to! What else do I have going on?"

"Okay, then." Fiona nodded. "Let me talk to her and sort out the details."

The server arrived with their cocktails and they touched glasses in a silent toast. Joan lifted the miniature plastic sword out of her drink and pulled the olive off with her teeth. "I'm thinking of going to a psychic."

"You are?" Fiona tore off a piece of bread and dipped it into the rosemary-infused olive oil and popped it into her mouth.

"She's supposed to be incredible. I got her number from a woman at the bereavement meetings."

"So why now?"

"I don't know exactly. It's over a year since Vinny's gone. I've been waiting for a sign… maybe he wants me to know something."

"Have you ever been to a psychic before?"

Joan shook her head no, sipping her martini that played dangerously close to the rim of the glass.

"If you think it's going to make you feel better."

"You want to go, too?" Joan asked.

"I'll wait till you let me know what you think of her. Come on, look at the menu. I'm starving."

Returning back to her sister's home in Long Island, Josie could smell the sharp scent of wood smoke from the beach house fireplace before she even turned into the street. Her car door slamming seemed like the only sound in the universe as it echoed, rising up with the thinning smoke pouring out of the stone chimney into the clear, cold, black sky.

As she shuffled around the patches of frozen slush toward the dark pool house Pharaoh's silhouette was in the window, propped up on his front legs waiting for her. He began to bob like a spring-loaded marionette as she struggled with the stubborn lock.

She knelt, letting him lavish her with his usual overzealous welcome while eyeing the soundless image of Marilla and Charlotte sitting at the table up in the golden glow of the kitchen window.

Josie rapped on the glass sliding door waving a wine bottle tied with a tangle of colorful ribbons around its neck. Charlotte held up a finger to wait and disappeared into the interior of the house. A moment later a Siamese padded across the kitchen, Charlotte in hot pursuit. Josie turned up the collar of her coat against the ever-present wind relentlessly battering the rear of the house while she waited.

"Quick little devil." Charlotte opened the door. "Come on, get in. March is definitely coming in like a lion." She slid the doors shut, ensconcing both Josie and Pharaoh in the cocoon-like warmth of their home.

"I hope we're not disturbing you. I could smell the fire a block away."

"Do you want some dinner, Jozette?" Marilla asked.

"Just ate."

"What do you have there?" Charlotte accepted the gift, peering at its label. "Whoo-whoo! This is the kind of bottle you bring to your wealthy, future in-laws. Look at this, Mim."

"I was in the city today doing some shopping with a friend. I bought it for you two at Reynard's in the Village."

"I know the shop. You overpaid there, you know, darlin." Charlotte reached on top of her head for her glasses and inspected the bottle further.

"You two deserve it. I like the way you live."

"I'm going to open this right now for us. We'll enjoy a glass by the fire."

"You two go ahead. I'm going to clear up the dishes." Marilla pushed up from the table.

Josie knelt on the Navajo-patterned rug in front of the lively fire scribbling shadows on the walls. She held her palms out to its warm breath, loosening in the inviting surroundings, Pharaoh leaning at her side.

Charlotte arrived with three glasses and the corked bottle in her other hand.

"I put your book back in the same spot."

"Did you enjoy it?"

"I did. I don't sleep much so it filled a few nights."

The older woman dropped into her chair and poured for them. "Marilla is not much of a drinker, so just a smidgeon for her."

"Smidgen," Josie repeated, letting the sound roll off her lips. "I love your use of the words."

"Glad to amuse you. Cheers. Here's to the art of language."

Pharaoh's ears twitched at the pitch of the expensive glassware clinking together.

"À votre santé," Josie echoed in perfect French.

"Very good," Charlotte said, chuckling. "Have you been practicing?"

"You inspired me."

"Merci. Relax, make yourself comfortable."

"Same seats?"

"Why not?" Charlee's legs rose as she pulled back on the lever of her cognac-colored leather recliner and took a delicate first sip from her glass. "Like a kiss," she said, gently closing her eyes.

"I'm glad you approve. I wanted you to know that we appreciate you preserving our dignity, and not making us feel like the charity cases we are, right now." Josie rubbed Pharaoh's head, who had taken residence against her chair near the fire.

Charlotte waved her off. "That's hardly the case. You're wonderful company. I look forward to our chats."

"Really?" Josie beamed. "I was afraid that maybe you were just being kind, someone as educated as you being pestered by all my questions."

"You do just fine keeping up your end of our conversations. You possess real intellectual horse power and your questions are thought-provoking."

"Good, because I have another one for you tonight," Josie said, listening to the sounds of the running water and Marilla busy in the kitchen.

"I thought you would." Charlotte gave an affectionate laugh.

Josie leaned forward. "What do you think of psychics?" Her piercing green eyes gleamed in the firelight.

"Are we talking psychics or mediums?"

"Either. Both."

"Frauds abound, but the allure still runs deep."

"You don't think there are any who are authentic?" Josie waited, accustomed to the pause the pragmatic woman took to arrange her thoughts before she spoke.

"There is scientific data that supports that there are individuals who possess elevated precognitive abilities, but being able to predict the future or contact the dead?" She looked dismissively over the top of her glasses. "I would argue, no."

"So why do you think they're so popular?"

"There are a lot of unhappy people out there."

"You think that everyone who visits a psychic is unhappy?"

"Studies have shown that a person's happiness correlates with the sense of control that they perceive possessing over their lives. A person resorting to a self-proclaimed psychic's advice is probably feeling pretty desperate."

Josie gave a pensive nod. "I agree."

"Why are you asking?" Charlotte peered at her.

"A friend of mine is going to see one."

"This *friend* of yours." Charlotte raised an eyebrow. "Is she in some sort of trouble?"

"It's not me," Josie assured her. "It's just that I like this woman; we hit it off pretty well. I just found it surprising that she would go in for that sort of thing. She doesn't seem the type."

"The type?"

"She's intelligent, even keeled, solid family. Pretty much has it all together."

"What's going on in her personal life?"

"Widow. Her husband died a year ago. She's a little flighty, I guess."

"There you go." Charlee held out her open hand. "Acute or prolonged stress can knock the neurotransmitters out of whack. Your otherwise together friend probably has suffered a biochemical imbalance set into motion by grief, which can reduce her emotional stability to that of a Ping-Pong ball."

"You're a smart one, Charlee." Josie wagged her finger. "That's why I like you."

"Tell your friend to recognize her feelings of desperation for what they are—deep-seated anxiety. And suggest she make an appointment with a therapist, not a fortune teller." She swallowed another mouthful of the velvety Amarone.

"I will. I'll tell her, thanks. But let me ask you this," Josie sat up in her chair. "How would you go about treating that type of a patient?"

"Talk therapy for starters and if her condition indicated, a regimen of antidepressants."

"A person can be talked out of a depression?"

"Listened out is more accurate. A skilled questioner can lead a patient to resolve issues thorough self-discovery. Think of it as getting desperately lost in your car. When you find your way yourself you've learned something, as opposed to just taking someone else's directions." Charlotte's voice trilled with optimism.

"Hmm. And what do you think about people who go for a reading out of curiosity or just for fun?"

"Fun, did you say?"

"You know, one of those psychic parties with a bunch of friends."

"What's fun about putting your destiny into the hands of a stranger? Have you ever heard of self-fulfilling prophecy?"

"Sure."

"Suppose this person posing as a psychic, whose objective is basically just to pad their bank account, offers some reckless information or insights? Either unintentionally or intentionally."

"Doesn't mean that it has to be taken to heart."

"Once something is in your head you can't unhear it. It would be like trying to unring a bell. Even if you think you've dismissed what you've heard, your subconscious hasn't. Now with that in mind, suppose your psychic has sadistic tendencies or is just plain twisted? Call me a killjoy, but the element of fun is lost on me. I don't believe in subjecting my peace of mind to that type of risk."

"Okay, okay," Josie stopped her. "But let's suppose that the psychic understood the effect her suggestions had on the subconscious and tailored a benevolent reading?"

"I'd say that sounds like a psychology practice." Charlotte's burst out in a contagious, hearty bout of belly laughter.

"So a psychic reading could be a good thing?" Josie asked through her wide smile.

"I suppose." Charlotte caught her breath. "Why are you so interested in this?"

"Do you remember when you suggested that I consider a career that would utilize my natural gifts?"

"Yes, I remember," Charlotte agreed cautiously. "You've consulted with a psychic?"

"Actually, I've learned that I have quite a knack for helping those who consult with me."

Charlotte put her glass down. "With you?"

"This is between you and me, of course?" Josie lowered her voice, her eyes shifting toward the kitchen.

Charlotte nodded.

"I've been seeing clients as a spiritual advisor," she whispered.

"Spiritual advisor?" Charlee's brow furrowed.

"Interested, aren't you?" Josie winked nodding with pride.

"How could I not be? Where are you getting your clients from?"

Josie suppressed a devilish laugh and shifted in her chair. "Let's leave that issue for another time." She placed her glass down on the end table.

"Well that's a big factor to leave for another time. I thought we established a sense of trust with each other?"

"We have. It's just that my methods are a bit *unorthodox*, if you will. I don't know if a person with your financial reference point could appreciate them."

"Well now you've really got me curious."

"Another time." Josie winked as she heard Marilla approaching.

"What have you two, old wash women been going on about?" Marilla dropped into the sofa, swinging her legs up.

"A little of everything," Josie said. "Charlee is interesting to talk to."

"And your sister is quite the conversationalist."

"Always has been. Even as a kid, she'd keep the two Jewish ladies next door entranced with her stories."

Josie laughed. "They were good to us, weren't they, Mim?"

"From what I remember."

"I would love to hear," Charlotte said, looking to Marilla for permission.

"Go ahead, Jozette," Marilla allowed, reaching to accept her glass of wine from Charlotte.

"Well, it was the only place we were allowed to go besides our own house. We'd fly off of the front steps to meet them as soon as they'd get home from work. They were spinster sisters, expert seamstresses. They worked in Manhattan, down in the garment district."

"I was petrified of the mannequin they kept in their sewing room," Marilla reminisced.

Josie laughed conjuring the memory. "They taught me and Simmy how to sew."

"And play the piano," Marilla enthusiastically added.

"And they would let you hold their box of beads when they were working on a gown," Josie reminded her younger sister.

"I remember. And what was the name of that singer who's records they would always play?"

"Edith Piaf," Josie said.

"And I remember you, Josie, sitting up on their kitchen counter reading your stories to Ruth—was that her name?—when she cooked for Sabbath on Friday afternoons."

"Ruth and Sylvia," Josie said with an affectionate smile.

"You used to write stories as a child, Jozette?" Charlotte pressed.

"She had stacks of them," Marilla answered for her. "It's a shame our mother wasn't interested enough to foster her talent."

Josie laughed. "It was just a hobby and Vera had her sights on her own ambitions. She was featured in a commercial for men's aftershave that ran on TV for a while."

"Why do you always let her off the hook?" Marilla's voice was peppered with scorn. "She was never home for us."

"Do you really want to get into this?" Josie tried to dismiss the subject."

"I think it's important that you finally come to terms with the effect her lack of support had on us."

"What are you talking about, Mim? She told us all the time how special we were."

"Because we were *her* daughters," she snapped.

"I can remember plenty of times when we'd sit on her bed and she'd read to us."

"From fashion magazines. I'll give you a little snippet of how I remember things. I remember Simone bumbling around trying to cook dinner for us and Martin sitting with a beer in his hand, staring at the door waiting for her to come home. And when she finally did float in they'd start in on each other."

"Martin didn't have a job?" Charlotte asked.

"He was an out-of-work photographer, turned drunk. That's how they met after she drove the husband before him, Jozette's father, out of his own house. So they'd have a screaming fight that would end up with Vera storming into her bedroom to pull out the suitcase she kept on the ready under her bed and she'd fling it onto the mattress and start packing. The three of us would hang on her in horror, begging her not to leave and he'd come in, swinging his belt down on us, scattering us all up to our beds."

Without any reaction from her uncomfortable, captive audience, Marilla persisted.

"…and we'd stay awake as long as we could, listening in terror, praying she wouldn't leave during the night. You crying the hardest." She gestured to Josie. "And that's what I remember about Vera."

"Ooo-kay." Josie rolled her eyes as she stood. "Thanks for that little trip down memory lane." She tapped her thigh.

"I'm just stating facts. Living in denial isn't healthy."

"And walking around seething with rage isn't so great either," Josie said. Pharaoh rose as if on cue and clipped after her. "Enjoy the wine."

Charlotte sat motionless waiting for serenity to reenter the room, but even the normally calming sounds of the low ticking antique clock and the crackling lazy fire took on an unsettling air in their quiet living room.

Marilla hopped up from the couch and knelt in front of the fire. "Jozette has always been in denial over our childhood." She angrily prodded the logs with the poker. "Maybe if she faces the reality that our mother didn't care about us, even risked leaving us in the care of that animal, maybe it would help her finally straighten her life out."

"Your sister's conception of your mother is her own. And Vera did eventually divorce your stepfather."

"Only after he murdered our baby sister, falling asleep with a cigarette burning the house to the ground while the rest of us were at school and she was out hawking acting work." Marilla let the iron poker drop heavily onto the hearth.

"I know the story, Mim. Don't do this to yourself."

Marilla rose. "It was you who encouraged the topic." She stalked out of the room.

Miles away, across the Atlantic Beach Bridge in Brooklyn, Tommy stood on Simone's front steps, his sledgehammer-wielding henchman at his side.

"It's a fake." Tommy glared through the storm door holding up the Rolex.

As soon as Simone unlocked the door he pushed past her, barging into the house, his accomplice standing guard as Tommy stormed through the rooms, hunting for Josie.

"What are you doing?" Simone shrieked, chasing after him. "You can't come in here!"

He flew up the stairs and came thundering back down. "Where is she?" he roared, punching a hole into the wall with his fist and then strode down the hallway.

The Jamaican aide spoon-feeding Vera her dinner at the table froze as Tommy burst into the small kitchen, Simone, Trixie, Darla, Raymond and Tommy's sidekick piling in after him.

"Get out of my house! I'll call the cops! I have a sick mother!" Simone shook her fist over her head, her smoker's voice raspy and cracking.

The confused, wide-eyed aide silently stood up to leave.

"Where do you think you're going? Sit down," the thug growled at her.

Tommy tossed the Rolex at Simone. "Where is she?"

Simone fumbled with the watch. "I would have never given it to you if I thought it was a fake."

"What the hell is going on?" Raymond insisted over Vera's babbling and the frantically barking dogs.

"Everyone get against the wall," Tommy bellowed and swiped a vase of plastic flowers off the counter, the crash sending nightgown-clad Vera into a shrieking fit.

"Not you," he told the aide who slowly lowered herself back down into the kitchen chair. "And shut the old lady up. And you," he yelled, pointing a blunt finger at Simone. "Shut those crazy mutts up."

Simone scooped up Trixie and Darla into her arms and obediently stood against a wall with the wriggling dogs next to Raymond who was barefoot and licking nervously at the sweat that had beaded above his lip.

Tommy towered over the hapless couple, leaning in with his gleaming cannonball of a head. "Now, for the last time…" he leered at them. "Tell me where she is."

"I don't know," Simone stammered. "I haven't heard from her since…"

MARY A. ELLENTON

With a heaving grunt, the thug raised the sledge hammer over his shoulder on Tommy's signal.

"No! No!" Simone and Raymond pleaded as the man swung it into the row of overhead cabinets, each additional blow further demolishing the kitchen.

Trixie jumped from Simone's arms and began to attack Tommy's ankles; Simone swung wildly at him when he kicked the small dog across kitchen floor with his thick-soled boots. Tommy deftly sidestepped her fist as Raymond struggled to restrain his wife, his other arm shielding his eyes from the flying debris. "Goddammit! Just tell him where she is!"

"Okay. Stop! Stop it," Simone conceded. "I'll call her." She handed Darla to Raymond and rushed over to a whimpering Trixie cowering in a corner.

Tommy grabbed his man's arm to stop him and an unsettled quiet fell over the room. The aide's arms slowly dropped from shielding her head and Vera stopped shrieking.

"Where's your phone?"

Simone pointed to the living room and Tommy signaled his brute. The panting thug wiped his forehead with the back of his arm and went off to fetch it.

The kitchen was silent as Simone dialed; a hazy snow of sheetrock dust lazily drifted down on the bizarre gathering as they all waited for Josie to pick up the call.

Lounging on the pool house bed, Pharaoh snuggling in the curve of her body, Josie turned down the sound of the television and picked up Simone's call. "Hey, Simmy." She held the phone away, grimacing from her sister's ear piercing voice. "Would you just give him the phone?"

Josie waited, holding the phone away from her ear again while Tommy ranted.

"Are you done?"

The calmness of her voice stopped him.

"So listen to this," she spoke matter-of-factly. "I have a grocery bag

98

filled with a year's worth of receipts for restaurants, lingerie, weekend
get-a-ways, and jewelry all billed to your credit card. It will cost me two
dollars in postage to mail it to your wife. She'll make sure that you'll
probably never see your kids again, not to mention what's going to happen when she hands it over to her divorce attorney." She sighed as with
boredom. "And here's the part I want you to think about: if you're so
worried about the few thousand dollars that you insisted I take from
you when you wanted to get into my pants while your wife was home
with your daughter and infant son, think about my little special deliv-
ery thrown into the equation when the judge rules on your eighteen
years of alimony and child support payments. Do the math, genius.
I'm letting you off easy. And… if the judge presiding over your case just
happens to be a female….Well, you can just kiss bye-bye to any hopes
of a life until you're done paying for your kids' college tuitions."

Pharaoh's ears went up and his head cocked at the sounds coming
out of Josie's phone.

"Relax. Take a breath," her voice rose in irritation, silencing him.
"Just one more thing; if they subpoena me, you can be sure that I'll
dress for the occasion—one of my short, tight little numbers you loved
so much."

"You conniving bitch– "

"Okay. That's enough. My favorite show is about to start, so let's finish this up. Here's what you're going to do, *baby*. Get out of my sister's
house and forget her address. If she bothers me just one more time
because of you, I'm licking those stamps. And you know me, Tommy.
You know I will."

7

$\mathcal{J}$oan's car rolled through the affluent suburban neighborhood as she peered out of the window, squinting at the house numbers searching for the address Mrs. Habbibi had given her over the phone. The neighborhood was a wooded area of sloping lawns and towering trees whose stature implied that they were residents long before the builders had arrived and placed houses among them. A cluster of cars parked along the curbs reinforced the certainty she'd arrived at her destination in spite of the remote setting.

The house was set back off the street and the grand, ornate lantern hanging above its entrance was dark. It made the odd experience of walking the winding slate path to the stranger's home that much more anxiety-inducing. A rusted, scrolled iron love seat was stranded out in the middle of the lawn and a stack of long forgotten, weather-beaten firewood piled against the mildew stained, cedar- shingled house tattled a sense of discord inside.

Joan could see others milling around through the open interior door and when the mechanized staccato of the doorbell ceremoniously announced another guest, a middle-aged, reed-thin woman in a sleeveless dress approached.

"Who are you?" she asked Joan through the glass door.

The woman's brusque manner took her aback. "Joan Bruno. I have an appointment with Mrs. Habbibi." Joan pushed an overgrown evergreen branch off to the side as the woman opened the door to her.

"I'm Miriam. You have your money?"

Joan began to fumble in her purse.

"Come in already, silly." Miriam Stemple stepped aside allowing Joan to enter the dated, 1980s contemporary-style décor of the damp-smelling house.

"Has she ever read for you before?" Miriam asked over her shoulder as she led Joan down the hallway.

"No. It's my first time." Joan navigated her way along a path stacked with cardboard boxes into the woman's home.

"She'll knock your socks off." Miriam turned and held the medallion hanging around her neck up to Joan's face; a gold oval with the image of a young man's face stamped onto it. "My son, Garret. She was able to contact him for me."

Unsure whether to offer condolences or congratulations, Joan managed an uncertain smile.

"I'll let you know when it's your turn—still a few ahead of you. There's wine and some sandwiches in the kitchen and the television is on in the living room. They're watching *Dancing with the Stars* I think." Miriam turned back to the activity in the kitchen.

Joan took a seat on an animal-print wing chair, relieved to be out of the uncomfortable company of the odd woman. She exchanged awkward pleasantries with two other clients sitting wide-eyed on the couch.

Her seat gave her a view down the hallway where she could see the next in line; a smartly dressed man in his early thirties, his arms hanging between his knees, also waiting on a chair outside the room where the readings were taking place. Soon, a middle-aged woman emerged; carefully closing the door behind her and the handsome client rose and waited to be summoned inside.

"You're next." Miriam Stemple excitedly waved to Joan glass in hand, and pointed to the newly-vacated chair.

"It's all yours." Its former occupant greeted her with an engaging smile while he waited admittance from the other side of the door.

"Come in, please."

And he disappeared inside.

"Hello. I am Mrs. Habbibi."

"I'm Jimmy. How are ya, Mrs. Habbibi?" He stood over six feet; a meticulously dressed Adonis.

"Sit, Jimmy. Turn your hands up for me, please."

"Cool accent." He held his large, neat hands open before her.

"There is a sense of panic and loss surrounding you. Broken heart, is it?" Mrs. Habbibi looked casually into his agreeable face.

He grinned with amusement. "I guess you could say that."

"And you want to know if she will come back to you?"

"Yeah," his toothy smile further enhancing his good looks.

"She is a pure soul. A keeper, as they say."

"My fiancée. She thinks I've cheated with one of my exes."

"Has she returned the ring back to you?"

He nodded.

"Surprising. This isn't the way with women today. She is of rare character. I can understand why you want her back so badly."

"She isn't like any other women I've ever been with. I'm crazy in love with her."

"Then why did you deceive her?"

"I didn't…"

"Oh?" Mrs. Habbibi raised an eyebrow with a mischievous smile.

He pulled his hands away and ran them through his flaxen hair. "This is too wild," he said, adding a nervous laugh.

"I need your hands back, please."

"Sorry. It's just such a mind fuc—"

"Yes. It is a rare gift. I treasure and cherish it. You are gifted yourself. A creative. I see many women around you. Hair stylist?"

He pulled his hands away again. "Really?" He rested his elbow on the desk and leaned in, his thick laughter disguising his shock at her accuracy. He slapped his palm down on the table. "Colorist," he informed her. "What a head trip."

"You own a dog, Jimmy?"

"Yeah. How did you know that?"

She pointed. "The short white hairs on your sleeve."

They both shared in a good laugh.

She cleared her throat. "So you claim you are in love with this woman, you respect her, and yet you deceived her with a former lover. Why? If you don't mind indulging my curiosity?"

He blinked and puffed out a breath. "Smokin' hot." He shrugged.

"You have caused your fiancé great heartache."

His lips pressed tight and a look of regret crossed his face as he met Mrs. Habbibi's eyes. "Will she forgive me?"

"The fiery clouds of anger still blur the outcome. I'm sorry I cannot say for certain at this time."

"Is there anything I can do to get her back?"

"Character is much easier kept than recovered. But I may be able to help you."

He pressed his palms together in prayer pose.

"Are you willing to put in some effort?"

"Anything."

"You mentioned that she returned your engagement ring?" She sat back in her chair, fingers in steeple position resting against her chin in thought.

He nodded with hopefulness.

"That is lucky for you. There are methods specifically for your situation—bringing back lost loves. And they are much more effective if invoked with an item symbolic of the union."

"You mean like, a spell?"

"I prefer to refer to it as a *treatment*." The psychic smiled modestly.

"I'll try it. Just tell me what I have to do?"

"Bring me the ring. We don't have much time. It is crucial to begin during a waxing moon phase. Do you live far from here?"

"No. I can be back in no time."

"Place the ring in a simple white envelope along with a current photo of the two of you together—prior to your transgressions. Leave the envelope with my hostess and I'll take care of the rest."

"How long does the treatment take?"

"Seven days. What is your fiancé's name? I see a V." Her forehead wrinkled as she feigned concentration, while, in fact, figuring out room in her schedule to visit a jeweler and swap his stone out for a zirconia. "Is it…Veronica?"

"Valerie."

"Valerie," she repeated. "What is Valerie's birth date?" She scribbled on the pad she kept nearby.

"Ah…March…" He struggled to remember. "March eleventh. How does this treatment work?"

"I cannot presume to explain my gift; the ability to summon the correct energies and direct them to a desired outcome. But if you the wish, I will describe the rudiments of the procedure."

The young man listened intently.

"First, I am going to smudge the ring."

"Smudge?"

"A spiritual cleansing to dispel the negative energy and influences that have tarnished the symbol of your union. When it is clear of all negativity, I will begin the prescribed invocations and recitations over the item. It will be submerged in a clear glass filled with rose water to which is added a sprig of ivy leaf, the symbol of marriage and fidelity, and an egg, the symbol of rebirth. Two candles will burn continuously on either side of the image of the two lovers, one blue, the color of opening blocked communication, and one red, the color of lust and passion. Is your fiancé employed?"

"She's a medical biller."

"This coming Friday send red flowers to her place of business. Now, there isn't anything mystical about that advice, but do it on a Friday. It is the day of the week ruled by Venus, love, and human interactions."

"Okay. That's not a problem. Got it covered. And when do I get the ring back?"

"Call me in seven days at the same number you used to make this appointment. At that time I will give you the address of where I will be holding my next readings. I will return the cleansed ring along with two crystals that I will have already prepared for you. Even if Valerie has come back to you by then, keep these crystals on your person at all times until after your wedding day."

"No problem. What are the crystals for?"

"The first is a garnet to stabilize your relationship; the other is a fire opal to empower your sexual energy."

"Okay. I'm in." He clapped his hands together, animated with renewed optimism.

Mrs. Habbibi joined his celebratory laughter. "I haven't told you the fee for the service, yet, handsome Jimmy the colorist."

"Whatever it is I've got to get her back. I feel like this is gonna work."

"It's fifteen hundred dollars. Cash, please. Include it in your envelope with the ring and the photo, please."

"Cash. Ring. Photo. I got it. I'll be back in an hour." He jumped up to leave.

"One moment." She stopped him.

"What?"

"You will live a long life. You will not die of sickness or a disease. It will be old age."

"Thank you. Thank you, Mrs. Habbibi." He kissed her hand and backed out of the room.

She reclined in her chair with a sigh, relieved to be alone in the space again.

"Whoops, excuse me."

She recognized the friendly voice of her next client on the other side of the door and then the soft knock came. Mrs. Habbibi immediately sat up and exhaled her previous client out of her system in short bursts and took in a centering breath. She wiggled her shoulders, rolled her neck and sat tall in her chair. "Come in, please."

Joan entered the calm of the dimly lit room and gestured to the empty chair.

The psychic nodded. "Please. I am Mrs. Habbibi."

"Hello, Mrs. Habbibi, I'm Joan. And you've come highly recommended from – "

"Please," she stopped her. "That is unimportant information." She lit the sage wand and began to sweep it in the space between them.

Joan placed her purse on the floor at her feet. "Sage?"

Mrs. Habbibi nodded. "But what *is* important is the very strong male energy that is here with us. Would you turn your palms up, please?" The psychic doused the wand.

Joan cleared her throat and obliged.

"Uncross your legs, please. That posture closes off reception." Mrs. Habbibi casually scanned Joan's upturned palms. "I'd like you to close your eyes and visualize calming, white light. Feel it all around you, peacefully surrounding you in Divine protection of the Christ."

Joan squeezed her eyes shut and after a feeble attempt, opened them with a sigh. "I can't. I'm too nervous to concentrate."

"I understand," the psychic sympathized. "Your husband has passed. Yes?"

"Yes." Joan immediately began to weep.

"He is here with us. Right at your side. Victor?"

"Vincent." Her voice was barely audible.

"Vinny. He's telling me, Vinny." The psychic's voice warmed.

Joan laughed affectionately through her tears.

"He wants you to know he is always with you and he loves you very much." Mrs. Habbibi tilted the box of tissues towards her client.

"Why hasn't he given me some sort of a sign in all this time?" Joan sobbed.

"He is busy. Your husband was a very dutiful man, yes?"

"Yes, he was."

"We are the same on the other side as we were in our mortal life. He is quite focused on his work in the spiritual realm," Mrs. Habbibi informed.

"Work?" Joan asked though her tears.

"I refer to it as work. There are many levels the soul needs to attain on its journey to perfection," she explained in her soothing, exotic accent. "It's almost as if he doesn't want to be distracted."

Joan's expression showed her confusion.

"Don't take offense." Mrs. Habbibi softly smiled. "Quite frankly, the realm of the living holds little interest for those who have crossed over." Her attention seemed to be pulled elsewhere and her hand rose into the air and began to move in a swirling motion beside her head. "I am getting someone else…another male energy—you have to acknowledge them as soon as they come through. They don't like it if you don't," she candidly offered and then stared off into an invisible world. "A dominant male energy… I'm getting an F… Faa...Fah…who is F?"

"I don't know," Joan shrugged.

"What was your father's name?"

"Phillip."

"That's our problem," she happily announced. "Same sound as an F." Satisfied, she returned her focus to the unseen visitors. "He loved your mother very much. Has she been ill, recently? He thanks you for taking care of her."

Joan's hand covered her mouth to control her emotions.

"Ha. You have several souls who surround you. Who is the female energy with an L? I'm getting an L…" She placed her hand softly at her chest. "An issue with her heart, breast?"

"That's my best friend Lenore." Joan's eyes glistened with tears, but she managed a small laugh.

"Her energy comes through with pink light. She had a deep affection for you—still has a deep affection for you."

"She died from breast cancer six years ago," Joan offered.

"She is at bliss. She sends her love to you. She says thank you for keeping in contact with her family."

Beguiled and completely pulled into Mrs. Habbibi's world, Joan edged forward with anticipation as the psychic's hand began swirling at an increased speed.

"What is it?"

"Vinny is back. Are you planning a trip? Is someone you know taking a cruise?"

Joan's eye's narrowed with concentration. "No."

"There is a vessel, a large ship. Is there a reason Vinny wouldn't want you to take a trip?"

"I don't know." Joan shrugged.

"Finished, finished..." Mrs. Habbibi squinted wiping her hands against each other. "He's telling me he's finished with something...."

"We own a boat," Joan said.

Mrs. Habbibi laughed with satisfaction. "That makes sense, then."

"What?"

"He wants you to know that it is no longer important to him."

"Oh my God." Joan gasped, covering her mouth. "I was so confused over selling it..."

"Well, you have your answer. And who is it that has just had surgery?" Mrs. Habbibi touched a hand to her midsection. "Was it a stomach issue? Digestive problems?"

"My mother. Diverticulitis," Joan called out, unable to control her astonishment.

"She is a resilient woman. She will recover completely. Is there a question you would like to ask?"

Joan tugged another tissue from the box at the corner of Mrs. Habbibi's table and dabbed at her eyes. "Will I ever be happy again?"

Mrs. Habbibi's expression was compassionate. "The answer is in the question."

"That doesn't help me much," Joan said, weary with emotion.

Mrs. Habbibi peered at her client and then reached down into a deep shopping bag, coming up with a small, brown velvet pouch. She slowly pulled at its gold string and removed a smooth marble-sized stone, deep green in color.

Joan watched as the candlelight reflected off of its sheen, held between the psychic's thumb and index finger.

"This is a Heulandite crystal. It comes in a variety of hues. The green ones are known for their power to restore positive energy, overcome grief, and realign the heart energy to reconnect with joy. Open your hand."

Joan let the psychic drop the distinctive bauble into her palm.

"Pretty, isn't it?"

"Yes."

"Keep it on your person, or in your purse."

Joan looked up from the polished stone sitting in her palm. "What do I owe you for it?"

Mrs. Habbibi shook her head. "It is yours."

"Thank you." Joan closed her hand around the mystical gem.

"We are our own jailers. You are a dynamic woman whose inner conflicts immobilize you."

Joan nodded with acknowledgement.

"Ask what it is that you are afraid of learning about yourself that is keeping you from walking out into your own life."

"I don't know." Joan dropped her head into her hands and was wracked with sobs.

The psychic remained skillfully silent for a time, allowing her client to reflect and then spoke confidently. "The cave you fear to enter holds the treasure that you seek."

Joan raised her head as if someone had called her name; Mrs. Habbibi's profound words a golden moment for her.

"Ah, hem." The psychic cleared her throat, summoning her client back to the present, not surprised at the effect the eloquent Joseph Campbell quote would deliver, a well-worn tool in her arsenal. "You will live a very long life. You will not die of diseases; it will be of old age."

Alone in her room again, the psychic exhaled with relief, light headed with mental exhaustion. She was aching to pull off her wig to scratch at the perspiration that tickled her scalp, but had to settle for reaching down into her bag and taking a swig of her bottled ice tea. The sugar would help boost her energy. And then the next soft knock came and then five more, as the arduous evening wore on, until the only person left in the house was its owner, Miriam Stemple.

"Mrs. Habbibi?" She knocked lightly on the door, anxiously taking the seat across from the weary psychic, sliding the bulging envelope across the table. "Here you go. More than the usual number of guests tonight."

"Yes. I can barely keep up with my popularity these days." Mrs. Habbibi pleasantly replied.

"And this." Miriam handed her a white envelope. The man who left it said that you'd know what it was."

"Yes. Thank you." Mrs. Habbibi pushed both envelopes down into her bag. "I'm happy to see that you look more rested than the last time we met. I could tell from just our phone conversation that you're a bit calmer. That's important. I'm pleased."

"I owe it all to you."

"Let's just say that we work well together." Mrs. Habbibi gave a knowing smile. "And thank you again for hosting the readings tonight."

"If that's what it takes to get an appointment with you, I'll host once a month."

Mrs. Habbibi laughed at the woman's enthusiasm. "Hmm. I'll consider the arrangement." She made light of the attractive offer.

"The house is empty. I don't mind the company and you said yourself that the room was perfect," Miriam persisted.

"If you insist. We can discuss that issue later, but I think we should begin. Are you ready, Miriam?"

She eagerly offered her upturned palms; Mrs. Habbibi hovered hers just above them.

"I can feel the energy already," Miriam said, peering into Mrs. Habbibi's eyes. "I think we will be able to make a contact tonight." She sat higher in her chair.

Mrs. Habbibi closed her eyes and her arm floated upward, swirling alongside her head. Miriam watched fascinated as the psychic's body began to sway, back and forth.

"I am getting a spirit," she squinted, "but it is not Garret. It is an older male presence… a father…a grandfather?" The psychic touched her hand to her chest. "Something in the chest area.."

"My father died of a heart failure."

"I'm getting an S… is it Sal… Sam?"

"Sam. His name was Samuel."

"Yes. He is coming through very strong. He wants you to know that he is with Garrett. They are together."

"Where is Garrett?"

"They are together, together in peace." Mrs. Habbibi seemed to be straining for more information, her hand still circling in the air.

Miriam gripped at the edges of the desk, zeroed in on the psychic's efforts.

"Garrett chooses to remain distant." The psychic slumped. "I tried, but he is intent on his work. He doesn't want to be distracted."

"What work? What are you saying?"

The psychic's dabbed at her forehead with a handkerchief she pulled from inside her sleeve. "I refer to it as work," she began to explain. "There are many levels the soul needs to attain on its journey to perfection and sometimes past life binds or energy chords from loved ones, here on the earthly plane hamper their progress. It is a distraction and…. well…unwelcome." She shrugged.

"What does that mean? You won't be able to contact my son for me again?"

"We just did. It was just through an alternate spirit. I suggest that we allow Garret to establish himself further in the other realm before attempting another contact."

Miriam released her grip on the desk and her arms went limp.

"Don't be upset, Miriam. You loved your son. I know that you wouldn't want to obsturct Garret's spiritual journey, would you?"

"No, of course not. But I wanted to be able to say some things to him. Some things that I never had the chance to…." Miriam's eyelids fluttered as she fought for control. "I worry about him, you know?" She ran her fingers along the edge of the Mrs. Habbibi's gold table runner. And I'm sorry if I'm distracting him, but I miss him so much." She wept.

"If that's what your intuition is guiding you to do, then go ahead and tell him, Mother. He can hear you."

Miriam looked up at Mrs. Habbibi.

"Go ahead, Miriam. Garret is waiting."

Miriam sniffled and took a deep breath. She swallowed. "Garr-Garr, I miss you so much, I love you. I miss seeing your beautiful face. I hope you are safe and happy; I'm going to be happy too. I'm sorry if I'm distracting you, I just want you to know that I'm sorry if there was anything I did... or didn't do, while you were here with me...tell grandpa Sam to take good care of you for me. " Miriam buried her face in her hands.

"That was excellent, Miriam. You followed your intuition. I feel the spirit energy retreating. It fades, peacefully. You handled that perfectly."

"I did?" Miriam raised her head, wiping at her tears.

"Perfectly. It was organic to you. Nature is always the superior. The only thing left to do is allow time to its task and keep your son in your prayers that he may continue on, unimpeded in his spiritual journey."

"What do you mean by unimpeded?"

"A complete transition to the highest level of his soul's evolution without being steered away from the light."

"Steered away from the light, how?" Miriam's face twisted.

"The spirit world is strife with negative astral influences, highly-evolved dark masters. All low vibrating energies that thrive on human suffering and hinder spiritual advancement," Mrs. Habbibi said with a subtle grimace.

"Stop! Stop!" Miriam covered her face with her hands.

"Unpleasant to think about, but wouldn't you rather know? And wouldn't I be remiss if I didn't advise you of their existence?"

"It's too upsetting to imagine. She clutched at the sides of her head. "I can't even think about it."

"If you like I can include Garrett in a daily ceremony that I preform for the deceased of many of my clients. It will offer protection from exactly that type of attack, ushering them safety along through their divine journey."

"How so?"

"It is a centuries-old, powerful ceremony, dating back to the Druids." She lowered her voice to a whisper. "Just before midnight, when these dark energies are on their ascent, it incurs the protective powers of the hierarchy of defenders of the light, they are compelled in the subject's name. In this instance, Garret."

Miriam blinked, listening in both horror and intrigue.

"These highly ascended powers all called upon in ancient utterances to convene and thwart the dark energies in the other realm, whose prime intent is to detour the departed on their spiritual journey towards divine transition. And considering the circumstances of your son's exit from this world …"

"Do it. Do it for him." Miriam leaned across the table emphatically.

"It is perpetual, meaning that it is a constant incantation." Mrs. Habbibi sat back, interlacing her fingers. The cost is two-thousand dollars each month. I recommend three lunar cycles.

"I don't care how much it costs. I want it for him. As long as there is anything I can do to help him…"

"Of course." The psychic scribbled on her pad. "I can include Garret in my petition this very night if you'd like. If possible, the first month's fee would be appreciated."

"I don't know what I'd do without you, Mrs. Habbibi. What Garret would do without you? I feel like you were sent from heaven for us." She pushed away from the table. "Let me get your money." She paused at the doorway, turning back to Mrs. Habbibi, the evening's mess on the kitchen counters in the background behind her. "The ceremony for Garret starts tonight, right?"

"This very night." She looked at her watch. "In fact, I need to be on my way." She began to clear away the items on the desk and place them into her shopping bag at the side of her chair.

Miriam disappeared out of the room and Mrs. Habbibi, herself, reached for a tissue, delicately dabbing the perspiration beaded at her forehead.

8

*J*osie emerged from the pool house on the warm morning greeted by Charlotte and Marilla doing yard work, clearing out the flower beds that lined the fence around the property. Moaning with joy, Josie held her arms in a V aimed at a pastel blue sky while Pharaoh pranced around her legs, sensing the anticipated change of seasons and reacting to his owner's light mood.

"Spring is here," Charlotte happily decreed leaning on her rake.

"Anyone care to join us for a morning stroll down on the beach?"

"No thanks," Marilla declined. "I want to wash up."

"I'll join you. We're pretty much done here." Charlotte slipped off her gardening gloves. "You don't mind do you, Mim?" She grabbed her jacket off of a fence post.

"Be my guest. I'll make us some French toast when you two get back."

"Deal," Josie said, headed down the stairs.

The beach was uninhabited except for the legions of seagulls dotting the wet sand, perched like contented hens, others poking near the lazy surf casually hopping out of the path of the three intruders on the nearly-deserted shoreline.

"I hope you're not upset with me. My curiosity started a conversation the last time we were together I didn't intend on." Charlotte tucked her hands inside her jacket pockets as they walked. "I meant no offense." She struggled to keep up with Josie's faster pace.

"No offense taken. There's a lot to be curious about." Josie picked up a piece of driftwood and threw it ahead for Pharaoh.

Further, along, they stopped at one of the jetties of jagged black boulders that presumed to partition the mighty ocean. Josie stepped up on a flat slope of rock, and watched the waves explode into spray as they crashed against the massive rocks.

Charlotte stretched onto the firmly packed sand. "It's heaven in the off season." She offered her face in homage to the warming rays of the April sun. "The masses don't consider coming down until Memorial Day."

"It is heaven," Josie agreed, looking out across the rolling blanket of glimmering sea, breathing in the freshness of the cool salt air.

They sat in companionable silence watching the ocean perform its eternal dance, indifferent to the size of its audience. The methodic crashing of the waves kept rhythm, the screech of a low-flying seagull, perfectly placed in the composition of the organic masterpiece.

"What are you thinking about?" Charlotte asked, watching her search the horizon.

"Life. The future. Vera." She stroked Pharaoh sitting next to her.

"I think it's interesting how all of you always refer to her by her first name."

"She was like a caricature," Josie said. "I didn't dare bring it up to Marilla, but Simmy just had to put her in the hospital—urinary tract infection or something. I've got a bad feeling. The last time I saw her, I hardly recognized her."

"Alzheimer's, right?"

"Yeah. Lethal injection for me if that happens."

Charlotte nodded in understanding. "People are living so much longer these days. It's a situation facing many families."

"I'll take the quality over the quantity any day."

"Who wouldn't?" Charlotte leaned back on her elbows. "None of us gets to choose. It's an insidious disease."

"Poor Simmy is the one who's been dealing with her."

"I'd been hoping that reconnecting with you would eventually prompt Marilla into reconsidering her stand."

Josie shrugged. "Leave it alone. Vera wouldn't know the difference anymore now, anyway and I think that being mad at her helps Marilla to cope in some weird way."

"You're a wise woman, Jozette. I'm sure you were a source of pride to your mother."

"Thanks, for saying that doctor, but I let her down, too."

"How?"

"It broke her heart when I dropped out of college."

"Why did you?"

"I fell in love for the first time."

"Really?" Charlotte sat up with a smile.

"He was a regular in the restaurant where I was waitressing. He would come in for lunch with other businessmen dressed in expensive suits, and leave me enormous tips. We started dating and he asked me to move into his loft in Tribeca."

"Did you?"

"I was twenty-three and broke, living in a furnished room. He was near forty, gorgeous and rich. What do you think I did?"

"And?"

"We had a great year or so together. I stopped going to school, we traveled, and he took me all over the city to places I never even imagined I'd get to see. We couldn't get enough of each other. It was the first time in my life that I looked forward to the next day. And then, just like that, he told me I had to leave."

"Oh, no." Charlotte wagged her head in sympathy. "What did you do?"

"Back to a furnished room in a basement; me and roaches the size of your thumb."

"You never went back to school?"

"I tried. But keeping up the grades, working to pay tuition, I ran out of steam. "

"So what did you do?"

"For the next few years I bounced around from job to job, and then I stumbled on the idea of becoming a spiritual advisor. I made enough cash to rent an apartment and eat a decent meal at least a few nights a week."

"How did you fall into it?"

Josie stood and brushed sand off of her bottom. "Let's walk." She picked up Pharaoh's driftwood and flung it for him. The two women pulled their jackets closer around their bodies, walking into the wind on the way back to the house.

"I was managing a boutique on Bleecker Street in the West Village. Most of the buildings down there are old, probably built at the turn of the nineteenth century, that's the charm of that area. There was a small alcove between the two stores that was rented by a fortune teller who sat in the front window reading palms. Miss Thea."

"You still remember her name?"

"I'll never forget her. She was a tiny thing, dark and wrinkled. She looked like an old Indian squaw. But oh, what an operator."

"A fake?"

"The best. She was a prop stylist and didn't know it. She had the place staged like an old time parlor. Candlelit, heavy, red velvet drapes, round table with Queen Anne chairs, everything but the crystal ball. She even had a cat skulking around the room. He'd sleep in the window most of the day until she'd get there at night."

Charlotte watched Josie's face as they walked, taken in with the story.

"The whole setup was kind of hokey. Completely over the top, but people ate it up. You could actually see them give themselves right over to it as soon as they stepped inside." Josie laughed, her eyes twinkling with memories. "Miss Thea sat in that store front reading palms every weekend, sometimes until 2 a.m."

"And she was a complete phony?"

"Completely. She had three basic scripts she worked with, peppered with only minor variations. I know. I listened to her every chance I had when there weren't customers in the store." Josie snatched the driftwood from Pharaoh's mouth and threw it again for him. "I saw people hand over cash to her to bring back lovers, break bad luck streaks, pick lucky numbers. They'd fork it right over and come again for more bringing friends back with them. And then she wasn't there anymore." Josie shrugged.

"What happened to her?"

"No one knew. Not my boss, not the landlord. But her setup was still there."

"You didn't!" Charlotte stopped walking her eyes wide, unable to suppress her shock and amusement.

"Oh, yes I did," Josie said laughing and tugged her along. "Come on. I've got to be at the salon in an hour. So one night, after I closed the boutique, I wrapped my head in a scarf and put on some false eyelashes and heavy makeup."

"You're serious."

"Once I cut my teeth I upped the prices. And within a few months I was in a sunny, one-bedroom with hardwood floors and windows that had a view of something besides a brick wall."

"How long did you do that for?"

"Until the space was rented to a shoe repair man."

Charlotte stopped walking again and gaped at her. "That's the un-orthodox method you were hinting at?"

"It's evolved since the days down on Bleecker Street. I'm working the private sector these days and my operation is a lot more sophisticated now."

They arrived back at the wood-framed staircase leading up to the house.

"Wait." Charlotte stopped her. "Sit. I want to hear the rest of this. "Sophisticated, how?" She propped one foot on a step.

Josie sat. Pharaoh dropped onto the sand, panting at her feet. "I do some research before I see my clients."

"Google them, take an inventory of their Facebook page?"

"Please, you insult me. When you're asking fees that are in my league, you better be delivering more than superficial observations."

"And where are you funneling these high-paying customers from?"

"The salons I've worked in and my newest source. Are you ready?" Josie gave a sly smile, her eyes gleaming. "Bereavement groups."

Charlotte blinked, her expression telegraphing her dismay and then distaste. "Are you telling me that you solicit personal information from unsuspecting people who are grieving and then disguise yourself to relay it back to them for cash?"

"Exactly."

Charlotte turned and started up the stairs.

"...Hey, you asked me." Josie stood, calling up after her.

Charlotte was collecting her gloves and water bottle when Josie caught up to her on the deck.

"You're looking at this the wrong way. I've given closure to more grieving widows than a seminary of priests. I've given people the courage to pursue life dreams that would have otherwise died on the shelf." She grabbed Charlotte by the arm. "My clients get results."

Their eyes locked in an angry standoff.

Charlotte shook her arm out of Josie's grip. "You're committing fraud. Not to mention this is depraved cruelty." She turned her back and continued up to the house.

"Put it that way, if it lets you feel superior, *Mrs. My Parents Started Saving For Me Since Before I Could Walk,*" she called after her. "And I'll pass on the French toast."

"What's wrong?" Marilla looked up from whisking at a bowl.

"Nothing." Charlotte strode to the sink.

"Where's Jozette?"

"She won't be joining us." Charlotte washed her face.

"She's still not making an issue of the other night in the living room, is she?"

Joan pulled her car into the gravel parking lot of Surfside Marine Supply, a pit stop on the sunny, Sunday morning before she and Fiona headed out for the day into Manhattan to stroll the Highline and lunch in the Meatpacking District.

"Aren't you coming in?" She turned to Fiona in the passenger seat.

"In a minute. I just need to confirm a few appointments before I forget."

Joan shrugged and left her to her phone.

Fiona watched her disappear into the store and reached into her purse for the burner phone she used for her psychic clients. She listened to a new message, jotted a name and date into a small journal and then dialed Andrea Petrakas. As the woman's phone began to ring, Josie slipped her feet back into her flats and sat up, clearing her throat.

"This is Mrs. Habbibi," she stated serenely in a perfect Middle Eastern accent. "Am I speaking to Andre Petrakas?"

"This is Andrea. I got your number from a woman at my salon. I wanted to schedule an appointment with you."

"Of course, Miss Andrea. This is a good thing that you have contacted me."

"Wh-why are you saying that?"

"It's just that I can hear the trouble in your voice. Perhaps I will be able to help."

"Oh. Okay…when will you be able to see me?"

"Tell me when it is convenient for you."

Fiona sashayed into the high-end boating supply store as if she were walking into a house party. The freakishly warm April morning had the specialty store buzzing with Long Islanders anxious for the start of the season. Joan stood in a long line of customers, some agitated and sweaty, waiting their turn to be helped by an overwhelmed, lone clerk.

"Looks like this is gonna be a while." She patted Joan's back. "I'm going to look around." She turned, making extended eye contact with the sophisticated-looking, well-groomed gentleman who had just joined the line behind them. "Guess spring has sprung," She flashed a smile with a carefree shrug. "Great hair, by the way," she flirted.

Joan watched her disappear down an aisle, touching everything as she passed like an unsupervised child.

"Next," The stone-faced clerk barked, wiping his forehead with the back of his arm as the line moved up a step.

"These plastic owls…they look so real." Fiona's voice carried over the rows of boating supplies and gadgets. "Ooh, look at this. What do they use these for?" Her question followed by crashing sounds. "I'm okay… I'm good. Nothing broke."

The clerk shot Joan a hard look and returned to his sale, and soon it was her turn at the cluttered counter.

"Hi, I guess it would be easiest if I just gave you my list."

He grabbed it from Joan's hand with impatience and scanned it. "What size engine is all of this for?"

"What size engine?" her voice revealed her confusion.

"You don't know what size engine you got?"

Joan stared blankly into the clerk's face. "My mechanic gave me the list. I didn't think to ask. He's getting it back into the water for me."

Someone tapped her gently on her shoulder from behind. "What type of boat is it?" the man Fiona had flirted with politely asked.

"A Sea Ray."

"I own a Sea Ray too. Do you know how many feet your boat is?"

"That much I know. Forty-eight feet. Diesel."

"That sounds like twin 500s," he informed the clerk.

"Okay. If you say so." And he disappeared into a stock room.

"Thank you," Joan said. "I should have thought to ask." She shook her head with embarrassment. "I'm out of my element."

"I'm Jay." He stuck out his hand to her. "New toy?"

"Joan." She shook his extended hand. "No. I'm selling it—my husband's."

Fiona appeared next to her wearing a white captain's cap accompanied by a new friend, an accomplished-looking older man following behind her with a fishing gaff hooked onto her jacket.

"Hey Jay, look what I caught," he called.

"Excuse me," the clerk chastised them from behind the counter. "You've got to put that down, sir. It's expensive. Someone could get hurt."

"Now there's an employee that's been taught the priorities." He unhooked his catch. "Jay, this is Fiona."

"Hi, Jay. And that's my friend Joanie." Fiona adjusted her jacket.

"I know. We've met," Jay said.

"And Joanie this is Bernie." Fiona swatted the price tag dangling from the cap she was sporting.

"Hello, Bernie," Joan said curtly, anxious to disassociate herself from the bizarre scene.

"I'll meet you outside when you're done, Jay." Bernie placed Fiona's captain's cap on a nearby rack.

Fiona shrugged at Joan with a devilish grin as Bernie led her away by the hand, leaving Jay and Joan looking at each other.

"Excuse me, Miss?" the clerk interrupted. "This is everything that was on your list. Anything else?"

"No. That's all." She handed him her credit card.

"I see we both have lively friends." Jay engaged her with a smile that gave him a boyish appeal.

"Lively. You're kind." She smiled back.

"I didn't think it was going to be this warm today." He held out a neatly-folded handkerchief towards her.

Joan looked down at the white cloth embossed with blue letters, J.B. "No, thank you, I'm fine." She signed for her bill. "Thank you again for your help." And mortified, she abruptly walked away.

When she got outside, Joan peeled off her jacket to quell the heat wave her body inflicted by turning up her thermosat without her permission again. Flushed and perspiring, she flapped her collar while she watched Fiona and Bernie leaning against a chocolate-colored Mercedes sedan in the parking lot carrying on as if they were old friends.

And then Jay was right beside her. "Excuse me. I was wondering if your husband would let me take a look at his boat. I may know someone who may be interested in taking it off his hands."

She took a step back, wiping the perspiration from her forehead as casually as she could with the back of her hand. "It's me who's selling the boat."

"I thought I heard you say it was your husband's?"

"It was. He passed." She watched his face become as flushed as hers felt.

"I'm so sorry. I misunderstood," he said visibly flustered.

Joan patted his arm to reassure him. "It's fine. You couldn't have known." She caught herself and abruptly pulled her hand away.

"I saw your wedding band and just assumed…" He held up his own banded finger. "My wife passed too." He shrugged in acknowledgement of their mutual situation, his soulful eyes reflecting loss.

Fiona and Bernie joined them.

Bernie extended his hand. "I'm Bernard Katz. My friends call me Bernie." His demeanor now far more subdued than the clown he had played inside the store. "Fiona tells me that your selling your husband's Sea Ray. First of all, my condolences."

"Thank you." Joan forced a smile, hating her classification of widow and the stodgy image she believed it conjured.

"At the risk of seeming too forward," he continued. "Jay and I have a close friend who owns a marina and brokers boats and I was thinking, if you're interested…" He looked to his friend for support, "What do you think, Jay, a good idea?"

"Good thinking" he agreed, grinning at Joan.

"Are either of you in the boating business?" Fiona asked, pushing her sunglasses up, then perching them on top of her head.

"I'm in real estate," Bernie pointed to himself.

"Family bakery business," Jay said.

"Joan and I are both merchandisers for the same women's accessory distributor."

Joan's brow knitted, taken by surprise by Fiona's embellished description.

"Why don't you come take a look at it now?" Fiona suggested. "Joan's house is just a few blocks from here. You can follow us over."

"Sounds good to me," Bernie said and looked to Jay.

Jay gave a shrug and then nodded in agreement.

"What do you think, Joanie?" Fiona asked.

"I guess..." she stammered.

Fiona clapped her hands together. "Fabulous. Follow us." And she took Joan's arm in hers and led the way to the car.

"What did you get us into?" Joan broke away, rummaging in her purse for her car keys.

"What did *I* get us into? You seemed to be keeping up your end of the small talk with *Mr. Not a Hair Out of Place*. What did he say he was, a baker? I was proud of you. It didn't throw you at all that he was married, either. Good girl."

Joan closed the car door. "What are you talking about? It never entered my head. You don't miss a trick, do you? And, for your information he is not married."

"But he's wearing a wedding ring." Fiona's eye's narrowed.

"Widower."

Fiona let out a scream. "Perfect!"

"Stop it." Joan clapped her hands over her ears. "I can't believe you invited these strangers to my house. And why did you tell them that I was a merchandiser?"

"You said you were interested in working a few days. And besides, it sounded good."

Joan tried to concentrate on pulling her car out of the lot as she glanced into the rear view mirror. "They're really following us," she said her voice revealing her discomfort.

"Of course they are." Fiona sneaked a peak in the side view mirror. " Oh goodie! It *is* Bernie's Mercedes."

"Why am I so nervous? I feel like I'm doing something wrong. My hands are shaking."

"Relax, would you?" Fiona brushed her off, straightening the fit of her jacket. "This is why it pays to always be dressed and carry a good bag." She applied lipstick and fluffed her dark hair in the vanity mirror.

"What are you doing? Are you actually interested in that guy? He's got to be in his sixties."

"Possibly. He is a little older, but I don't mind. He's fun. He's got style. And that Jay, he made sure you didn't get away. He was out the door right after you. I saw the whole thing."

"What are you talking about? He's interested in my boat, not me."

Fiona turned Joan's head in her direction by her chin. "Joanie. That Jay guy was interested in you. Trust me. Stop buggin and just go with it."

"*Buggin?* You need to work around some people your own age." She turned the car into her street.

"He's very sophisticated looking, a John Forsyth type," Fiona approved. "Did you check out what he was wearing on his feet? Driving shoes—the leather strip up the back of the heel— easily six hundred dollars."

"Fiona! Stop talking." Joan pulled the car into her driveway. "What should I do?"

"What should you do? The same thing you have been doing. Just be yourself. That Bernie is kind of cute, don't' you think? He's got that teddy bearish kind of appeal."

Joan put her hand to her forehead. "What if this Jay thinks I'm trying to pick him up? How mortifying. I was sweating like a barnyard animal in front of him…what am I going to do, now?"

Fiona pulled her hand away and looked into her face. "You didn't ask him. He asked you. Stop being such a baby and start thinking business. How great would it be for you if these guys are able to take that boat off of your hands? Think of the time and money it will save you. It's business. So get yourself into business mode and let's just work from there. Business."

"Business," Joan repeated. "Okay. Thank you. That helped." She unconsciously fluffed her own hair. "How did you get so nervy?"

"It's natural."

Joan forced a smile at the two men as they stepped out of the car and began to follow her across her lawn and up the walk at the side of her house.

"Why do I feel like a sneaky teenager whose parents are out of town for the weekend?" she asked Fiona under her breath as she reached over the top of the fence to unlatch the gate to her backyard.

9

By the time all of the negotiations and paperwork were completed for the sale of the Sea Ray, Fiona had been dating Bernie for over a month. Once she discovered that he was the wealthy owner of a chain of Manhattan parking garages he didn't stand a chance of slipping through her fingers. She was the only other woman Bernie had ever fallen in love with besides his wife who'd unexpectedly filed for divorced after thirty-two years of marriage and three grown children.

"She did the right thing, staying away," Fiona said as they stood on Joan's deck watching the Sea Ray's new owner maneuver the impressive boat out of its slip. "It is kind of melodramatic."

The boat's powerful engine roared churning the water in the narrow canal into an angry, bubbling whirl, as Vinny Bruno's boat pulled away from his dock for the last time.

"Yeah, poor guy." Bernie shook his head with his arm around Fiona's waist. "But life goes on. You have to enjoy it when it's good, baby," he said playfully nuzzling Fiona's neck.

She turned his plump face towards hers with a delicate touch and lightly kissed his cheek. "I am." She sweetly smiled looking deeply into his eyes.

Standing in silence, arm and arm, they watched the boat make its way out into the open water.

The empty boat slip was the last thing Joan saw each night before she fell asleep and the first thing she opened her eyes to each morning.

With her husband's boat gone, she would linger after waking considering the new view, grappling with the mixture of guilt and relief its absence brought.

With her bedroom awash in morning sun, she would lie propped against pillows, replaying every word the psychic had said to her, fingering the green crystal she now wore as a pendant, determined to find the courage to get her life back on track again, inspired by the visit to the wise seer.

She could almost hear Mrs. Habbibi's exotic voice, flushed with gratitude toward the stranger for allowing her see that she still possessed the ability to experience life beyond her past. She also felt grateful for her friendship with Fiona which pulled her from the bleak vacuum her existence had become; grateful to her sister, Francie for prodding her to the bereavement meetings where they'd met. Now in retrospect, it all seemed somehow predestined.

There seemed to be a new force in her life, unseen, but setting events into motion that were moving her forward—her mother's recovery, the chance meeting of Jay Barrett and Bernie Katz, the effortless sale of the Sea Ray. And then she thought about Vinny and what Mrs. Habbibi said about him being focused on his journey to move on. She felt the warm tears stream down her face and she smiled. It was so like him. She felt thankful for all the years they'd had together, having him to rely on, trusting his judgment in the decisions he'd made and now, even with him gone, he was still showing her the way.

And a great appreciation for simply being alive filled her and for the first time since her husband's death she felt eager to get out of bed in the mornings.

Fiona pulled up in front of Joan's house after work, radio turned up, horn honking. The late-afternoon sun painted Joan in an elongated shadow across the new growth of emerald on her lawn as she locked her front door.

"No. No. Stop. Hold it." Fiona stuck her head out the car window.

"What?" Joan looked back at her, key still in hand.

"You can't wear that. Go back inside." Fiona hopped out of the car in her platform sandals, gathering her peasant-style skirt at her thighs and stalked towards her.

"Why?" Joan looked down at her khaki-green, capri pants suit with a mandarin collar.

"Are you kidding me?"

"What? This was expensive. I bought it at Nordstrom."

"Where? In the Chairman Mao section?" Fia ushered her back into the house following after her as Joan stomped through the rooms like moody adolescent into her bedroom.

"I look fine. I don't want to change."

"You have to." Fiona grabbed Joan by her shoulders. "You have to do better than that. Haven't you noticed the way Jay is always dressed? He's got it all together. Let's see what you've got in here." She began to slide hangers across the bar of Joan's closet. "And I'm redoing your make-up."

"For what? I just agreed to a quick, polite *thank you* drink for taking the boat off my hands. I don't want to send the wrong message."

"Trust me. That outfit is doing it for you." Fia held up a casual, knit dress against Joan squinting at its possibility.

"You and Bernie have really hit it off and I think it's great. It seems like the two of you are having a ball together, but I want it to be clear that I'm not trying to make this a double date."

Fiona rolled her eyes. "Yes, yes. We know. You made that clear. Several times. It's not a date. But it doesn't get you off the hook for dressing like you're going to a PTA meeting." She evaluated another outfit she held out at arm's length.

"I should have never agreed to this." Joan flapped her arms down at her sides.

"Yes you should have. It's the right thing to do. They came back to your house three different times to see the sale through and you told me yourself that you thought Jay was a real gentleman."

"I don't care what I said. I've been anxious since you arranged it. The thought of my sons and family finding out what I'm doing gives me stomach cramps. I'd just as soon get undressed and get into bed."

Fiona's eyes darkened. "Then go ahead." She dropped the blouse she had just pulled out of the closet down to her side. "Get in." She whipped back the bedspread. "A summer of long days is on the way and you can stay in your bed until it's winter again and no one will care. Your sister, your sons, all of your former friends, they all have their own lives."

Joan stood in the silence of her bedroom ablaze in the orange glow of the June afternoon sun flooding in from the window.

"That's right." Fiona glared at her. "You heard me. No one will care. Just like no one cared about all the days and nights you've cried your eyes out in here alone. Do you know how many single, widowed and divorced women there are out there, your age and younger, who would give anything for the chance to be invited out for a nice evening with a normal man?"

Joan blinked as her friend continued her tirade.

"Not to mention, a good-looking, fit, classy one. Just for the sheer sake of preserving your femininity you should jump at the chance. Unless maybe you're in a hurry to become a crone?"

"Alright. Alright. Shut up already. Let me see what you've got there." Joan snatched the hanger out of Fiona's hand.

They arrived at Prime, one of the North Shore's most popular hot spots and from the encouraging number of cars already parked in the waterfront restaurant's lot, it was clear that Long Island was eager to celebrate spring after a cold, gray winter. With the sun showing no signs of setting and the air fragrant with blossoming trees, there was a natural anticipation in the air. Summer was back in town and was preparing to unpack its bags.

"You can thank me for making you change your outfit later," Fiona said under her breath through her brightest smile as they walked towards Jay and Bernie waiting for them at the outdoor bar that overlooked the harbor. Both men looking very eligible in smart, thought-out, attire.

Fiona glided directly into Bernie's open arms leaving Joan standing awkwardly before Jay.

"You're a little late." He smiled and handed Joan her usual drink.

She accepted the Cosmopolitan Martini from him with puzzlement.

"I had Bernie ask Fiona." He grinned. "I'm glad you decided to join us. I've always preferred a drink and a good conversation with a lady over a night out with the guys. A sophisticated lady, that is." He held his glass up tilting it towards her. "Most times these days I'd rather stay at home then listen to their same, old, worn-out stories."

"I know just how you feel. I consider myself lucky to have a great sister for company...until she starts getting on my nerves, that is."

They both burst into laughter and simultaneously sipped at their drinks.

"My daughters do their best to make sure that I'm not alone on the weekends. They're great that way, but after they pack the kids up and all head back home, Sunday nights can be long."

And the happy hour get-together was off to a smooth, interesting start.

"Anyone else have spring fever besides me?" Bernie asked the group as they finished their second round of cocktails. "I took the Bentley out tonight. Look at that sky." He gazed up to the pink-hued blanket of magical twilight.

"I'm in." Fiona perched on her bar stool gave a wiggle.

"And so are you, right, Jay?" Bernie answered for his buddy. "Well, that makes three of us."

Fiona furiously nodded at Joan while the men waited for her reply.

"I guess...."

The parking valets had the slate-gray Bentley displayed in front of the restaurant alongside the other expensive, North Shore adult toys.

Bernie held the driver's door of the luxury car open for Fiona and dangled the keys. "Why don't you drive, baby?"

She did a happy dance for him and hopped behind the wheel of the attention-demanding machine, leaving no other choice for Joan except to slip into the roomy backseat with Jay.

"Where are you going to take us, Fia?" Bernie asked from shotgun position, as he let the convertible top drop down and turned up the volume of the sound system.

She thought for a minute, her hands poised on the walnut burl steering wheel. "Okay. I've got it. Everyone up for an adventure?"

"I am!" Bernie's arm shot above his head. "And so are you, Jay."

"I guess I am." He said, laughing and raising his hand up too.

"That a boy. Well, that makes three of us."

They all turned to Joan.

"Do I have a choice?" She asked hunching her shoulders as she timidly wagged her hand in the air.

The other three cheered her reluctant renegade spirit and the supercharged engine purred with restrained power as Fiona pulled away from the restaurant and headed west into the swirling orange and violets of the sherbet sunset.

A breezy, exhilarating cruise later, stars arriving in the impossible periwinkle sky, Bernie turned down the music and squinted at the green exit sign as Fiona pulled off the parkway. "Shore Road. Coney Island?"

"The Cyclone, baby. It's my annual pilgrimage to usher in summer. It's the perfect night for it."

The chatter inside the car abruptly stopped.

"Come on guys. When's the last time you lost your breath?"

The car rolled down lively Surf Avenue, passed the unmistakable, iconic green and yellow striped facade of Nathan's that took up a block in either direction, and then turned into the street that the famous wooden framed roller coaster had resided on for almost a century.

"I can't remember the last time I was here." Bernie said sizing up the landmark from inside the car. "Maybe with my kids, twenty-five years or so ago?"

"That sounds about right," Jay hesitantly agreed.

Silence fell inside the car as Fiona turned into a parking slot and turned off the engine.

"This is going to be great!" she pounded on the steering wheel with the excitement of a teenager.

The others sheepishly climbed out of the car after her, gaping up at the notorious first drop of the rickety structure.

"How cool is this?" Fiona turned back to them; her arm locked in Bernie's pulling him along towards the ticket booth.

Jay and Joan silently followed, being shoved from behind by their pride when a melee of shrieks and screeching metal streaked past them as a train of coaster cars whipped around the street side, outer track and disappeared back into the bowels of the wood-framed monster.

Fiona was already bouncing in her seat next to Bernie, excitedly waving them into the car behind them, again leaving Joan no option, but to ride with classy, self-contained Jay Barrett. Joan returned Fiona's enthusiasm with narrowed eyes, as she tentatively stepped down into the tattered, red upholstered, antiquated car with the reluctance of a dog entering a vet's office.

As soon as Jay wedged himself down into the seat next to her an attendant brought down the restraining bar, crushing them yet even closer together, pinning Jay's arm against Joan's breast. Trapped, emotions swinging between terror and humiliation, Joan suffered in silence and by the whiff of antiperspirant rising up between them, it was clear that Jay was having issues of his own.

With a wave of the attendant's hand the train of cars lurched forward and made a slow right turn, abducting the cattle cars of thrill seekers out of sight. Joan cringed as some of the adrenaline-drunk riders squealed with delight, flailing their arms overhead, as the ominous click, click, click, of the ancient pulley system began its tortuously slow ascent, dragging them higher and higher into the abyss of open sky over Surf City, Brooklyn.

And then there was silence. Perched high, in the cooler air at the summit of Coney Island, before falling into its famous eighty-five foot plunge, the coaster took a sadistic pause. Joan clamped her eyes shut and started to take a final bracing breath, but the car was already in free fall. The last thing she remembered was Jay Barrett's hand clamping over the white- knuckled death grip she had on the roll bar—and then the screaming.

When the Cyclone was through having its way with its passengers it innocently rolled back into the loading zone. Some hopped out of the cars charged with euphoria, others clamored for the reride option offered at a discounted rate, but Joan did not move. She sat motionless, waiting for her cognitive abilities and most of her motor functions to return from the place in her aching skull where they had been shaken to. Slowly, she dared to raise a trembling hand to her temple where Jay's head had cracked against hers like a set of Klic-Klacs throughout the violent turns of the hell ride.

"Are you okay?"

She heard his voice and when she finally summoned the coordination to turn in his direction, she was relieved to see that he looked as battered as she felt. His lips were dry and colorless, wisps of his hair stood on end, and his jacket sloped unevenly across one shoulder.

"Wasn't that great!" Fiona's appeared looming over them, bouncing with energy. She held her hand out to Jay who was struggling to climb out of the car, and then the two of them pulled Joan up and onto her feet.

"Where is Bernie?" Jay asked smoothing down his hair, holding his back, then steadying Joan by her elbow.

An attendant ran up behind them returning Joan's purse.

"He went ahead. He said he needed to walk. I think he may have gotten a little nauseous—are you guys okay?" Fiona pushed out of the turnstile into the throbbing, neon-lit street, bustling with clusters of excited visitors.

"Take me to the restroom," Joan stammered.

"I'll wait with Bernie." Jay staggered to the chain-link fence that Bernie was propped against.

"I could just kill you." Joan pulled herself along the railing as she hobbled up the ramp to the boardwalk. "Where is the fucking bathroom?"

"I don't think I've ever heard you curse before," Fiona hooted with amusement, steadying Joan with an arm around her shoulder. "You're almost there; it's just to the right."

"I think I'm going to throw up. I hate you."

Fiona laughed at her. "You're fine. Come on, it was fun."

"I think I wet myself. Check the back of my pants; don't make it obvious. Can you see anything?"

Fiona took a peek and dusted at her bottom. "No, you're good."

"I think I farted too. I'm so mortified. Do you think Jay heard?"

"No. You were screaming too loud."

Lemon ices and a stroll along the boardwalk arcade slowly healed the ravages the Cyclone had exacted on its unwilling victims.

"I have a suggestion," Fiona offered.

The others instantly shot her the same death stare.

"Relax," she said, laughing at their expressions. "No more rides. You all need something to eat. There's this fun restaurant a few minutes away. I'm starving. The best pizza you'll ever eat."

It was after ten when they arrived at Spumoni Gardens, a Bensonhurst landmark renowned for its pizza and great people watching. The restaurant was known to attract the occasional celebrity, but the colorful crowd was entertainment of its own.

A dirty aproned, jean-clad waiter ceremoniously set down a steaming plank of Sicilian-style pizza in front of the foursome at their street side table.

Fiona lifted a square onto a plate. "Hmmm…smell that basil," she closed her eyes as she passed a slice under her nose on its way to Bernie. "You'll all feel better once you get something in your stomachs."

"I hope so." He took his slice. "I was a little wobbly for a while there," he admitted, now a safe distance from the experience.

"I feel like I have boater's fatigue." Jay refilled Joan's wine glass, his chest softly pressing against her arm as he leaned in.

"You'll never catch me on that thing again. It was like going over Niagara Falls in a barrel," she said, Jay's jacket draped over her shoulders.

"Chickens," Fiona laughed at them, licking tomato sauce from her fingers.

"You don't feel jostled?" Bernie asked her. "That thing really throws you around and that first drop… I haven't screamed like that since my stock spilt in '87. What would you say that was, Jay, a hundred feet?"

"I don't know, but it sure gets your heart pumping."

"That's the whole idea." Fiona beamed. "It's exhilarating—changes your prospective. It's like getting rebooted."

"Rebooted?" Joan rubbed her neck. "I'm just thankful to be alive."

"Exactly," Fiona confirmed with a punctuating nod.

Bernie pulled Fiona's hand to his lips and pressed a kiss against it. "I loved it, Fi." He raised his glass to her. "Here's to being alive."

Wine splashed onto the tabletop as the four glasses enthusiastically clinked together, high in the June night sky over Brooklyn.

10

*F*eet together, hands folded over her purse in her lap, Andrea Petrakas sat alone on an ottoman in the stranger's overcrowded living room waiting her turn with the psychic, Mrs. Habbibi.

The house was shrill with an assortment of giddy women talking over each other and noshing on store-bought hors d'oeuvres, their collective anticipation charging the house with an errant, tense energy all its own.

An introvert by nature, Andrea kept to herself, taking in the overlapping snippets of conversation similar in content; long waits for appointments, astonishing accounts of accurate revelations from friends and acquaintances who had previously met with Mrs. Habbibi, and tales of some requests for a reading being turned down by the gifted clairvoyant with no explanation given.

Slowly Andrea's ambivalence was giving way to a sense of relief and soon she began to feel fortunate instead for having secured an appointment with the revered psychic whose popularity had seemed to have grown to near-celebrity status among the privileged North Shore crowd.

The middle-aged hostess, a stranger in tight jeans and heels turned mistress of ceremonies for the evening broke away from a huddle of clone-like friends in the kitchen and signaled to Andrea. "You....your turn, you're next." She waved Andrea into a chair across from the room where the readings were taking place and collected the fee.

"How long is a reading?" Andrea handed over her tightly-creased bills, looking around at the woman's noisy, standing-room-only kitchen. "The psychic is going to see all of these people tonight?" she asked.

"No, they just came to hang out, hoping for a spot from a no-show."
She vamped away, Zinfandel sloshing in her glass as she hurried to return into the fold.

Andrea rapped on the door and was invited in by the psychic's serene
voice on the other side.

The sixty-four-year-old, foreign-born widow inched the door open
with her head tucked low as she crept inside, cautiously scanning the
dimly-lit room, its walls alive with trembling shadows from the flickering candles on either side of its solitary, mysterious inhabitant.

"Sit, please. I am Mrs. Habbibi."

"I'm Andrea."

"Hello, Andrea. Are you feeling well?"

"Yes. Why are you asking me that?" The smallish woman slowly lowered herself into the empty seat, her eyes never leaving Mrs. Habbibi's.

"May I have your hands please?"

Andrea placed her purse on the floor next to the chair and tentatively
offered her upturned palms.

Mrs. Habbibi took them in hers and scanned the woman's strong
hands and thick fingers in silence and abruptly let go of them.

"What? What's wrong?"

The psychic lit a sage stem. "I am going to be direct with you. I realize what I am going to tell you will be difficult to hear, to say the least."
She stood and purposefully passed the smoking stick around her own
head and shoulders. "The density of dark energy that surrounds you
alarms me."

"What are you doing? What is that?" The confused woman twisted
in her seat as the psychic circled behind her and then proceeded to hastily trace the outline of Andrea's body with the smoldering stalk.

Mrs. Habbibi returned to her seat. "Sage." She passed the smoking
wand over herself again for good measure before stubbing it out. "Used
throughout the ages for dispelling negative energy." She looked into the
woman's face. "You have many spirits around you. They are strong. Not
the kind you want."

Andrea leaned back, away from the desk. "What are you saying?" Her voice was edgy with fear.

"Your husband has passed. Something with an S-Steven…Stephen…"

"That's close enough. His name was Stephanos." The woman turned slightly sideways with a suspicious smirk.

"Step-han-os." The psychic slowly repeated, exaggerating each syllable. "He is here, with us. Him and many others. Their energy is anxious."

Andrea's eyes shifted cautiously around the room.

"Your husband, Stephanos…he passed suddenly…an accident of some type—a tragic accident."

The woman remained silent.

"Your husband spoke with an accent much like yours. You both were from the same town in a foreign country."

Reluctantly intrigued and frightened, Andrea slowly nodded. "Corfu, Greece."

"You loved it there. You regret ever leaving."

The woman's lips pressed tightly together, bracing against emotion.

"Did I say something that upsets you?"

Andrea began to tear up. "My husband wanted to raise our children in America. We planned on spending our time between both countries. It never happened once he became so involved with business."

"With your permission, Mrs. Andrea, I am going to open lines of communication to the other realm. I am hoping for information to help me understand the urgency of the energy I'm feeling when I sit before you. From the very day of our phone conversation, in fact. May I proceed?"

"Go ahead."

"I just ask that you remain silent during my attempt," she lowered her voice with warning. "…No matter what the results may be. And keep your hands down turned, atop this desk." she warned.

Andrea swallowed hard. "I understand."

Mrs. Habbibi cleared her throat and her right hand rose into the air and began to slowly rotate beside her head. Her eyes squeeze closed in concentration and she began to rock to and fro.

Her client reflexively recoiled as Mrs. Habbibi began to softly groan in concentration, her hand swirling faster and faster.

"My back." The psychic reached around, clutching her lower spine, sliding her hands down her legs. "My back." She grimaced. "My legs."

"It's my husband! His spine was crushed in the fall."

The psychic stopped her with a raised hand. "There are others." She said straining in concentration. "Voh-ee-thee-se-mas Voh-ee-thee-se-mas." (*help us, help us*) She moaned, her face contorted with anguish and suddenly her eyes abruptly snapped open as if she had been startled and she blessed herself and reached to relight her sage.

"My God." Andrea hastily made the sign of the cross in response, and then her hand went over her mouth.

"What do those words mean?" Mrs. Habbibi asked while waving the smoldering wand around her body.

"Help us," the woman said stiffly.

"I believe that you have been cross-hexed Mrs. Andrea."

"Cross-hexed?"

"From your husband. And by the age of some of the discarnate souls who have presented themselves, it tells me that this hex has been in place for quite some time. Generations in fact—on your husband's side of the family."

Speechless and spurred by the revelation, Andrea fanned the lingering smoke in her direction.

"It won't help you. The hex is too established. It has a firm foothold on your spirit, too."

"Mine?"

"Through the energy chords you shared with your husband. And worst of all, they prevent him and decades of his deceased family members from crossing over to other side. They're trapped." Mrs. Habbibi shook her head in empathy dabbing out the stalk.

"Why should I believe you?" Andrea picked up her purse from the floor.

"I'm not asking you to. It is you who appeared before me and I delivered the information that presented itself."

Frightened and at a loss, the woman began to weep.

"Mrs. Andrea I realize what I've told you is difficult to accept, but you're an intuitive woman, ask yourself—what force drew you here?" She offered the box of tissues.

"I'm not sure...but I felt like I needed... some help," she blurted, visibly rattled.

"Mrs. Andrea..." The psychic sat back in her chair, returning to her signature composed demeanor. "You have been plagued by more than your share of strife over the years, isn't that true?" Her voice was tender with pity.

"You're right about that," Andrea admitted.

"Surely you have sensed a force greater than yourself working against you throughout your married life? As early as the deep resistance you felt leaving your country with your children? And I sense that there have been several untimely deaths on your husband's side of the family including his own. And many painful estrangements from family members, as well."

The color drained from Andrea's face.

"That is one of the most favored tactics of these dark forces. They thrive on the chaos and self-destruction that dissension among family can wreak on a life."

Andrea's arms wrapped closer around her small frame.

"And like most, we prefer to stay in denial, dismissing our sacred intuition. Instead, quick to blame ourselves or cursed luck, when all the while, our deeper intelligence whispers the truth." She paused. "At the very least, I hope you feel a sense of relief, Mrs. Andrea. None of it was your failure as a wife or mother."

With growing sobs, Andrea began to open up. "I haven't seen my sons or my grandchildren since the argument with their father. They became enemies overnight. My boys vowed that they'd never let their children see either of us again."

"It's an unhealthy way to live ."

"And all because of money." Andrea dabbed at her nose and blew into the tissue.

"What was the nature of the disagreement, if I may ask?"

"Their wives were pestering our sons to have mine and Stephanos' names taken off some of the business that the family managed. We wouldn't agree to do that. If something happened to one of our sons why should we have a stranger as a partner?" She stated her case with practiced outrage.

"You viewed their wives' concerns as unfounded?"

"They didn't work for any of our money. One of them wasn't even a Greek. They never wanted for anything—we wouldn't have let them go hungry. We were protecting our sons; they just didn't want to admit that we were right. And what good did it bring us? I'm all alone now." She snatched another tissue.

"Hmmm. Most unfortunate for all. More of the dark brotherhood's handiwork—keeping disharmony prevailing through blocked communications. Would you like me to explain how you can lift this burden from yourself, your husband, and grandchildren—present and future? The hex is of a consanguineous nature."

"I don't know what you mean."

"Through blood—the curse travels through the blood. It has spanned generations.

"How could you know these things?"

Mrs. Habbibi smugly tilted her head at the woman. "And it will continue, propagate, unless it is severed."

"I don't know what that word means."

"Grow more powerful." The psychic crossed her arms.

"I don't care about myself. Can you help my sons and their children?" She clutched at her heart.

"Yes. I can help them."

"Oh, thank God." Andrea's body slumped with relief.

"But there isn't any time to dally. The demons…they know that they've been identified. They already know of your intentions. We would be wise to get started." Mrs. Habbibi pressed closer to Andrea. "There is a centuries-old ceremony to release this type of hex. It is involved, time-consuming, and it will require both your cooperation and participation. Do you understand?"

Andrea nodded.

"When it is lifted, you will feel like your old self before the affliction, light-hearted, and full of the joy of living. Do you remember that woman, Andrea?" The psychic asked her voices soft with tenderness. "And you will be reconciled with your children."

The woman shook, sobbing deeply. "Please. Please. That's all I wanted for my life." She tugged another tissue from the box.

"I'm going to need to invoke your husband again. I need more information to know how to proceed in my work."

Andrea nodded, shrinking further into her chair.

Mrs. Habbibi's eyes closed and her hand rose, swirling in circles, then she swayed in her chair and soon began to murmur incoherently. "He is here with us. Stephanos is here with us. He is easily contacted because he is just below the surface, desperate for help from this side…." she said and began to squint into the beyond. "Se a gap-o, Se a gap-o" Mrs. Habbibi struggled with the strange word.

Andrea gasped, her hands covering her mouth.

"Do you understand that? Does it mean something to you?"

"It means *I love you*."

"Your husband wants you to know that he loves you and he misses you. I sense relief from him."

"Oh, Stephanos, poor Stephanos." Andrea buried her face in her hands.

"Him and the others." Her hand continued to swirl. "They are grateful, relieved that you are here. They are hopeful and pray that your intuition will guide you to avenge them, release that which keeps them at unrest."

Andrea whimpered burying her face in her hands. "I can't. I can't do it."

"Andrea! You need to summon your courage if we are going to be successful in severing these hexes and avenge your family. You are a strong woman. You are blessed with good health. Your faith in the power of the light will support you."

"Why did this happen to us? How could I not have realized it sooner?"

"They are clever. Their work is done covertly."

"Covertly?"

"Secretly. Only a person such as myself would sense their demonic presence."

"What are you going do?" Andrea pleaded.

"What are *we* going to do?" Mrs. Habbibi corrected her. She sat back and looked squarely at her client. "To begin with, I need you to understand that lifting this type of curse is not a simple procedure. It calls for precise readings of a complicated incantations, and decrees spoken aloud in tandem with, methodical steps over a specific time frame."

Andrea shook her head, impatient and overwhelmed. "When can we start?"

"I haven't finished." Mrs. Habbibi clasped her hands over each other and rested them on the table. "Lifting this hex will be time-consuming, three lunar cycles to be exact and, to be quite blunt... costly."

Andrea's brow's furrowed.

"Allow me to continue, please..." She took a breath. "Performing these ceremonies, I put myself at risk for absorbing the wretched karma of the dark forces or at worst...having the hex transferred onto me. The highly-evolved dark masters delight in attaching themselves to pure energies." Mrs. Habbibi relit the sage and stood.

"What are you doing?"

"They already know. They gather..." She hurriedly passed the smoking stick around her torso and then flailed it through the air.

The woman let out a wail of fear scanning the ceiling.

"Shh—hh." Mrs. Habbibi glanced at the door. "Take hold of yourself," she whispered. "Pay attention to what I am going to tell you. You need to understand what we will be up against. They will try to thwart my intervention in any way they can...attempt to absorb my energy and turn it against me, invade my auric field..." She returned to her chair and pressed her palms protectively against her heart and paused. "Which is why my fee is five thousand dollars."

"Five thousand dollars?"

"For each ceremony. There are nine of them over the course of three waxing moon phases."

"That's almost fifty thousand dollars!"

"Payment is due at the start of each ceremony."

"That doesn't' sound right... I'm not sure..."

Mrs. Habbibi laughed revealing the gap between her front teeth.

"There must be another way to get rid of this... hex."

"None that I know of. And as far as seeking out other practitioners who may let you haggle with them for their services. Hacks." She held up a warning finger. "Know that short cuts and omissions in any procedure are sure to yield less than desired results. You know that Andrea; you are an excellent cook. It is your most enjoyed passion."

The woman's head jerked, startled at the psychic's intimate knowledge of her.

"Think. Would you expect optimum results from a recipe with inferior ingredients? And could a guest leave the table satisfied from a cook who took no pride in her craft?"

Andrea blinked.

"I won't mislead you, as I said before—timing is crucial, but I don't want you to enter this endeavor with ambivalence. Why don't you go home and rest? Allow your higher self to guide you through your trepidations."

"No. I don't want to wait. I need my sons in my life. Too much time has passed already. I'm all alone now."

"Hmm. I'm pleased that you understand the urgency. So be it." Mrs. Habbibi shifted her position and held up two fingers. "Two things that

I need you to know before I commit myself to your problem. First, I will require an intermediary to act as a buffer. She will retrieve and deliver all items that pass between us—the payments and the personal items I will be requesting. Once we have begun the ceremony nothing must pass directly between us—it would be a portal for the dark forces to thwart our mission. I work with Ms. J."

"Ms. J?"

"She is a most capable and trusted associate. Her fee is two-hundred dollars each time she acts as an intermediary for the items that pass between us. You can include the payment in each package. She is discreet and most importantly understands the seriousness of my work."

Andrea listened intently.

"She will not discuss the nature of our business with you and you are not to discuss it with her either—no one is to know of our intentions. Second, be advised, you are not to contact your sons or any other estranged relatives, send or accept any correspondence from them until the cleansing is complete. Do not doubt that the dark spirits of the other world travel among us. Any contact can serve as a porthole for reattachment. I cannot accept responsibility for that nature of breech. Do you understand, Andrea?"

She nodded. "I do."

"I will contact you in a few days with the address of my next readings. Please have your first payment in a sealed envelope. I will give you the first instructions at that time." She leaned back in her chair. "All will turn out well, take comfort. You higher self is guiding you. " Mrs. Habbibi glanced down at her watch. "My next appointment is waiting."

Andrea Petrakas wearily stood to leave.

"And one more thing, Andrea."

The woman turned around to face her.

"Until we meet again, I advise that you state your allegiance to the keeper of the white light aloud. And often."

Joan knelt on the floor with Fiona unpacking the inventory for the new retail space in Salon 99's new, partner salon, Panache. The shop was much smaller, but renovations were underway while stylists worked on their clients amid distracting hammer strikes and the unnerving whining of a table saw. Wendy Waxman, riding the wave of her newfound ability to attract success, had offered Fiona free rent until the merger developed a solid clientele.

"Do you think I'm going to be able to remember all these names?" Joan ran her hand over a black velvet tray of sterling silver birthstone rings.

"You're going to do just fine. You're a natural with people and these items sell themselves." Fiona stood and began arranging the new stock of costume jewelry in the display cases. "Whatever the customer asks to try on just gush over how perfect it looks on them—in a sincere way."

Joan laughed, as usual, amused by Fiona's blunt personality, "I'll take a few of the wholesalers' catalogs home with me and brush up."

"Don't obsess. Until this place gets busy, I don't plan on having you here more than a few hours a week. So, get me up to speed on you and Jay. You've been out on three dates with him–any fireworks?" Fiona devilishly winked at her."

"We were with you and Bernie all three times. What fireworks?" She began to unpack a box of stylish reading glasses from their plastic wrappers.

"You can't fool me. The two of you didn't watch a single inning of the Mets game the other night, and they were field level seats."

"We have a lot in common, that's all."

"Has he put any moves on you?"

A grin spread across Joan's face. "No." She looked away.

Fiona shrieked and tossed a ball of packing tape at her. "You better tell me!"

"No, nothing yet, I swear. Neither one of us is ready for that sort of thing."

"Don't you have…*needs?*"

Joan shrugged. "I'm not even sure. I've felt like I've been dead from the waist down ever since Vinny's been gone and even if I felt otherwise I'm so self-conscious."

"Self-conscious? Of what?"

Joan grabbed the pesky roll around her midsection. "Menopause." She made a face. "I'm perfectly happy with just being friends and if things develop beyond that—with anyone— it'd have to be somewhere where the lights were down real low."

"Don't let the body image thing keep you from getting some. All boats look the same when they're upside down."

"Oh, Fiona!"

"It's true," she said. "And none of us are twenty-one anymore. I'm sure Jay's not a perfect specimen either when he's naked."

"Would you stop, please? Nothing like that is going to happen." She began to gather shipping cartons and packing material that were scattered about. "And I have guilt. I think we both do."

"Guilt? You're both single. What is there to be guilty about?"

"When you've been with the same person for as long as we have and they die on you, there's a lot to sort out in your head when you think of yourself being intimate with someone else. We're both perfectly fine being just friends. Let's talk about you and Bernie."

"What would you like to know?" Fiona bounced her hip and squeezed her breasts together, lightening the moment for her friend.

Joan held her hand up. "Please. I can use my imagination."

Fiona flung her head back with laughter. "Come on, that's enough for today. I want to get over to the bank before they close." She lowered the glass lids on the display cases and clicked closed the small padlocks that secured them. "I wanted to ask you something. Are you okay with adding your name on the business account for this place? That way you can make transactions when I'm not here."

"Sure, that makes sense."

"Oh, and another thing you can take care of for me …" Fiona said to her as they walked through the salon.

"Name it." Joan followed Fiona out the door.

"I have this very wealthy client, Andrea. She prefers that her orders are dropped off to her at her home. She spends a ton of money with me so I never say no."

"No problem," Joan assured her as they strolled down the busy avenue together, the streets crowded with people enjoying the return of the warm weather.

"I'm always sending her samples and new pieces to try on as they come in. Money isn't an issue for her, but she's on the eccentric side and doesn't like to make small talk. So when you're making a drop, don't speak to her."

"Not even hello?"

Fiona shook her head. "Nutty. I know. But just go with it. And after you're in this business for a while you'll be wishing all of our clients were like her."

Joan shrugged. "Whatever you say, boss." She held open the bank's heavy glass door.

Fiona stepped in. "I'm really looking forward to dinner tomorrow night. I'm thinking of wearing a slinky little black number. How about you?"

11

Simone could hear the water running in the shower when Josie picked up her call.

"What is it, Simmy? I'm trying to get ready to go to dinner."

"Same senior citizen?"

Josie laughed. "Bernie is just in his early sixties but he's got more energy and style than any of the thirty-year olds I've been with. I'm actually enjoying myself."

"What kind of condition is he in?"

"Workable—and the only ailment he has is one that I like...swollen wallet. I'm talking to you from my new rental that he set me up in a block away from the ocean."

"How'd you get that out of him?"

"Gave him a sob story about getting wiped out in Hurricane Sandy. Plus, he thinks I'm a riot."

"Sounds like true love to me."

"Very funny. Actually, I really do like him. Maybe an older man is what I needed all along. I could see it being something long-term."

"Where's he taking you tonight?"

Josie bent to shave the other leg. "Ever heard of The River Cafe?"

"Of course I have. How out of the loop do you think I am? That's the place down under the Brooklyn Bridge."

"It's DUMBO, these days," she informed her. We're meeting our friends there."

"How cute, a double date. That same white toast, Long Island woman you've latched onto?"

"Hey, it's working for me. We're planning to sail out to Montauk to her boyfriend's summer home for July fourth."

"Really? How nice for you. You're spending your summer on boats and country estates and I'm here in the sweltering city eating takeout, babysitting our elderly mother."

"You love the heat and aides are taking care of our mother, I know because I'm footing the bill," Josie said. "Come on, Simmy. I'm having a good time and recreation helps my readings. I've opened up a bank account and making weekly deposits so I'll have legitimate money when I'm ready to buy a place."

"I'm proud of you. This is the first time in your life I've ever heard you talk about saving money."

"We're not getting any younger— I just started the Andrea Petrakas job. By the way, thanks again. Your setup was Oscar worthy. And be glad for me because I'm taking you with me when I finally make it."

"I'll start packing my bags. The reason I called is because I had to put your mother back into the hospital again. She started acting crazier than usual—looking up in the corners of the room; talking to people who weren't there, and then she started running a fever."

"Is she okay?"

"They tell me that it could be just dehydration, but since the fever was so high, they're keeping her there for a few days on an I.V. and running some tests."

"Okay, so you've got yourself a little vacation."

"Right. Listening to Raymond and his eighth grade-educated buddies play five bucks-a-hand poker in my kitchen, drinking supermarket beer."

"It could be worse, Simmy. He could be looking to spend time with *you*."

Her laughter echoed in the shower after Simone hung up on her.

A mere pane of glass separated the choppy waters of the East River shimmering under the silver moonlight from the elegant world of The River Cafe restaurant on the other side. Fiona and Bernie sat facing each other, noses nearly touching, enjoying cocktails at the bar to the tinklings of the tuxedo-clad pianist and the sweeping view of the city skyline twinkling at them from Lower Manhattan across the water.

Giddy from the magic of the room and their second cocktail, Fiona crossed her leg at the knee treating Bernie to a better view of her strappy stiletto and suntanned thigh while they waited for their friends. Neither of them could hide their delight when Joan and Jay arrived, arm in arm, looking very much like a couple.

"Sorry we're late," Joan apologized. "I just had to get a few pictures of the view from the dock and those floral arrangements in the lobby— absolutely breathtaking."

Jay guided her onto the seat at the crowded bar that Bernie surrendered to her.

Fiona sipped her drink, silently observing the subtle clues that their relationship was progressing: Joan's lighter demeanor along with the new, flattering glow she radiated; Jay casually handing her his phone to keep in her purse.

The candle-lit dining room was alive with the low roar of buzzing conversation and the attentive presence of the sophisticated wait staff, alert to every need of the Manhattan elites. They were escorted to a coveted corner table that bestowed an unsurpassed view of New York, the Brooklyn Bridge above, and Lady Liberty in the distance looming ever-present and proud in New York Harbor.

Two seasoned waiters in black tie arrived at the table accompanied by a silent team of subordinates to assist them in artfully delivering the five-star meal to the cheerful foursome.

"Oh, boy, look at that." Bernie honed in on the porterhouse that was set before him, thick and adorned with a calculated pattern of diamond-shaped grill marks. "How can you resist, Fi?"

"Easily." She dropped her head in reverence over her branzino, her lips moving, eyes closed in silent prayer.

"I have to know. What are you saying to your fish?' Bernie asked, glass of aged Quintarelli Reserve in hand.

"I'm thanking it for giving its life for me."

"So why can't you do the same for a cow?" he questioned her near-vegetarian status, his fork and knife poised above the pricey cut on his plate.

Joan and Jay listened on with amusement at the usual entertaining banter that went on between the unlikely couple.

"I would. Not a factory farmed one." Fiona speared a piece of braised fennel.

"What's the difference?" he asked, enjoying his first forkful of steak.

She laid her utensils on the edge of her plate. "After a lifetime of existing in cramped, unnatural surroundings, ingesting feed that has been doctored with antibiotics and chemicals, it's off to the slaughter house. They can smell the fear from the other terrified victims as they're transported in dark, overcrowded trucks. They're sentient beings; they can experience anxiety.

The others blinked with discomfort as Fiona continued.

"And as they wait their turn on the conveyer belt to be beheaded in the noisy warehouse filled with the sounds of animals in distress and loud machinery, fear surges adrenaline through their bodies. Unused adrenalin becomes toxic in their tissue which you are about to ingest along with the terror of that innocent animal's final moments."

Reacting to Fiona's commentary, Joan's fork landed with a clink when she dropped it onto the expensive china.

"Oh, good God." Jay picked up his white, starched napkin and wiped his mouth, equally disturbed.

"You asked. Bon appetit." Fiona shrugged and happily returned to her meal.

Bernie belly laughed at Jay and Joan's reaction, taking his usual delight in anything Fiona said or did.

Sated from the heavy meal and lighthearted from expensive wine, they watched the waiter's flamboyant tableside performance as he prepared Bernie's dessert, cheering with approval when the Bananas Foster burst into flames further adding to the grandeur of the evening.

"Ah, excuse me, you two." Bernie interrupted Jay and Joan who were deep in conversation, sharing samples of each other's desserts.

They looked up from Jay's Crème Brûlée and Joan's chocolate replica of the Brooklyn Bridge, the restaurant's signature dessert.

"Thought that you two forgot that Fia and I were still here."

"Sorry, buddy," Jay said laughing.

"So I've convinced Jay to visit the psychic," Joan cheerfully announced.

Fiona picked up her water glass and took a long sip.

Bernie looked over to his friend. "Really?" He pulled his head in with disbelief.

"Joanie talked me into to it." He looked down into his after-dinner scotch, gently sloshing it against the sides of the weighty tumbler. "I don't really put any stock in that sort of thing."

Loose from the wine, Joan continued to cajole him. "Come on, honey. Be a little open. Why not? Do it for me." She sipped at her cappuccino.

"I just don't buy that anyone has the ability to predict the future," he shrugged.

"I think we all do–in varying degrees," Fiona disagreed. "Some just more than others."

"Fiona's right," Joan said. "Have you ever been thinking about someone and then out of the blue, you run into them? Or sensed being looked at from behind? Or what about that, 'something told me so' feeling?"

"I guess those are arguments, but I just can't see myself taking predictions about my life from a total stranger, seriously. I know others do. I guess it's just the latest fad."

"People have been consulting psychics and spiritual advisors since recorded history," Fiona said.

"There were suckers, way back then too." Bernie sipped at his Grand Marnier.

"You can laugh, but I think there's something to it—*Caesar, the Ides of March,*" Joan defended her point. "Consulting with an oracle or a soothsayer was an everyday event for the royals and leaders of all the ancient cultures. They relied on them."

"Using chicken entrails and tea leaves?" Bernie smirked.

"No, Bernie," Fiona corrected him. "Astrology, divination, runes, palmistry. The Mayans, the Egyptians, the Chinese. They were some of the most advanced civilizations in human history."

"Hold it. Stop!" Bernie hushed them. He closed his eyes and drummed his fingertips on his forehead. "A spirit is contacting me right now—it says there is another Grand Mariner in my near future." He opened his eyes, "Oh, waiter." He snapped his fingers over his head, sending the rest of his over-served tablemates into hysterics.

Josie cupped her hands around her eyes, watching Charlotte work at the counter, shafts of noon sunlight stabbing across the kitchen from the skylight and the wide-paned windows. The sun rallied above, coming into its season. It heated Josie's back and shoulders through the thin material of her blouse. Charlotte jumped when she rapped on the glass.

"Hi." Josie waved her arms wildly.

Charlotte wiped her hands and opened the door to her.

"It's been a while. You just missed Marilla."

"What a shame." She walked around to the other side of the counter. "What ya making?"

"Avocado, tomato sandwich. Would you like one?"

"Sure." Josie dropped into a seat.

"I'm glad to see you in good spirits. We haven't seen much of you. I was a little concerned; seems like you haven't been spending nights here."

"That's what I came to talk to you about and to visit too, of course." She picked up a slice of avocado and popped it into her mouth. "I miss our late-night chats."

"Speaking of chats. The last one we had has been weighing on me. I've been wanting to discuss it with you."

One of Charlotte's Siamese jumped onto the counter and pressed his head into Josie's hand. "And who is this?"

"That's Mr. Wu."

"Hello, Mr. Wu." She scratched under his chin. "He's really adorable, but I don't think anything compares to a dog. I'm sorry, I know you're a cat person, but I have to say…"

"Grab one." Charlotte licked a finger. "I was planning on eating out on the deck."

"Outside it is." Josie rose and took one of the plates.

"This really is the place." Josie gazed out on the ocean, her sandwich and iced tea set before her, listening to the happy gurgling of the water flowing off the rock fountain into the turquoise blue of the in-ground pool. "I sure picked the wrong season for my little stopover here."

"You're leaving us?"

"I am. Don't tear up, Charlee." Josie pulled the crust from around her sandwich. "I've got myself a cute little rental down the shore a ways, in Long Beach. This Long Island living is easy to get used to."

"I'm glad to hear that you've gotten back on your feet."

"Well, to be honest—you know that I can't lie to you Charlee…"

"I'm touched."

Josie grinned. "The guy I've been seeing set me up in the new place. I love it. It's a little doll house of a bungalow on the west end. It's perfect for me."

"How long have you been dating him?"

"Three months. Give or take."

"Is he living there with you?"

"No. He has his own place, a few of them, as a matter of fact."

"Wealthy man, is he? He must be smitten with you."

"To say the least." Josie threw her head back when she laughed. "But who can blame him?"

"Tell me about him. You're not repeating history are you?"

"Not at all. Bernie is older than me—he's got nothing to prove. Nothing like the last few."

"Is he married?"

"Listen to you. Always focused on the line of questioning."

"Is he?"

"Technically, I guess. But his wife moved out and hit him with divorce papers after thirty-plus years of marriage. Out of the blue. Just like that." She snapped her fingers. "She rented herself a town house and enrolled in college. Can you believe it?"

"Societal epidemic. Gray divorce."

"I don't know what color it was— but it works for me." She held up her triangle of sandwich and took a bite.

"So does this mean that you'll stop your criminal activity, defrauding widows out of their money?"

"Soon, if things go according to plan. I'm not home free, yet. And is that how you see it—criminal activity?"

"That's what it is. But if you enjoy it so much and think you have a knack for helping people, as you say, why not develop your skill and skip the false identity?"

"You're so cute." Josie tilted her head at the older woman with fondness. "Always trying to champion me. No one is going to fork over two-hundred bucks for generalizations. These store front palm readers charging five dollars a pop would have to give forty readings for every one of mine."

"But they're not putting in any research time. That's work. It's got to be time-consuming."

"What work? All I do is listen. Most people can't stop talking if they wanted to. And if they're bored with their own lives, there are always their friends."

"Point taken. Have you considered a social work degree?"

"Who has the time?" Josie took another bite.

"What about life coaching? It's a certificate program. You could take it online"

"Come on, Charlee." Josie flopped her head to the side. "Would you hire me as a life coach? You want to talk about ripping people off? I'm an honest fraud and I'm actually getting results for my clients."

Charlotte looked down at her plate.

"Go ahead. It's okay to laugh."

"I'm trying to help you." Charlotte sipped her iced tea.

"I know. That's why I love you. But even if I did do it your way and got a certificate or a degree or whatever they want you to buy, then I'd have to..." she struggled for words. "What do they call this thing you need to do these days on top of everything else—develop a platform for myself." She held an imaginary gun to her head.

"I think what you're doing is more difficult. Extracting information, the risk of being found out, the disguise."

"Even a sports car salesman has to put on a suit when he goes to work."

"What does that have to do with it?"

"My disguise is not a lot of effort for the return. A Corvette is a novelty; the customer already wants the car before they even get inside the showroom. It basically sells itself. Once a client is sitting across from me, they're ready to believe whatever I tell them. You just have to know how far you can push."

"Does it concern you that your influence could produce negative consequences for your clients?"

"That's up to them. I go in assuming the reading will be helpful."

"So you assume no responsibility?"

"Responsibly for what?" Josie shrugged and pushed her plate away. "Everyone's story has an unhappy ending. The hero dies at the end."

Charlotte closed her eyes in frustration. She picked up her napkin. "Your ability to deflect accountability is daunting." She wiped her fingers.

"Any other questions?"

"And what about what you're charging these poor unsuspectings?"

"For my part, I know that my clients leave with exactly what they need to move them along, so my fees are on par. Have you ever seen what a New York advertising agency charges or a publicity agent? You want to talk fees for unguaranteed results?"

"You've got this whole situation justified to yourself, don't you, Jozette?" Charlotte wiped her mouth with her napkin and stood. She moved a lounge chair into the sun's angle. "What about the karmic aspect? You obviously studied the occult and supernatural phenomenon to play your role. Aren't you concerned that your dabbling could put your own soul in jeopardy?"

"I'm very careful that I don't get myself into trouble. I say a prayer of protection before and after each reading—white light and all that." Josie passed her hand though the air with a wink.

"If you don't dabble, you won't need protection. Would you like to hear a story?"

"You're not going to try and scare me straight, are you?"

"You can make of it what you like, but it is a true story."

Josie moved to the foot of her lounge chair. "Make it quick. Bernie's taking me furniture shopping for the new place. I just stopped by to grab a few things until I get some time to move my stuff out of there." She nudged her chin across the deck.

Charlotte crossed her arms. "I had a thirty-two year old patient, attractive woman. Pleasant enough. She believed she was being haunted by a spirit. She came to me to rule out that she was losing her mind."

"What made her think she was being haunted?"

"As teens, she and her sister picked up an Ouija board at a garage sale. The sisters and their friends fussed around with the board every now and again, but after one night at a pajama party, even though they were just kids, they knew to stop when the board started performing some unnerving antics."

Josie sat riveted.

"She hadn't made the connection until years later, but it was from that very night on, she experienced regular nightmares and told me that she sensed that she never felt that she was alone." Charlotte pushed herself higher in the chair. "I worked with her for about eighteen months. Our sessions seemed to provide comfort and we made some headway with her long-standing bulimia issues, but her *haunting* as she referred to it, was only resolved when she went to a psychic."

"What did the psychic do for her?" Josie shifted in her seat, crossing her legs in the opposite direction.

"It seems her problem wasn't unique. He told her to burn the board."

"But you said she was a teenager when she had messed around with it." Josie squinted in interest.

"She was. She was damn lucky. Her parents still lived in her childhood home. The board was still in the house; stowed in a forgotten pile of other board games in the basement."

"And what happened?"

"She burned the board."

"And?"

"Two sessions later she stopped seeing me."

The gurgling of the fountain spilling over into the swimming pool seemed louder in the silence.

"She never felt the presence again," Charlotte concluded.

Josie blinked in silence. She stared off in thought and then her fingers danced in the air. "Whoo-ooo." She burst into laughter.

Charlotte nodded, letting her have her fun.

"Come on, doctor, I'm surprised at you. That wasn't very scientific sounding." She tugged Charlotte's big toe. "Are you telling me that you believe in evil spirits?"

"I didn't say that. I believe that a troubled person's mind is very malleable. And we've both agreed that those who frequent psychics, mediums, or fortunetellers are more than likely troubled."

"Who isn't?" Josie brushed at the wedge of her platform sandal.

"What I'm trying to get across to you is that if you plan to continue your activities I urge you to be very careful. Don't underestimate desperation. Of the living *or* the dead."

"I don't." Josie pulled her jeans at the thighs as she stood. "But bad times are good times in my business." She shrugged with indifference. "I accept it as an occupational hazard."

Charlotte remained silent, clearly frustrated with her.

"You worry too much, *mon amie.*" Josie knelt, taking both of the older woman's hands in hers. "Thank you for everything, Charlee. It really meant something to me, having time with you." She leaned forward and pressed her lips fervently against the older woman's and stood, swaying across the deck to her former home. "Mimi is going to be ecstatic when she hears that she's getting get her pool house back just in time for the summer," she called over her shoulder.

Charlotte watched her disappear inside.

12

*J*ay stepped into the darkened room lit only by a corner lamp and two candles on either side of the olive skinned, older woman sitting motionless in the flicker of lazy candlelight.

"Kind of spooky in here. No lights?"

"No hocus pocus, here," the psychic pleasantly replied. "I have never found anything that induces calm as immediately as candlelight. In my business, calm is the weapon of choice." She unabashedly displayed her flawed smile. "I am Miss Habbibi."

"John Barrett." He dropped into her chair heavily with restrained impatience.

"You are not here by your own will, but it doesn't mean that you won't benefit from your visit, Mr. Barrett."

"You're right about that much. I don't buy into this sort of thing." He crossed his legs.

"How about some emotional freedom? Can I sell you that?" She grinned, waiting for his reaction.

"Do you have some?" He shared in her candor, drawn into the charm of the curious character with the exotic accent. "Why the two different color candles?"

"You have natural inquisitiveness; it has served you well throughout your life. A valuable companion to your money attraction power."

"My money attraction power?" Jay gave a cavalier laugh.

"You don't put much credence in my abilities, Mr. John Barrett. I'm not offended. I appreciate that you are a pragmatic man. Your wife has been around me for the last three days. I realize who she is now that you're here. The white for purity, the purple for spirituality."

"What?"

"The candles. You inquired about the color of my candles."

John nodded, swallow hard. "Right."

"I like to offer a prayer of protection before I begin. There are always lower forms of spirit energy present when we delve into the other realm. We need to guard ourselves. We don't want to make it easy for them to attach. May I have your hands please, and would you kindly close your eyes and think of the highest good that you are capable of?"

Jay felt his heart begin to thud in his chest, but he remained stoic and followed the psychic's instructions, beginning to take Mrs. Habbibi far more seriously than he had expected to.

"I find it is helpful to close *both* eyes John." Her voice was playful. "I want you to visualize yourself surrounded with the protective white light of the Christ. Breathe it in. Imagining it filling you, surrounding you. That's very good. Now, exhale. Open your eyes." She was smiling at him. "Thank you."

He watched skeptically as the psychic raised her hand, swirling it in sweeping circles at the side of her head, her eyes narrowed in concentration. "There are many around you. Their light is white. They protect you…." She swayed. "I'm getting a J-J… your wife's…"

"Judith." He needed to swallow again.

"Jude" she said, her voice satisfied. "You called her Jude?"

Jay nodded, wiping at tears that rolled down his cheek with his knuckle.

"She is happy that you are here. She says she loves you and thanks you for taking care of her."

To his great dismay, Jay began to weep.

"Ahhh." Mrs. Habbibi sighed with compassion and pressed the box of tissues toward him.

"Thank you," he struggled, dabbing at his eyes.

Mrs. Habbibi laid her hand at her chest. "Breast cancer?"

"Yes," he whispered.

"You have unsettled guilt over her passing. No good, John. It impedes her spiritual progress and keeps you bound in grief."

"I didn't know what to do for her." He broke down. "I'm not sure I did enough." He covered his eyes with his hand.

"Cancer is a greedy thief. There was nothing you could do for her. There was nothing that anyone could do."

"I know. I know. That's what made it so terrible."

"It was her soul's time. And so now, by depriving yourself—renouncing pleasure do you expect to avenge her fate?"

He shrugged helplessly like a small boy.

"You're wracked with fear. The fear of losing again. Although fear is a protective measure, it can also become our jailer if we allow it to rule. I want you to know that your wife is at peace. Her soul is radiant; blissful to be on its spiritual journey."

"I always hoped she'd give me a sign, or something to let me know she was alright." Jay sobbed pitifully before the stranger, the only person he had ever bared his pain to. "I'm sorry. I'm sorry." He buried his face in his trembling hands.

"You've done nothing wrong." Mrs. Habbibi soothed her client. "I've come to learn that most are unable to see what is contrary to their own beliefs, but you are a broad thinker. Would you at least, consider what I'm about to explain to you?"

"Go ahead." Jay began to regain his composure.

"Sometimes the intense grief of loved ones left behind can distress the departed."

He looked soberly into Mrs. Habbibi's eyes.

"Your relentless mourning distracts Judith from her work."

"Work?" He plucked another tissue from the box.

"I refer to it as work." Mrs. Habbibi said with compassion. "There are many levels the soul must aspire to before it reaches perfection. Our human form is just one of them and quite frankly, once a soul has crossed over, the realm of the living holds no interest for them."

"How could I be affecting her if she's no longer here?"

"The same way she is affecting you."

He paused in thought.

"The bond of love between souls is divine. It isn't broken merely because one has transitioned to enter the next dimension. The concept transcends our human comprehension, but just consider the divine love a mother has for her unborn child, a soul she has yet to lay eyes on and yet the profound effect the two have upon each other is irrefutable." She abruptly held up her finger and squinted, her attention appearing to be pulled elsewhere.

Jay watched with renewed respect.

"Someone else is coming through. I'm getting someone else, also with a J." She struggled. "No, it's your wife, again…I'm sorry…I'm confused. It is your wife, but she seems to be trying to be showing me a name. A name with a J. Someone close to her or in her good favor. It is a woman. Do you have a daughter?"

"Yes, three, but their names don't have a J in them."

Mrs. Habbibi struggled, her face creased with puzzlement. "I'm not sure, what message Judith is trying to send you, one can only speculate, dealing with the spirit world, but what I can say for sure is that, your wife is adamant that this J female is acknowledged by you." Mrs. Habbibi touched her fingers to her temples, straining. "And she fades." She slumped with puzzlement.

Jay found himself shaken and struggling to keep his face neutral, sitting across from the incredible woman who abruptly popped up in her seat.

"Ah. Others are here." Her hand rose into the air and danced above her head. "You have to acknowledge them as soon as they come through or they get angry," she informed him. "I'm getting a very strong male. A father or a grandfather presence. John? Jack?"

"That would be my father. His name was John, too."

"He has a very strong energy." She grinned with amusement. "Very take charge. He wants to be sure that you know he is here."

"That's him," Jay said and laughed through his tears, dabbing again at his eyes.

"Were you in business together? Something with food. A restaurant?"

"Bakery," Jay said.

"He's happy you still do this work—I'd like to take a look at your palms. Sometimes the information they offer can round out a reading. Would you turn them up for me, please?"

Jay extended his hands.

She studied them in silence for a time. "You're right-handed?"

He nodded.

She took his hand in hers and began to examine it closely. "You have an earth hand. It indicates a practical nature. Your lifeline here, the one curving around your thumb, it indicates health and vitality. Yours is nice and solid, uninterrupted." She looked up, peering into his face over the top of her glasses. "That's good, John."

"Good." He was able to share in her candor. "I could use some good news."

She returned to his upturned palm. "There is a prominent break in your heart line," she studied further. "The line curves and then falls off abruptly then proceeds beyond. Was there a previous marriage before your wife who passed?"

"No."

"Hmm. Now, your head line…"

"No, no, go back to the heart line—the break."

"It can be interpreted in several ways." The psychic shifted her position, peering closer at the line. "I would say another partner is in your future, but lines on the hand can change over time, which is why I use the information on the palm as only part of my practice." She cleared her throat. "Now, your fate line, this is the line that runs from the base of your palm to where the fingers begin, it signifies the path through life, also indicates career and money attraction."

"I'm not interested in that—is there anything else you can tell me about this other *J* person?"

The psychic closed her eyes for a long moment. "No. Judith is gone." Mrs. Habbibi looked soberly at her client. "Her essence has faded. If you like, we can try again at another time."

"No. No, thank you." He turned on a hip and reached into his back pocket.

Mrs. Habbibi watched him pull two, one hundred dollar bills from his wallet and placed them on the table as he rose to his feet.

"That's for you," he said.

"Wasn't your fee collected before your reading?"

"Yes it was, but I want you to have that."

"Thank you." Her dark hand lifted the bills off the table and tucked them down into her blouse. "Tips are always gratefully accepted." She smiled widely.

"Thank you, Mrs. Habbibi." He turned, walking tall out of her room.

The psychic sighed with relief, slumping forward when he was gone. The next knock came abruptly. She swallowed a gulp of iced tea. "Come in." She stuck the bottle back down into her bag and straightened her spine.

It was after two more clients that Andrea Petrakas hurried across the room and pressed into the chair across from her.

"Hello, Mrs. Habbibi," she whispered, clutching her purse and pushed an envelope at her across the desk.

"Thank you, Andrea. I would like to get started right away." She tucked it down into her bag. "The moon is about to enter its waxing phase. We can begin the first of the three treatments the night after next if all is in order."

"I'm ready."

"First, I'm going to teach you the Tower of Light. It's a method of spiritual protection and a means to strengthen your aura. Even under the best circumstances, whenever we delve into the other realm there are always low vibrating energies lurking. We do not want to make it easy for them to attach and hamper our efforts. I would like you to stand, please."

Andrea began to weep. "I don't know if I can go through with this."

"Pull yourself together. The dread that you are feeling is the dark forces at work against you. They attempt to wear you down, dissuade you from your intentions. You have nothing to fear anymore as long as you follow my instructions. And remember you will always have the ability to protect yourself."

"I haven't slept since I saw you last. I'm exhausted." Her lower lip quivered.

"I understand, but you must summon your courage. You're on your way. The power is in your hands to finally rid yourself of this insidious curse that threatens your legacy. Your husband is gone; you're the only one who can release his soul from torment and save your family from the same fate."

"Oh, my God. It's all just so horrible." Andrea whimpered, her face turning pale..

"You owe it to yourself and to your family. You have all suffered enough. I need you to be strong. I cannot proceed successfully without your help."

Andrea slowly rose to her feet.

"Stand with your hands at your sides."

Andrea hesitated.

"Do it," the psychic firmly instructed.

Andrea stood in the shadowy room; arms held at her sides, her eyes squeezed shut in desperate concentration.

"Visualize a bright blue light, a protective force field all around your body, encapsulating it, and extending one foot beyond–above your head and below the level of your feet. Can you see it, Andrea?"

"Yes."

"I want you to feel it, too–the well-defined blue light surrounding you, protecting you. Concentrate on the image and when you feel ready, I want you to imagine a globe of brilliant, bright, white light, hovering just above your head. You don't have to look up, just know that it's there."

"Okay," Andrea confirmed its presence, her eyes still tightly squeezed closed.

"You are making the image of this orb to represent the light of your higher self. Concentrate on it, aspiring to the highest good that you are capable of. You are doing excellent. Keep focusing on the shining orb and when you feel ready, imagine that glowing, bright orb sending brilliant sparkles of light down, flooding your aura, coursing through you, until it becomes part of you."

"I feel it."

"You're doing, wonderfully. Now, slowly let this image fade from your consciousness knowing that even though it fades, it is ever-present and ready for you to access whenever you feel the need. Now, slowly open your eyes."

"That was marvelous," Andrea said, her gaze meeting Mrs. Habbibi's beaming face.

"Now we can begin. Sit. We must stay on schedule." She pressed towards her speaking in a whisper. "Throughout the ages, the number three has held mystical significance. The Holy Trinity; past, present, future;- birth, life, death. The human form itself is comprised of three parts; head, upper and lower. And the sacred practice that I am going to evoke to remove your hex will also be in three parts." She reached down into her bag and placed two glass vials on the table. I have prepared each of these vials for you. Take the vial that contains the amber crystals and listen carefully to my instructions, Andrea."

Andrea held the small glass cylinder in her palm.

"Tomorrow morning fill a large bucket with two parts distilled water and one part white vinegar, add half the contents of the vial and then leave the combined solution out in the sunlight for the afternoon." Mrs. Habbibi's raised her voice. "Do you understand?"

"Yes, yes. I understand," the woman assured her.

"The following morning, add the other half of the contents in the vial to the solution. Open every door and window in your house–this will give the evil spirits I will have disavowed on your behalf ample opportunities to flee once the treatment takes effect. And then starting on the first floor, swab the threshold of every door and its frame with the treated water. Do the same for every window in your house. Any of this solution left when you are done is to be poured into the earth. Are you following the instructions? Easy enough, yes?"

Andrea nodded.

"Next," she gestured for Andrea to take the vile containing white crystals. "This is sea salt that I have prepared for you in a purification ceremony. On the night of the full moon, at nine o'clock, add half of the contents of the vial to a bucket of clean water and scrub your bathtub in preparation. Make sure you will not be disturbed when you bathe so be sure to turn off your phone. Rinse the tub thoroughly before you fill it with hot, water, as hot as you can tolerate and then add the other half of salts left in the vial into the steaming tub. Climb in. Soak for a moment and then completely submerge you entire body, including your head. Sit in the tub for a full five minutes, sweating out your impurities into the water. Drain the tub as you are still sitting, feel the pull of gravity drawing the water and its impurities away from you and down the drain. When the tub is empty, quickly shower in hot water and climb right into bed. When you wake in the morning, shower again and wash all of your bedding."

Andrea stared, wide-eyed.

"Do you understand these instructions?"

"Yes," Andrea nodded. "I understand."

"It is most important that you begin the soaking ceremony at precisely nine 'o clock because this will be the time I will begin the clearing incantations. It is crucial that we work in unison."

"Nine. I understand."

"Now, since the hex that is attached to you is through energy lines that passed between you and your husband throughout your married lives, I will need to sever the chords of attachment."

"How can you do that if he's not here?" Andrea panicked.

"Symbolically. I will need your wedding bands, engagement ring and any other tokens representing your sacred union that you have given each other over the course of your marriage, including wedding anniversaries, birthdays and so forth."

"What are you going to do to them?"

"I'm going to perform a ceremony invoking the legions of the light to cleanse all of the dark energy that has attached to the items and then symbolically cut the chords of energy that connect to you."

"I don't understand any of that. I'm uncomfortable handing over my valuables."

"If you like we can work with just a few pieces at a time if that will make you more at ease. Remember, the masters of darkness thrive on your anxiety, so perhaps that is the proper way to proceed. Does that make you more comfortable?"

"Yes. Thank you."

"Of course. Above all, I need you to stay calm and remember that it is only you and your devout resolve to do what's necessary that will rid you of this curse and release your family, being held as hostages. I am merely an instrument."

"Okay. Okay. I understand. Let's get on with it." Andrea straightened and wiped her red-rimmed eyes.

"Gather the personal items that we discussed starting with your engagement ring. Put it in a sturdy envelope with the first payment—in cash, along with Miss J's fee. Miss J will be at your home to pick up the sealed envelope tomorrow afternoon. She will return the items to you within one week, totally cleansed and cleared of all negative binds. And you will be on your way to your new life, reunited with your family."

13

*P*haraoh was staying at Joan's house for the day while Fiona's new bungalow was being painted. He chivalrously escorted Joan to the door when her bell rang. Jay was taking her to lunch and a vintage car show on the sunny July afternoon.

"Wow. Look at the size of him," Jay said, standing in the doorway.

"He's as gentle as a puppy. Just come in. You're making him nervous." She stood on her toes and kissed him on his mouth.

"I'm making him nervous?" Jay cautiously stepped inside.

"Pet him. Tell him something nice."

"Nice Pharaoh. Good boy." He patted the dog's head.

Pharaoh jumped up on his back legs to return Jay's greeting.

Jay screamed.

Joan laughed at him. "Just go inside and put on the game. I just have to feed him before we go." She gave Jay a playful peck on his cheek and headed to the beeping microwave.

Jay took the remote and plopped down in front of the television. "Don't tell me that you're heating his food?"

"It's the only way he'll eat it."

"Life doesn't begin when the kids are out of the house; it begins when the dog dies." He mumbled, flipping through the channels to find the Mets playing at home at Citi Field.

Pharaoh patiently waited as Joan spooned his warmed, boiled chicken and rice mixture into his bowl.

"Hey, Joanie, I've heard that Dobermans are notorious for turning on their masters," Jay teased her from the living room.

"Thanks. Sure do appreciate that," she said walking across the kitchen, Pharaoh's black toenails clicking on tiled floor as he pranced alongside of her.

"Time for nums-nums," Joan sang, setting his dish down. She popped her head into the living room. "Just give me a couple of minutes and we're outta here."

Jay gave her a thumbs-up.

"Ugh!" Her voice carried from the other side of the house. "He pooped in my bedroom! Jay, can you get in here with some paper towels?"

"Nice." Jay soon appeared in her bedroom doorway holding a roll of paper towels and the trash container staring at the gift Pharaoh had left on the champagne-colored carpet. "Let's get that window open for you."

A low rumbling sound began to rise from behind them. They gaped at each other and slowly turned to see the massive Doberman teeth bared, front legs parted in attack stance, filling the doorway with his broad, heaving body.

"Don't make a move." Jay became a ventriloquist. "He'll charge."

Joan nodded in terror.

Jay motioned to her open closet with a nudge of his chin. "On the count of three," he urged under his breath, the blood-draining growls growing louder at their backs.

"One," he mouthed the words. "Two…."

Her eyes widened in anticipation.

"Three!" Jay shouted and gave Joan a shove that sent her crashing into the louvered doors, tumbling onto her closet floor. He snatched up an armful of folded laundry from a nearby chair and flung it into the dog's face just as it leaped, lunging toward him. Jay dove into the closet, crashing on top of Joan, pulling the doors closed.

They both screamed as the enraged animal pounced, pressing the doors inward, snarling and snapping as they huddled together on the floor.

"What are we going to do?" Joan cried in desperation, her limbs wrapped around Jay as if they were drowning at sea while Pharaoh scratched frantically at the base of the door.

"Get my phone out of my pocket." Jay braced his palms against the doors to keep them from being pushed in by the angry dog's powerful thrusts. "Call the police."

"I'm not going to do that. They'll shoot him." Joan fumbled with the phone. Its light illuminated both their terrified faces in the cramped space. "I'm calling Fia. What is wrong with him? He's never acted like this before," she whimpered, stabbing the number into the phone, waiting for Fia to pick up.

"Territorial. I don't think he wanted me in your bedroom."

"Maybe you should have bonded with him more."

They both flinched as another threatening pounce reverberated.

"Too late now."

"Fia! Thank God, you picked up. Pharaoh has me and Jay trapped in my bedroom closet!"

"What?"

"Jay came in to help me clean up his poop and he barricaded the doorway."

"Is he okay?"

"He's a little shaken up, but…"

"Not Jay—Pharaoh?"

"He's pacing outside the door. I've never seen him act like this. You need to get over here, now!"

"I have someone in my chair, I'll leave as soon as I finish up with her. I'll be there as soon as I can."

"Hurry!"

"Just, whatever you do, don't open the door. He's in protection mode," Fiona warned her.

Joan ended the call and the phone's light faded out. "I'm so sorry I got you into this," she said in the darkness of the closet.

"It's not your fault. We're both safe. Everything's going to be all right." He touched his lips to her forehead. "Sounds like he's stopped pacing. I think he may be getting tired."

They heard him sigh, and there was silence.

"Shh, I think he's sitting down. Maybe he gave up," Jay whispered against her cheekbone.

"Thank God." She let her body go limp against his.

"That was close. We make a good team," Jay said, the low grumblings on the other side of the door seemed to be turning into throaty snores. "I can hardly see you," he said, his reassuring caresses at her back becoming slow, rhythmic stokes.

"I'm here," she whispered.

"I know. You're cutting off my circulation."

"Sorry." She giggled, allowing the enticing spice of his aftershave to lead her away.

"We just have to wait it out until Fia gets here," he whispered back.

"That's not going to be for at least an hour."

The next morning Joan sat on her sofa sipping her coffee beside a contrite Pharaoh.

Fiona poured herself a glass of grapefruit juice at the kitchen counter. "I'm so glad that the two of you made up and you aren't holding it against him."

"I don't ever remember being that frightened of a dog before. It was like he was a different animal."

"He was just trying to protect you, Joanie. Jay was a stranger to him."

"I realize that now. I did try to get Jay to warm up to him, but I guess it wasn't enough."

"Pharaoh considers you one of his own, that's why he pooped in your bedroom."

"I'm honored." Joan rolled her eyes, pushing up from the couch and poured herself a second cup of coffee.

"So let's hear more about those two hours in the closet—and not the nap part. I've been dying for the details all night."

Joan fell into a kitchen chair with a sigh and stared into space holding her coffee mug close to her chest. "It was...I don't even know what...." She twirled on the swivel kitchen chair.

"That good, huh?" Fiona laughed at her. "Well, are you in love?"

"I think I have been all along... I'm not sure..." She stood. "I don't know what I am." She glided across the room, staring out the patio doors at the water.

"It was just a lay, Joanie. It's not really that big of a deal."

"That's what you think." She turned around toward her friend. "There's more to tell."

"That really must have been some good time in that closet."

Joan waved her off. "It was after the closet...later that night, when we were at dinner. Are you ready?"

Fiona held her arms opened, her face etched with impatience.

Joan put her mug down on the counter. "You've heard of Barrett Brothers Bakers, haven't you? Those blue and gray striped boxes in all the supermarkets?"

"Of course. They've been around since we were kids. Choc-Alots, Coconut Clouds..."

"Right. Orange Sponges, Strudel-Doos..."

Fiona's eyes twinkled with anticipation. "Yeah, so?"

"Jay *is* Barrett Brothers."

"*The* Barrett Brothers?"

"Yes." Joan's eyes sparkled with excitement. "The business has been in his family for generations. Jay and his brother own the entire company."

"Really?" Fiona's eyes began to narrow as the news sank in. "Bernie, that sneaky hold-out. He never said a word."

"Jay is very protective of his privacy. So listen— here's the exciting part."

"How much more exciting can it get than finding out that your boyfriend is the owner of one of the biggest companies in the country?"

"He invited me to the picnic that the company hosts for the local employees every year at the fairgrounds. You and Bernie can come too. And his family is going to be there."

They both screamed, twirling each other in circles around the kitchen.

"He wants me to meet his family!"

"Good work, Joanie! We are definitely going shopping to buy you a new outfit."

14

The next week Joan arrived at the salon on a Friday morning, happily ridding herself of the balancing act of managing her purse and the clumsy cardboard tray that held two coffee cups.

"Good morning, gorgeous," Fiona looked up at her from fussing with some of her stock.

"There's your chai tea, two bags." Joan said settling in, stowing away her purse. "And there's Andrea's return." She slid the sealed manila envelope across the top of the glass display cases toward Fiona. "That lady is not a happy camper," Joan said, straightening her blazer and patting down her hair.

"I told you she was strange," Fiona said, easing the lid off of the steaming cup.

"Strange is one thing, that woman acts as if she has the weight of the world on her shoulders. You'd figure that someone who lived in such a beautiful, big house with all that money would be just a little more cheerful," Joan said, uncapping her cappuccino.

"Who knows what goes on in people's heads?" Fiona pressed her teabags against the inside of the plastic lid, draining them into her cup.

"It's Friday, we're probably going to be busy, you think?"

Fiona looked up to answer her and abruptly put her cup down. "And what is *that* around your neck?" She beelined over to Joan bringing the striking diamond sparkling at her throat closer for inspection.

"Last night. Jay surprised me. I was speechless. I didn't know what to say."

"How bout, *come to mama!* Joan, that is magnificent——it's got to be at least four carats." She delicately ran her fingers over the smaller stones that adorned the impressive piece.

"You think? I didn't know that you knew about that kind of stuff."

"Eh-h." Fiona shrugged. "Joanie, this is more than just a necklace. This is marking territory."

"I know. That's the problem."

"Who can make a problem out of receiving a giant diamond necklace?" Fiona glanced up at the ceiling as if searching for answers.

Joan sighed as she began to explain. "I've never mentioned Jay to my sons. And the few times that I mentioned him to Francie, just in passing, I could tell she wasn't comfortable with the idea. She and Vinny had known each other since we were kids. He was like a brother to her."

"What does what Francie is comfortable with have to do with how you and Jay feel about each other?"

"My husband's only been gone a little over a year. What will people think of me getting involved so soon?"

"I didn't know that they handed down a minimum sentence for the grieving process." Fiona walked back around to the counters. "So just don't wear it when you're around your family."

"That's another problem. As Jay was clasping it for me, he told me that he never, *ever* wants it to leave my neck."

Fiona walked back around the counter and wrapped her arms around Joan hugging her tight. "I hope that they're tears of joy that you're crying, Joanie."

"They are." She sniffled, then brushed at her tears with the back of her hand. "But you know how crazy I can make myself—I'm going to be meeting his daughters for the first time next weekend at that picnic. I don't want to start off on the wrong foot—I'd be so uncomfortable if they suspect that the diamond is from, Jay."

"Seems like it doesn't matter to him."

Joan dropped her head into Fiona's shoulder. "I love you, Fia. You always make everything right for me."

The fairgrounds in Flushing Meadow Park was the site of The Barrett Brother Bakers' tri-state area, annual picnic. It was a cloudless, Sunday July afternoon. The kind of day northerners dream of in February while waiting out its cold, gray dreariness. Fiona and Joan sat at a picnic table enjoying the sounds of a Reggae band and watching Jay and his older brother, Harry play host to five-hundred employees and their families who had been invited to share a day of food, music and games on the grounds that had once hosted the 1964 World's Fair.

"Burger for you, Joanie. Veggie burger for Fi and two hot dogs, extra kraut for me." Bernie returned with their food, swinging his leg over the picnic bench.

"Jay's like a celebrity to these people." Fiona said twisting around to the table top.

"They love him," Bernie said. "He treats all of his people like family. He footed the whole bill for one of the trucker's wife's kidney transplant. But you'd never hear it from him." He tore open a packet of mustard with his teeth and squeezed it onto his hot dogs.

"It's really wonderful to see all of the families out together, enjoying themselves," Joan said.

"When are we gonna get to meet Jay's family?" That's what I want to see." Fiona flicked at the burger, unimpressed and twisted away from it, straddling the bench.

"They'll be here. Be patient. You're such a yenta," Bernie told her.

"What's a yenta?" Joan asked.

"It's Yiddish for a woman who has always got her nose in other people's business." He playfully held his hot dog up to Fiona her for a bite.

"Yuck." She pushed his hand away.

"I'm not in such a hurry to meet them. I'm so nervous." Joan fanned herself with a paper plate."

"Why? You're making too much of it. We're all just hanging out, listening to the music. Relax. Enjoy. And that wrap-around dress looks fabulous on you. Teal is your color."

"Fia is right. Don't be nervous, Joanie," Bernie said pushing the last bite of a hot dog into his mouth. "I've known Jay's kids since they were in high school. They're sweet girls."

"Don't look now," Fiona said, pulling her sunglasses down lower on the bridge of her nose.

The family entourage moved in a pack. A few grandchildren broke away, anxious to be the first to greet their popular grandfather. The daughters were blondes, fashionably thin, and dressed like they'd just stepped out of a Ralph Lauren ad. All were striding toward them with the same air of confidence and privilege. The three women were trailed by their husbands who carried their smaller children and all of the gear required for a summer day outdoors.

They surrounded him, grandchildren tugging at his waist, hugs and kisses from his daughters, hand-shakes and hugs from his sons-in-law. Jay pointed across the way to his guests and the entourage closed in on the picnic table, losing some of the older grandchildren along the way who scattered off to the rides and games stationed throughout the picnic grounds.

"Bernie!" The young women squealed as he stood to receive their warm greetings.

Jay redirected their attention. "Allison, Stephanie, Carly, meet Fiona and my good friend, Joan Bruno," he casually introduced his guests.

The undertones of the introductions were camouflaged well enough until one of Jay's daughters lifted her sunglasses presumably to get a better look at the women who were with her father and his longtime friend.

"Grandpa are you going to play horseshoes with us?" A grandson tugged at his wrist.

"Of course, I am." Jay mussed the boy's hair. "Why don't you girls get settled in? I had this nice group of tables set up for all of you right here next to Bernie."

"That was so nice, Dad. But a few of the guys are already setting us up across the way at some tables under the shade."

"Oh... well, that's fine. I'll be by as soon as I make a few more rounds."

"Don't be too long." His youngest daughter, Carly, lovingly flattened out the collar of Jay's polo shirt.

Allison planted a kiss on his cheek and headed back in the direction of their outpost, the rest of the entourage following.

"Make sure you have enough sunblock on, Dad," Stephanie called back to him.

"The girls look great." Bernie said. "And the kids are getting so damn big."

"Your girls are stunning, Jay. You're blessed. You have a beautiful family," Joan told him.

He took her gently by the shoulder. "Come, Joanie, take a walk with me. I have to say hello to some people on the other side of the park."

"That went pretty well," Bernie said tipping the last of his Diet Coke out of the can into his mouth. "You have to give Jay credit. This was the perfect occasion to introduce Joan to his girls."

"I don't like them," Fiona said twisting around on the bench, her forehead was furrowed as she faced him.

"How can you say that? They weren't here for more than a minute."

"It's the little things that people do that tip off their real feelings. Did you catch how the middle one made no effort to hide that she was giving me and Joan the once-over? And the other one treating Jay like he was one of her kids, fussing with his clothes. That was all to let it be known that there was a definite wall between Jay and any outsider. And *they* were it."

"You got all of that out of the fifty seconds that they stood there?" He searched her face.

"Of course. What are you laughing at? You think that I'm crazy, don't you?" She laughed herself.

"No, I don't. I caught all of it, too," he admitted. "I've been watching those girls fend off the Pot Roast Brigade since the week after Judy died."

"Pot Roast Brigade?"

"The steady stream of women doing everything but standing on their heads to be the next Mrs. Jay Barrett."

"It's not their father they're protecting, it's their pocket books."

"And you're right about that, too." Bernie playfully slapped her soundly on the thigh of her faded jeans. "Come on, dance with me. Let me show you my Caribbean salsa." He tugged her off the bench toward the music.

Jay's daughter, Allison was hosting a fortieth birthday party for her husband the following weekend. It was not clear if the invitation that was extended to Joan, Bernie and Fiona was initiated from the hostess, but Jay assured them that they were all welcome and he was adamant that they join him at the outdoor celebration at his daughter's home.

High above the East River, crossing the expanse of the Throgs Neck Bridge, the sound of the tires speeding over the road grates vibrated inside Jay's Audi on their way to Connecticut on the Sunday afternoon.

"So explain to me again, why isn't Bernie joining us?" Joan asked Fiona.

"I'm not even sure—something last minute with his daughter." She answered from the back seat. "He was being annoying. I just hung up on him."

"I hope everything is okay. I'm just so glad that you're still taking the ride with us."

"Of course. Why wouldn't I? It's a gorgeous day and it sounds like it's going to be a fun time."

"It will be. Allison throws a great party." Jay said, making sure to give his nervous girlfriend a reassuring smile.

In the town of Greenwich they drove through a tunnel of graceful old trees, their natural canopy spreading over the ribbon of narrow, sun-dappled road. They cruised into a neighborhood with a wall of tall hedges and gated driveways slipping by on either side that sequestered the opulent homes that lie beyond. Jay made the sharp right turn though the stone pillars into the winding driveway lined with Range Rovers, Escalades and other expensive cars that belonged to the family's guests.

Joan and Fiona exchanged awed glances as they stepped out of the car in front of the breathtaking home perched on a rolling hill, the Long Island Sound the backdrop at its rear.

"This is just magnificent," Joan said.

"Wait until you see the view from the decks. It's a winner," Jay said as he followed them up the wide stone stairway.

They stepped into the refreshing coolness of the home. The festivities were taking place on the wrap-around balcony and waterfront backyard at the opposite end of the house, leaving the airy entrance hall quiet and still.

"I don't know where to look first," Fiona said gazing up at the vaulted ceiling above the fresh floral arrangement in a massive Ming vase in the center of a circular table that dominated the space.

As they continued into the home, Joan stopped to admire the black-and-white photographs of Allison's children that hung all along the walls of the wide, long hallway.

"My daughter took all of those pictures," Jay told her.

"Does she do it professionally? She's got a great eye."

"Just a hobby. She's a lot like Judy. Good at everything."

As the words left his mouth, Judy herself, stared back at Joan from an oversized family portrait of her and Jay sitting under a tree on a grassy hill, joyfully surrounded by their grandchildren who sat all around them in matching overalls.

"Give me a minute, girls. It was a long ride." Jay stepped into a hallway bathroom.

Joan and Fiona stood before the large, colorful portrait.

"Pretty lady," Fiona said.

"Hmm," Joan agreed. "Elegant."

"Judy had a lot to live for."

Joan nodded. "Yes, she did."

"Nobody knows when they're going to be yanked out of this life. It doesn't matter how much money you have—you can't bargain with fate."

"She seems like she was a happy person." Joan continued to study the poised matriarch.

"She does," Fiona agreed. "You can tell that she knew how to be in the moment."

"You can only imagine the void her children are suffering without her."

"It doesn't excuse them from taking it out on other people." Fiona turned her attention to the other artwork adorning the walls.

"Dad! You're finally here!" Jay's daughter, Stephanie and her young son approached from the other side of the hall just as Jay was emerging from the doorway.

"You know what the traffic is like getting out of the city on summer weekends."

They embraced and Jay tried to grab for his grandson as he darted past him into the bathroom.

"It's a full house in there. All the other bathrooms are occupied. He couldn't wait." Stephanie leaned in and gave Joan and Fiona each an anemic air kiss at their cheeks. "It's so nice to see both of you again. Where is Bernie?" She asked her father. "He's not with you?"

"He got caught up with something or other... See you, inside."

The spreading kitchen was alive with the joyful chaos of close friends and family and a small team of uniformed help scrambling to keep the privileged class of attendees and their employer happy.

"Dad!" Allison stepped away from a semi-circle of chatty friends gathered around a counter top and threw her arms around Jay. "And Joan and….wait…wait… I remember. Fiona!" She blurted.

"That's right." Fiona cracked an exaggerated false smile.

Joan presented the hostess with a gift. "I made them just this morning." She lifted the lid of the container showing perfect rows of bite sized, custard-filled tarts topped with colorful berries and kiwi.

"You made these?" Allison gushed with exaggeration.

"Wow. They don't even look real. It must have taken you hours to get each one so uniform," Fiona said.

"I've always loved to bake. They need to be refrigerated," Joan said offering the box to her hostess.

"Thank you so much. You didn't have to do this. There's so much food here. Almost everyone brought some kind of dessert. Dad, the birthday boy is down at the water showing off his new Jet Ski. Go down and say hello and don't let him try and talk you into getting on that crazy thing. I'll be down in a bit."

There were enough guests at the party to get lost in the crowd. It was obvious that Jay's daughter and son-in-law's younger friends had a genuine affection for Jay and they were considerably warmer and more engaging to Joan and Fiona throughout the day than his three children were.

Midway into the party, on her return from a visit to the rest room, Stephanie and Carly signaled Joan to join them and a group of women gathered in the active kitchen. After preliminary small talk, Stephanie singled out Joan with a question. "Did our father invite you to our mother's charity walk next weekend?"

"Ah, no. I don't remember him mentioning it."

"Oh," the woman said, doing a poor job of hiding her relief. "Just thought I'd ask."

Joan squeezed onto a bench next to Fiona who was enjoying a plate of lobster salad in front of an outdoor fireplace.

"I know that look. What's wrong?" Fiona asked her.

"Those girls are just downright rude."

"What happened?"

"Nothing—and do you know that my fruit tarts are still sitting out on the counter. Allison never put them into the refrigerator. Should I say something? There probably a soggy mess by now."

"No. Don't you say anything. Just go back out there and enjoy yourself with Jay. I'll take care of it."

Fiona followed after Allison on the hostess' next trip into the kitchen. She sashayed right up to her while she was in the middle of ticking off instructions to the catering staff. "Excuse me, Allison. I just want to say what a wonderful party this is and wanted to know if there was anything I could help you with?"

"I think were in pretty good shape." She coldly dismissed the gesture.

"Are those Joan's fruit tarts still sitting on the counter? I think she mentioned that they needed to be refrigerated."

"Oh. I thought that I told one of the girls to take care of that." She called over to no one in particular working in the noisy kitchen. "Would someone put that box into the refrigerator, please?"

And as the air cooled and the sun sank in the sky to the west, the grand, tennis racquet-shaped birthday cake was carried out of the kitchen and set down among a vast array of tempting desserts; many of them homemade offerings from guests, but curiously, Joan's fresh berry tarts were not among the selections.

"Do you think that she forgot? Should I say something?" Joan whispered to Fiona.

The candles were lit and the balcony full of party guests crowded around the glowing cake sang a zealous rendition of Happy Birthday.

"Does that shrew seem to be the type that forgets anything?" Fiona eyed the three sisters clustered together looking back at them across the noisy, celebration. "They're messing with us, Joanie. Testing you. Don't give them the satisfaction. Just keep smiling."

15

*I*t was weeks later and Joan and Jay had decided to stay in for the night. They were snuggled in bed, a bowl of popcorn between them, binge watching *Game of Thrones* when Jay's phone rang. He untwined himself and reached to take the call.

"Don't answer it," Joan murmured.

And seconds later a text pinged through.

"Let me see who this is," he said rolling onto his side, grabbing his phone off of her night table. He peered at the text from Bernie. PICK UP YOUR PHONE! And it rang, seconds later.

"Jay! Are you with Joan? I need you two to get over to my house. I had an argument with Fiona and she trashed the place and then locked herself in the bathroom. I think she took some pills."

"Is she okay?" Jay sat up, swinging his legs over the side of the bed.

"I don't know. I can't get her to come out."

"We're leaving now."

Bernie yanked open one of the double doors of the elegant entry of his ostentatious waterfront home. He was holding his bleeding hand against his Tommy Bahama oversize, button down.

"What the hell happened?" Jay asked as they stepped into the elaborate house, clothes and other personal items strewn across the salmon-colored, Italian marble foyer. "And what happened to your hand?"

"She bit me!"

"What?" Jay and Joan asked in unison.

"The crazy bitch bit me. Come on and take a look at her. She's in the den." He pointed with his other hand.

His confused friends looked at each other and followed.

"I finally got her to come out of the bathroom," Bernie explained as they trailed him into the other room. "I had asked her to come over so we could talk. I wanted to explain that I needed to stop seeing her and she went berserk." The burly man stopped and turned, his eyes pleading like a frightened child's. "I was actually scared. In my whole life I've never seen a woman act like that."

"It's okay, Bernie," Jay tried to calm him with a reassuring hand on his friend's damp back.

The three of them stood before the sofa gazing down on Fiona. She was lying face down in the cushions. One of her legs dangled off its edge, her foot out of her platform sandal but still strapped at her ankle, the wall-sized, pop art portrait of Bernie's wife, Shelia, hanging above her.

Joan gasped.

"She's not dead. She was babbling to me a little while before you got here. I think that she just needs to sleep it off. But I need to get her the hell out of my house."

Joan knelt and gently turned Fiona onto her side.

"Joanie." Fiona groaned, and her head flopped to the side, a trail of drool dribbling out the side of her mouth.

"What did she take?" Joan looked up at Bernie while straightening Fiona's halter top.

"There's a bottle in her purse. It looks like Valium."

"She seems okay. Let's try and get some coffee into her." Joan stood.

"Come in the kitchen, Bern. Let me wrap up that hand up for you. You're bleeding all over your shirt," Jay said as they followed after Joan.

"It looks like there was a brawl in here," Jay took in the violent scene.

The mosaic backsplash above the six-burner stove was sprayed with purple splatters, shards of shattered glass and a broken bottle lay in a puddle of wine that had dripped down one of the cabinets. Fiona's purse and its random contents littered the kitchen floor.

"What'd you say to her that set her off?"

Bernie collapsed into an upholstered swivel stool at the black and gold veined granite counter. "The scotch is right over there, Jay. Would you pour me another one? I'm still shaking." He ran his hands under the flow from the curved, gold leaf faucet. "My daughter told me that her and my son-in-law are expecting their first child. She's been stopping by the office the last few weeks, and working on Shelia too. So her and I met a few times over dinner and she wants to move back home. I wanted to explain the situation to Fiona like a gentleman. That's why I asked her over. We sat, I opened a bottle of cab, everything was fine and I started to tell her and she went nuts." His voice started to crack as he ran his uninjured hand through his hair in distress.

Joan rested her hand on his shoulder.

"Take it easy, buddy." Jay poured him a generous refill of Black Label.

"It was a fling. We were having a great time. What? Did she think that I was going to marry her?" Bernie took a belt of the liquor and popped up off the stool, stomping across the kitchen to an overturned box and began gathering the clothes and toiletries strewn all around it. "She kept some things here for when she'd spend the night. I got them together and packed it up for her and when I tried to give it back, she threw it all over the place, knocked the wine glasses off the counter and then she came at me. I put my hands up and she grabbed my wrist and took a bite out of my finger!"

"Oh, jeez." Jay's voice revealed his shared disbelief.

"I shoved her away. I didn't mean for her to fall. And she got up and grabbed her purse and took off into the bathroom." His face was flushed and he seemed on the verge of tears.

"Oh, Bernie." Joan sighed, standing stiffly at his coffee maker.

"It's my fault. I should have never gotten so involved. It just took on a life of its own…" He bent, frantically snatching up clothing and shoes, firing them back into the box. "I just want it all the hell out of here. And her too!" He became unhinged.

"Your hand, Bernie." Joan rushed over to stop him. "Just sit." She pried a red bikini top from his fist.

"I'm done. I've had enough!" He waved his arm violently through the air and slumped back at the counter, propping his forehead in his palm on a bent elbow.

"Settle, down. We'll take care of it." Jay took his hand and began to bandage it for him. "Joanie, get all of her things back into the box and put it out in her car. I'll clean up the glass."

The acappella chorus of crickets harmonizing from their hiding places in the lush shrubs and trees of the property's manicured landscaping echoed in the still mid August night. Joan walked out across Bernie's circular driveway, around the three-tiered fountain that lazily spilled over into itself and popped the trunk to Fiona's car. As she dropped the box down inside a strange object caught her eye. She leaned in further and zeroed in on what looked like an auburn-colored wig sealed inside a plastic Ziploc, stuffed into a canvas shopping bag.

Curiosity getting the best of her, she reached for it and noticed the two large, previously- burned candles rolled in a gold cloth. Her brows furrowed, not yet registering what she had discovered and she rummaged down further. Carefully, she opened a plastic case with unsteady hands and mounting horror. She dangled the mouthpiece it contained between her fingers, and realizing what it was, flung it as though she had picked up a tarantula.

She felt her face twist as she tried to comprehend the implications of her discovery and though the sense of dread stupefied her, she continued to dig in the bag. She found eye glasses, shoes, a case holding a rubber prosthetic nose, and a bottle of adhesive. She was panting when she reached for the black and white marbled covered notebook, glancing back at the house before she dared to open it. Fiona's unmistakable looping script filled the pages with what was becoming apparent; a collection of personal information from bereavement groups at various locations. Heart pounding, ears buzzing, Joan whisked through the pages, following the entry dates until she reached the previous autumn and scanned the entries, searching for her own name.

11/13 Crestwood Community Center
Kathy Pranza paralegal /husband Bill-58 financial advisor heart attack painting dining room- golf, county club president, always said that he knew he wouldn't live to see 60 just like his father
daughter 32 son 35 four grandchildren

Janice Gordon bank teller /husband Paul 55, wholesale beverage center complications from staph infection, after three week hospital stay -fishing, practicing guitar to be able to play Beatle songs -four children, son in marines

Terry Farber-insurance agent- /second husband Steven 59, insurance adjuster- heart attack having dinner at brother's bday party
three daughters ,always wanted a son, Jack Daniels, Texas hold-em tournaments
sister died just one month earlier, time share in Orlando-Disney trips

Peter Hanover NYC fireman- /wife Jennifer 46/breast cancer/bank teller daughter 17, son 21 family party thrower, ladies bowling
Gave up on chemo treatments

Evelyn Grabel- housewife /husband Robert- 58 crane operator lung cancer- ski trips to Vermont always wanted a house
there
2 sons 1 daughter was trying to stay alive for daughter's
wedding

11/20 Temple David
Susan Blust housewife/son-Josh- 14 -lukemia, Jefferson High
School, science award, soccer team, town held fundraiser,
school tree planting
 21 year old daughter,Rachel Alton University
 Betty Krammer- retired /husband Robert 55 -brain tumor-
accountant-bridge player, fly fishing trips w his brothers
ask her never to remarry after he was gone
2 daughters, 1 son

Carol Simmons teacher-/sister, 38 car wreck, life support 3
days -ashes to be scattered at beach, spa weekends, beach
volleyball
8 yr old daughter 10yr old son-
had a bad feeling that night about her sister

Susan Haig -jewelry store clerk /-husband Robert- 58 lung
cancer realtor 3 sons, Yankee games, loved his dog Scoop,
grandfathers ring for one of his sons

Saint Cecelia's 12/3
Debra MeKenner court reporter-/husband, Kenneth-ac-
countant 62 pancreatic cancer, chamber of commerce di-
rector-
golf tournaments, loved his vacation home Naples, Fla,
1daughter, 1 son, 2 grandchildren

Pat Nickerson retired secretary/widow-mother Lucy, 86, lots of friends, card player, sandwich generation, two brothers out of state

Renee Connolly waitress -/husband, Howard, 48 massive stroke
appliance salesman, Steelers fan, annual trip to Hawaii/ honeymoon spot daughter 18, 2 sons, 16,12 Worried about finances/kids college

Marie Caputo dental assistant-/husband Carl 66/colon cancer
Dept. Public works remission, one of six brothers, Las Vegas trips,
would not listen to her about going for his check-ups

Joan Bruno /retired -husband Vincent 56/ heart attack in kitchen, mechanic, worked w him in shop -tennis player - cartier watch, 50th birthday, pressured by sister to meet- ings
2 sons 27 & 31

The entry seemed to throb at her as she stared at it, reading it over and over. She clapped the book closed, and instincts guiding her, she hurriedly stuffed the items back into the shopping bag and slammed the trunk shut. She scurried over to Jay's car and tucked the notebook into her purse that she had left on the floor in front of the passenger seat and zipped it closed.

"Are you okay, Joanie?" Jay asked as she arrived back in the kitchen.

"I'm fine. Just a little upset about the whole situation, I guess. May- be I'll pour myself a drink too," she said walking over to Bernie's bar across the room, careful not to make eye contact with either of them.

"Go for it, Joanie," a more relaxed Bernie said resting his arm on the kitchen counter, his bandaged finger held in the air. "Who could deal with this scene from a Wood Allen movie sober?" He finished what was left in his glass.

She kept her back to them, her hands shaking as she poured and then took a long sip of vodka and tonic.

"I brought some coffee into her," Jay said. "She wouldn't drink it."

"Let me see if I can try," Joan said swallowing another mouthful of alcohol and gratefully disappeared out of the room.

Holding the tepid mug, Joan stood a reluctant distance from the sofa. One of the men had covered Fiona with a blanket and she watched her snooze, curled comfortably on her side, snoring on her inhales.

"Fiona." Joan moved towards her carefully as if she were approaching a stray dog. "Fiona." She nudged her shoulder with a cold a poke, and again with increasing force. "Fiona. Wake up."

Fiona stirred, smiling up at her through one, half-opened eye. "Hi, Joanie," she slurred and then slipped back to where her self-induced slumber had taken her. Joan bit down on her bottom lip and walked out of the room.

"Get anywhere?" Bernie asked.

"She's still out of it." Joan dumped the coffee into the sink and began rinsing the mug.

"I don't think you're going to get any more problems from her to-night," Jay said to Bernie, sitting across from him, finishing up his bottle of San Pellegrino water. "And it doesn't make sense to try and move her."

"You're right. It doesn't. But now what?"

"Get some sleep. Your kitchen is all cleaned up, all of her things are out of your house, and I bandaged you up pretty good," Jay said. "Do you want to hear what I think?"

"Of course I do. I didn't know what I was going to do if you two didn't come over."

"You'll be awake hours before her in the morning. When you hear her get up, just walk outside. If she wants to be civil, try and smooth things out between the two of you, that's fine. If not—just call the police on her. What else can you do?"

The next morning Joan's phone rang startling her when it broke the silence. She'd slept little the previous night and rose at dawn. She started her coffee maker and stared unseeing out at the usually soothing view for hours, her thoughts swirling, still struggling to wrap her head around her discovery.

"Hi Joanie. I heard that you and Jay got roped into witnessing that horror show last night over at Bernie's house." Fiona's voice was light and casual. "I really wish he hadn't called. He made more of it than it needed to be, but it turns out he's just a little boy with a lot of spending money—whatever. I know you have my notebook, even though you had no business going through my things. I hope you didn't mention your Sherlock Holmes act to Jay."

"No. I haven't told anyone. I'm not sure what I've found yet myself."

"That tells me that you understand the delicateness of our situation."

"*Our* situation?"

"Why don't you bring the book over? I'm home. We should talk."

"We should talk. I'm leaving now."

Fiona answered the door wearing a loosely tied, pink silk bathrobe. Seeing her without a thoughtful application of make-up, her hair tightly pulled back from her puffy face, it was all Joan could do not to gasp at the shocking contrast of the finished product Fiona always presented to the world. The stark pallor of her skin gave almost a ghoulish effect to the dark circles and sagging skin around her eyes.

"You don't look so hot, this morning Joanie. Didn't get much sleep last night?" She stepped aside for Joan to enter. "Come on in, sit down."

"I'll stand," Joan said, acknowledging Pharaoh with placating pats on his head as he wiggled with joy greeting her.

"Yes, baby, Joanie's here," Fiona cooed to him as she walked across the room. "He loves you, so much Joanie. So do I. Come, sit with me."

Joan didn't budge, her posture rigid, her purse clutched to her side.

"So stand." Fiona shrugged and fell into her new couch. "You're always over dramatic about everything, anyway. Afraid I'll bite?" She clacked her teeth at Joan and burst into laughter.

Joan watched from just inside the doorway, struggling to mask her growing alarm at an unsettling version of Fiona she had never witnessed before.

"Bernie. What a clown." She rested her bare feet on the coffee table, examining her toenails. "Taking his busted-up old wife back after she's completed her research to see if it was just her, or forty years of monogamy that dried her out. He's going to be a grandpa, did ya hear?"

"I heard. I don't care about Bernie and his wife; tell me what I'm dealing with here Fiona. If that's even your real name." Joan produced the notebook from her purse.

"Let me have my book."

"Take the disgusting thing." Its pages fluttered in the air as Joan lobbed it across the room at her. "How do you know I haven't made copies of the entries?"

"I don't. But why would you want to do that? To provide duplicate proof of your detailed knowledge of our business?" She casually inspected its condition.

"What do you think you're trying to pull? I'm ready to go straight to the police as soon as I leave here."

"No you're not. Just the fact that you haven't even mentioned it to Jay already tells me you realize you're in deep with a lot to lose."

"You're wrong. I'm here because I just want you to tell me face to face what you've been doing to me and God knows how many others who believe that you're someone else."

"What *we've* been doing, Joanie. *We.*" Fiona leaned over to the end table and wiggled the mouthpiece into place. *"Do you have a question you would like to ask me?"* She cocked her head, speaking in the exotic Mrs. Habbibi's voice.

The genuine horror on Joan's face sent Fiona into a fit of wild laughter and the mouthpiece dropped out of her mouth. "Whoops." She caught it deftly. "Don't worry. That can't happen during a reading, I use really expensive adhesive—horrible tasting stuff." She clucked her tongue. "Almost as nauseating as tongue kissing Bernie." She set the mouthpiece back onto the table. "And I'm telling you right now, you even mention the police again and it will be you sitting right next to me answering their questions. Uh, huh." She bobbed her head. "Andrea Petrakas? Do you think anyone will believe that you thought that you were running eye shadow?"

Joan burst into tears, unable to keep up her facade of bravado any longer. "What did you have me doing to that poor old woman?"

"What the fuck are you crying about?" Fiona screamed at her.

Joan dropped her purse and her legs wobbly, slid down the wall, her face dissolving into tears.

"Nothing's happened to you. And that miser bitch has more money than she can spend in ten lifetimes. Spare your sympathy. Money was more important than her own children."

"I feel sick." Joan clutched her stomach and began to rock herself.

Fiona shot up off of the couch and stood over her. "Pull yourself together. You still have your million dollar baby. I set you up with a cream puff pitch and to your credit; you knocked it out of the park. I was proud of you." She returned to the couch. "Now you're wearing a rock around your neck the size of Bernie's prostrate and you're on deck to become the Cinnabun heiress. So tuck your balls up and get with the program before your damsel-in-distress bit gives you up to

Jay, yourself." She sank down on the couch again and shoved a stack of magazines off the coffee table with her foot.

"He knows me. He knows that I could never be in on something so depraved," Joan shrieked at her from her perch on the floor.

"Hmm." Fiona looked up in thought, putting a finger to her chin. *"Oh, come on, Jay, I went for a reading, now you have to go. Do it for me,"* she mimicked Joan coaxing Jay across the restaurant table.

The color drained from Joan's face.

"You did sell Mrs. Habbibi pretty hard to him." Her eyes glittered with a hard light. "And even if you got him to believe you, what about that coven of potential daughters-in- laws?"

"What do you want from me?" Joan demanded her voice shrill.

"Oooh. You can get nasty." Fiona howled with laughter.

"Just tell me what you want from me so I can get away from you."

"No, no. Let's back it up first. Let's pull apart that scene. And I don't want to get too far ahead of ourselves, but I'd say that Jay is the old fashioned-type. A formal proposal of some sort is probably not totally out of the question somewhere down the line—and that's from me, not Mrs. Habbibi." She added a thumbs-up gesture.

Joan listened, wiping her cheeks with the back of her shaking hand.

"Just imagine if those bony daughters of his ever found out. It will be an eleventh hour gift from heaven for those greedy parasites."

Joan began to push herself up to her feet.

"That's right. Think of the tap dancing you'd be doing to explain yourself when that bomb dropped." Fiona flung her head back in a now-familiar gesture, roaring with laughter. "They'd be on you like a school of piranhas. They'd tear you apart until there was nothing left of you."

Joan glared at her, eyes blazing though she remained tight lipped.

"And old faithful, straight-laced Jay. He'll think it was retribution from above, serving him right for taking his old wiener out of storage to cheat on precious, dead Judy. You'll be history so quick it'll seem like the whole AARP Cinderella story was just a really good dream." She broke into belly laughter falling back on the couch, kicking her feet in the air.

Joan exploded with anger. "You're an evil cun—"

"Hey, now." Fiona sat up, cutting her off. "Dooon't you say it," she warned, stopping Joan with a chastising finger. "I really have been a horrible influence on you haven't I?" She resumed her unnerving laughter.

"I'm not listening to any more of this. You're sick." Joan bent to pick up her purse.

"You're making me late for work, anyway, so let's just tie up our loose ends."

"We don't have any loose ends."

"We do. I just need you to make a few cash withdrawals from our business account and your usual pick-ups from Andrea for the next two weeks and then we can say good-bye. Not a lot to ask, for all I've done for you, is it?"

Joan studied Fiona's face, not sure if she believed her.

"If things would have worked out with me and drugstore hard-on Bernie, we all could have been travel buddies for the rest of our lives. But, shit happens as they say, which is why one should always have a plan B."

"What Plan B?"

"It's been a rough year. I'm tired. I'm thinking of spending the winter some place warm to figure things out. Courtesy of Andrea and other fine residents of lovely Long Island I can pretty much choose where I'd like to settle down now. Don't get me wrong. It's not that I don't like it here, but, if you ask me, you people are getting shaken down, paying these crazy taxes. The beaches are great, but, please…"

"How do I know you won't resurface and blackmail me for the rest of my life?"

"Listen to me, Joanie. I like you, you and your painfully-dull family. We had a fun little ride together and I'm not looking to hurt you unless you try and hurt me. As long as you keep your mouth shut, I see nothing but good things in your future." Fiona cupped her hand over her mouth, holding back a laugh. "Oops. There I go again."

"Asking for your word would be pointless." Joan turned, ready to leave. "But at least tell me what possessed you to act on such a heartless scheme?"

"I'm a Libra. I need stuff." She shrugged.

"You're sick. What you need is help."

"No, Joanie. I give help." She slowly rose from the sofa and began to move towards her.

Joan cautiously stepped backwards, not knowing what to expect from the creature she so trustingly had thought was her friend.

"I helped every single person who ever sat across from me." She inched closer. "All of them were better off after their visit, including you."

"How wonderful of you, Fiona. And here I was thinking it was the cash."

"It wasn't all selfish. I'm paying for around-the-clock aides to keep my mother out of a state-run nursing home."

"You said your mother was dead."

"Did I?" She scratched her head. "Well, no. She's very much alive—a ruthless wanna-be who made no effort to pretend I was an unwelcome distraction while happily drinking herself to death with a parade of losers she let defile everything they could get their hands on when she wasn't looking."

"That's not a reason, it's an excuse. I suppose it what makes you able to stomach what a disgusting person you are." Joan glared at her.

"Get out," Fiona snarled, her face morphing into a brewing, dangerous storm. "What are you standing there for? Get the fuck out!" she shrieked firing the notebook at the door as it slammed shut.

Later that afternoon Josie met Simone in the parking lot of a supermarket in Queens.

She pulled up next to her car and hopped into the passenger seat lugging a black, plastic garbage bag inside with her.

"You look like hell, Josie."

"And your car smells vile."

Simome flicked her cigarette out the window. "So that's the baby, right there?" She stared at the bundle covering Josie's lap. "Can I take a look?"

"Be my guest."

Simone pulled the clumsy sack across the console and stuck her face inside. "Holy smokes." She popped her head up. "How much is in there?"

"Upwards of six-hundred thousand."

"Where did you get it all?"

"It was a very good yearrrr…" Josie tilted her head back and crooned a line of the Frank Sinatra tune. "I made five grand just this morning for doing nothing."

"How?"

"It was *get out of my life and don't come back* money from that Viagra-munching, ATM machine I was letting schtoop me for the last five months."

"What happened?"

"It doesn't matter." Josie snatched the bag from Simone's lap, tying a loose knot at the top of it. "Hide this down in the basement, up in the ceiling over the washing machine. It's not safe at my place anymore."

"Why not?"

"Bernie rented it for me from a friend of his. And with the latest turn of events, I may find the locks changed and my clothes out on the front porch at any time."

"You think he'd do that to you?"

"He's a man. I know how they operate. Once they're not getting any from you anymore they cut you right off—like they never even knew you."

"Sorry, Jo."

"Thanks. Don't waste your energy. I want you to go straight home with this." She pointed at her sister. "Call me when it's in place so I can exhale."

"Don't worry. I got this."

"Good girl. It won't be up there for long. I feel big changes coming on."

16

*W*ith the last reading of the evening about to begin; drained and eager for her final performance as Mrs. Habbibi to come to an end, Josie had begun clearing off the desk when she looked up to see Miriam standing in the doorway, the house quiet and darkened behind her.

"Our guests have all left?"

Miriam stood slump shouldered in silence, the candlelight making it difficult to read her expression.

"Aren't you coming in?"

"No."

"Is something wrong, Miriam?"

"Nothing is wrong. I'm just so tired," she slurred.

"Yes. It has been a long night. Let's get started." Mrs. Habbibi arranged the items she had just placed down into her shopping bag when the unmistakable sound of a trigger clicking froze her in motion, shattering the lull of the candlelit room.

Josie's heart stopped in midbeat. She swallowed and slowly began to raise her head to meet the blood-draining sight of the revolver wavering in Miriam's hand.

"I'm just so tired of living without my son."

When Josie was able to produce words they were in her natural voice although Miriam didn't seem to notice.

"No, no, Miriam. You don't want to do that," she stammered, palms raised. "You don't have to do that."

"Yes. I do."

"You can always speak to Garrett through me whenever you want."

Miriam leveled the gun at Mrs. Habbibi's head and locked her elbows. "That's why I'm taking you with me."

"No!" Josie screamed as she sprang up from the chair, yanking off her wig. "Don't! I'm not a real psychic!"

Miriam's face wrinkled; preparing for the blast and Josie hurled herself to the floor.

There was a flash of light followed by a high-pitched pinging sound. It dulled into a mechanized buzzing in Josie's ears as she lay face down in the thick nap of the rug. She lay motionless; suspended in a brief eternity where the consciousness is separated from the body while its systems convened in a biological code red before rushing to their battle stations. For the infinite moment she floated within the surreal limbo until there was another horrible blast followed by a thud, as if someone dropped a large duffle bag onto the floor. Josie heard herself shriek at the sight of Miriam Stemple's bulging eyes level with hers beneath the desk, her face a distorted mask of surprise and the blank expression of death.

Josie shrieked again when the corpse's tattered skull came into full focus, a jagged eggshell bathed in blood and gore. Her screams served to unite her brain with her body and her hand instinctively went to the side of her head, finding an unfamiliar mush. Her stomach churned at the vision of her open palm, dripping red as if she had been finger painting in blood.

I can think. I can't be dead. Just get out of this house. She summoned her courage and patted at the side of her face with a trembling hand to assess the severity of her wound, screaming in pain and horror when her fingertips found the row of her top teeth where there should have been flesh, and higher up the remnants of an ear.

Nausea and chills seized her when she struggled to all fours. *You're alive. It's just a flesh wound. You're going to be alright. You have to get yourself out of here.* She grabbed at her gold table runner Miriam's body had pulled down as it hit the floor and she pressed it against the side of her head, bending her neck to the opposite side to stanch the torrent of blood running down her arm and trickling down her back. She clawed at her belongings spilled onto the floor, scraping them into her bag and then began crawling across the room, clutching at the skirt of the sofa and struggled up to her feet.

Shopping bag in hand, heaving for breath, she propped herself against the doorway and took a frantic last pass of the scene and spotted her wig laying on the rug at the other side of the room.

She glanced at her escape through the kitchen door just feet away before taking a dizzying, first step back into the shadowy study when the startling whoosh of the drapes bursting into flames sent her tumbling over Miriam Stemple's lifeless legs, her brow catching the edge of the solid wood desk during her fall.

After the blissful, dreamlike passing of an unclear amount of time, Josie reluctantly felt herself blinking as the sounds of popping and crackling roused her. Slowly she was able to turn onto her side. Straining to push up from the floor, her stomach lurched up a stream of bitter vomit from panic, pain and the acrid smell of burning synthetics. As the smoke thickened, rising into the glowing shadows, Josie watched the ceiling fade as the flames devoured the room, smiling contently at her younger self, reading a story she had written to the delight of Vera and her handsome daddy, relaxing on a summer day on the front porch of their home on St. John Street.

The next morning Joan was on her way to the salon after making her last pickup from Andrea for Fiona. It was Friday, nearly two weeks since she had learned the truth about her friend and her diabolical psychic impersonation scam.

Throes of distress and raw wounds of treachery had kept her struggling to remain calm and cheerful in front of Jay. She had been tempted so many times to unburden herself from the strain of carrying Fiona's secret and confide in him, especially on those nights when they would be lying together, and she was being held safe in his arms. But when he'd start hinting at getting a place of their own, telling her that hers was the only voice he wanted to hear each night before falling asleep, instinct and common sense choked off the impulse.

The dilemma owned her; her mind in a continual tug of war. *And what if he didn't believe her version if she did decide to confess to him?* That's when the image of Fiona, sadistically imitating her appeal to Jay across the restaurant table, those magical months ago, shamelessly pitching a visit to Mrs. Habbibi, would flash in her memory. Then she'd know for sure she was going to stick with the route she was going. It was Jay's consequential visit with Mrs. Habbibi that jettisoned his guilt, streamlining their romance.

And why did she deserve consolation? She would admonish herself— *wasn't she to blame for the whole situation, anyway? She should have known that someone like Fiona was trouble, there had been signs.* But she'd been having so much fun in the whirlwind of new excitement being with Fiona created that she didn't care to know—the same reason that she couldn't confide in Francie. She just wasn't up to the merciless, brow beating, *I told you so* lecture her alarmist sister would unload on her when what she really needed was someone to console her. Someone with street smarts to advise her if her decision to stay compliant was the right choice, or just to go to the police and get it over with. Joan sighed at the latter prospect, not only because she was embarrassed of her naivety, but the real possibility of prosecution as an accomplice. She knew firsthand how convincing Fiona could be.

She parked her car outside the salon, and dropped her head onto the steering wheel. *It was almost over.*

Joan walked through the quiet salon returning greetings as naturally as she could muster on her way to Fiona's station. At the sight of the pile of mail on top of the glass cases and their small padlocks still unopened, a stab of panic seized her. Fiona was always in the shop by no later than ten every morning. Joan instantly grabbed for her cellphone thinking she might have missed a call from her. *No missed calls.* She streaked back to the front of the salon without knowing how she got there to ask the receptionist if Fiona had called in or left a message.

The sense of foreboding she felt was visceral. It numbed her thinking until it occurred to her that Fiona's absence could be part of a setup, some kind of a double cross in progress. The possibility hit her like a lightning bolt, stopping her in midstep. The worst part was she had no way of knowing for sure, the situation reducing her to the likes of a captured animal; all frantic energy, but no way to escape.

Her breathing was becoming shallow. She paced the floor in front of Fiona's station, gawking out the windows, waiting for the sight of her car pulling up to save her from phoning Jay. Struggling to control her breathing she knew every second she put the call off was a gamble on their future together. No matter what, if he found out through some other turn of events, things would never be the same between them.

Not knowing what else to do, Joan sat behind the counter trying to act as pleasant as she could manage while fighting the urge to cry. *Maybe I'm over reacting.* Her hands shook as she unlocked the cases. *Maybe it has nothing to do with me—maybe she left town already, there are probably one hundred reasons she had to leave. Maybe some other fool she swindled got wise to her and has her on the run.* Her thoughts rambled and caught on possibilities as she set up the display items. *What would she get out of hurting me? I was good to her; my family was good to her. Fiona said so herself.* She glanced over at her phone, just lying there waiting for her to make the call. She picked it up, but lost her nerve, and poked again at the redial button to try Fiona's number.

She dialed every fifteen minutes, the calls routing straight to voice mail and by two o' clock she couldn't stand it any longer. Joan locked up the cases and left, taking the envelope she had come to deliver with her. She could only wonder what had been extorted, sealed inside, from the duped widow.

On her drive home, she was nearly incapacitated with anxiety, her throat tight and her hands shaking on the steering wheel. She needed to swerve back into her lane, nearly sideswiping another car as she envisioned her street swarming with flashing police cars waiting to cuff her and haul her away if Fiona had decided to beat her to the punch. It wouldn't take much to convince them. It was her name on the bank accounts and Andrea Petrakas had never even seen Fiona.

She was dizzy with relief as she turned into her block, neat and serene as any other afternoon. She waved, returning her retired neighbor's friendly greeting as he stood idly watering his lawn.

She went straight into her living room and poured herself a vodka to fend off the breakdown that was bucking just below her thinning sense of control, waiting to take her down. She dropped into an armchair listening to her heart beat in her ears and looking around her neat comfortable home, she cursed herself for ever taking its stable simplicity for granted. She shook her head; she needed to get out of victim mode. She needed to start thinking clearly about what she should do next instead of waiting around like a sitting duck for whatever it was Fiona had up her sleeve. She knew now who she was dealing with and that absolutely nothing could be put past the vindictive, viper of a woman.

She allowed her eyes to close. She hadn't eaten all day and could feel the warm stream of alcohol burn as it trickled down into her system, mercifully en route to anesthetize the panic that had gripped her since the morning chewing relentlessly at her innards over the hours.

She swallowed more of her drink and exhaled heavily before she reached for her phone and dialed Jay. She closed her eyes bracing for the worst as she listened to the sound of his phone ringing.

"Joanie!" The tone of his voice held its usual, merry enthusiasm whenever he picked up her calls.

He didn't know anything yet. Her heart throbbed with relief and she forced herself to smile before she spoke. "Would I disappoint you if I stayed home, tonight, love? I've had a pounding headache all day and it just seems to be getting worse. I left the salon early."

"That's fine. You don't sound like yourself. Do you want me to bring you over some dinner?"

"You're sweet. I don't want you to do that. I just need to crawl into bed. We'll make up for it tomorrow."

"I have some papers I've been putting off looking over. It will give me a chance to get it out of the way. I'll miss you, tonight."

"I'll call you in the morning." She pressed her hand to her forehead, exhaling an anxiety-laced breath of relief and dropped the phone down on the table. She felt miserable lying to him. She loved how he never asked questions or pressured her; he was such a trusting person. And then her mind switched to imagining his reaction if he ever found out the truth about the magnitude of the deceit she was intentionally keeping from him. *Would she ever be able to gain back his respect? Would he even give her the chance?*

Through the night she called Fiona's phone to the same maddening outcome and finally, after a tortuous and sleepless night, she couldn't stand it any longer and realized she needed help. She waited until six the next morning and desperate, called Bernie. While his phone rang she prayed he was alone, that his wife wasn't back and sleeping next to him. He agreed to meet her at Fiona's rental within the hour.

When Joan pulled up to Fiona'a bungalow and spotted Pharaoh already standing tall on his hind legs waiting in the front window she knew with an icy certainty that something terrible had happened. At the sight of Joan's car, the frantic dog darted out of sight, reappearing at the front door. She sat motionless inside her car for the moment, sealed from the cool morning air and the fate awaiting her.

Bernie arrived in the next seconds, his car coming to an abrupt stop behind hers. She watched him in the rear view mirror, stepping out of his Mercedes and bolstered herself before she opened her own door, knowing her life would never be the same, one way or the other once she stepped out of the car.

She threw herself into his arms. "Bernie," she whimpered into his shoulder.

"What is it, Joanie? What's going on? When was the last time you saw her?"

"Day before yesterday."

"Did she seem okay?"

"She seemed fine. Everything seemed fine," she added nervously.

"Do you think this could have anything to do with me?" He looked somberly into her eyes. "I didn't mean for it to end the way it did."

"No. I don't think this has anything to do with that."

They stood looking at the house Pharaoh barking frantically from inside.

"Did you ring the bell?"

"No. I waited for you."

Joan followed up the stairs behind him with heavy legs. Two newspapers lay on the wooden porch, the plastic wrappers dotted with condensation and morning dew. Bernie looked into Joan's ashen face for a fateful second and pressed the doorbell, sending Pharaoh into a frenzy running in circles in front of the door.

"It's okay, boy. It's okay." Joan bent, trying to soothe him as he pounced at the squares of the glass-paneled door. He scurried backwards in fear when his pouncing pulled Fiona's brocade curtain and its rod down on top of himself.

Bernie walked up to the window and cupped his hands around his eyes. "Doesn't look like anyone is in there."

Joan followed him around the back of the house where he peered through the bedroom window and then gestured for her to have a look at the few cartons she'd begun to pack and the bed, not slept in, still neatly made. They looked at each other and Bernie took out his phone.

They waited on the front porch after he put in the call.

"Should I break a window and let him out? The poor bastard's going crazy in there."

"Don't, Bern. Wait for the police. It will just complicate things. It won't be long."

A V-formation of honking geese passed over the explosion of autumn colors reflected in the lake. Joan and Jay sat on Adirondack chairs their hands linked watching a lone swan silently glide past on its way home, pausing briefly to consider them.

"No," Jay's authoritative voice halted Pharaoh as he jolted forward.

Pharaoh let out a whimper of defeat and settled back down on the blanket Joan had spread for him between them.

"Mr. Barrett," the voice of the construction foreman called from the scaffolding that surrounded the lakefront home.

"Let me go see what they need." Jay pushed up from his chair. "You coming?"

"You go ahead. I'll be along." She smiled up at him.

"Take your time, Joanie." He kissed the top of her head and started up the hill to the house.

She let her head rest against the back of the chair. With her eyes closed, the nostalgic smells of her favorite season seemed to intensify. She breathed in their sacred scents; the carpet of golden leaves mulching the ripe earth, flowers past bloom, preparing for the turn.

It had been almost three months since the fire. What happened in the Stemple house that night was still a mystery. The cause of death of the two bodies that were pulled from the scene had been ruled a homicide. In spite of the detectives tracking down and questioning everyone that they could find who had been present for a reading that night from the psychic, Mrs. Habbibi, no arrest had been made yet.

Jay and Bernie were suffering from loss and guilt almost as badly as Joan. Each of them blaming themselves in part for Fia's death. Jay for boasting to Fia about the incredible reading Mrs. Habbibi had given him and Bernie for breaking her heart, driving Fia to make the fateful appointment with the psychic out of desperation over their break-up.

Each of them along with the authorities could only speculate on what had transpired. The consensus was that poor Fiona was caught in the middle of a confrontation between Miriam Stemple and Mrs.

Habbibi or Miriam Stemple and her estranged husband who was also named as a suspect. It was believed the murderer set the fire before fleeing the scene in attempt to destroy any evidence. Until the psychic, Mrs. Habbibi was apprehended no one would ever know for certain.

Joan pulled her sweater up around her neck as the shoreline across the lake began to darken, the November sun, anxious to turn in early, dropping low in the afternoon sky. She rested her hand on Pharaoh's back, the fingers of her other hand, stroking the Heulandite crystal she'd resumed wearing soon after Fia's death.

As hundreds of times before since the fire, the thought of disposing of the gift flitted across her mind. The bottom of the deep lake would always be a strong contender, but strangely there was a side of her still compelled to keep it. It was tangible proof of what was once an impossible dream come true. And a costly reminder that the power to rechart the course of a life resides wholly within its owner.

She hoisted herself out of the chair. She had time to think about if she would keep it or not. Joan patted her thigh and Pharaoh hopped to his feet, trailing after her as she walked up to join her fiancé.

The End

Acknowledgements

No one writes a book alone.

I do not know where the quote originated but I do know it to be true. The following are the individuals who assisted me in transforming an idea into the book that you are now, holding in your hands.

Barbara, Regina and Debbie for sharing their insights on becoming widows; their brave and generous personal accounts were invaluable. The amazing psychic(s), palm reader(s) and tarot card reader I sat with during my research; your intuitions and revelations were enlightening. Talented Justin for a wonderfully moody book cover, kornfeldstudios@aol.com, steady Andrea for her book design, andrearaiola.design@gmail.com, and enterprising Deanna at D Connection Social Media Marketing, deannatabone@gmail.com, Bonita, the best cheerleader that anyone could ever hope for, her unwavering support was more sustaining than I think she realized.

And the deepest gratitude to my esteemed editor, Jessica Morrell and all of her kind; the wise and patient wordsmiths who loyally stick by their writers, helping us land the plane even when we have veered way off course or become lost in the clouds of our imaginations.

ABOUT THE AUTHOR

Mary A. Ellenton returned her focus to a lifelong passion for writing after motherhood and a successful career in her own fitness business. Her 2012 debut novel, Flipping, a view into the world of the predatory lenders, became an Amazon top selling title among independent authors. Mary was also the first publisher in Ingram's independent publishing program to achieve a top selling status.

Mary is a native New Yorker who lives on Long Island with her husband and their dog, a Boxer named Brunell.

www.maryellenton.com